YOU
BELONG
TO
ME

YOU

BELONG

TO

ME

HAYLEY KRISCHER

G. P. PUTNAM'S SONS

AUTHOR'S NOTE ON CONTENT:

*This book contains mentions of child sex abuse, scenes depicting
predatory behavior, drug and alcohol abuse, and death.*

G. P. PUTNAM'S SONS
An imprint of Penguin Random House LLC
1745 Broadway, New York, New York 10019

First published in the United States of America by G. P. Putnam's Sons,
an imprint of Penguin Random House LLC, 2025

Library of Congress Cataloging-in-Publication Data
Names: Krischer, Hayley, author. | Title: You belong to me / by Hayley Krischer.
Description: New York : G.P. Putnam's Sons, 2025. | Audience term: Teenagers
Audience: Ages 14 years and up. | Summary: Frances Bean, a self-proclaimed goth outcast, gets swept
into a whirlwind romance with popular Julia, who introduces her to the luxurious world of DEEP,
but Frances begins to question everything when events take a dark turn at an exclusive party
Identifiers: LCCN 2024040053 (print) | LCCN 2024040054 (ebook)
ISBN 9780593698389 (hardcover) | ISBN 9780593698396 (epub)
Subjects: CYAC: Cults—Fiction. | Friendship—Fiction. | LGBTQ+ people—Fiction.
LCGFT: Thrillers (Fiction) | Novels.
Classification: LCC PZ7.1.K748 Yo 2025 (print) | LCC PZ7.1.K748 (ebook) DDC [Fic]—dc23
LC record available at https://lccn.loc.gov/2024040053
LC ebook record available at https://lccn.loc.gov/2024040054

ISBN 9780593698389

1st Printing

Printed in the United States of America

LSCH

Design by Rebecca Aidlin • Text set in Iowan Old Style

To Andy

1

You could say it all started with this invitation, a thick white card popping out of my locker door:

FRANCES BEAN ELLIS

deep *requests your presence*
On the fall equinox
When the sun shines directly on the equator
The Patterson Home
Dress code: white

Girls like me don't get invitations to Deep events. Girls like me aren't supposed to be interested in beauty serums, namaste hands, mindfulness apps, crystal water bottles, and the expensive white lace dresses that everyone wears who is adjacent to wellness guru Deena Patterson. Especially not me, Frances Bean Ellis, the teacher's daughter.

Yes, I'm named after *that* Frances Bean, as in Frances Bean

Cobain, Kurt Cobain and Courtney Love's daughter. My mom liked, at least according to legend, that they graced her with a middle name after a character in *The Beans of Egypt, Maine,* by Caroline Chute, which, according to my mom, is an excellent book on poverty in America. My friends call me Bean.

Most of the girls in my school *and* their mothers want to be in close proximity to Deena and her daughter, Julia. Deep is a multimillion-dollar wellness company with international recognition, a billionaire fan base, *and* a flagship store right here in South Brent because Deena Patterson, who lives in a palatial home in the estate section, wanted a short commute. But Deep isn't just wellness. It's clean beauty products, organic clothes, detox brushes, salt therapies, and new ways to heal yourself.

Then about five years ago, Deena Patterson launched Femme, an exclusive offshoot for young girls. Femme girls host parties, or "gatherings" as they call them; they intern at the local Deep store and are regulars on the Deep Instagram account. All of them in their white dresses and lacy skirts, draping their glowy legs on white ruffled organic linen sheets, surrounded by an endless supply of cosmetics and products. Girls with huge smiles on their faces, looking like someone vacuumed the brains out of their skulls.

I could barely afford a hair tie from the Deep store.

The reason I want to be in close proximity to Julia Patterson has nothing to do with Deep or Femme. It's because I've been crushing on Julia long before we became partners in Nineteenth-Century Lit. Yes, me, with my overdyed platinum-blond hair, my red lips, my white, ghostly skin. My unplucked, messy dark brows. My black velvet skirt, my embroidered top with the lace sleeves, my fishnet stockings.

I'm supposed to rebel against such things.

Yet I have a crush on Julia Patterson. A wild, out-of-control crush.

"I heard about these invitations, but thought it was like folk-lore or something," Brooks says, and plucks the card from the crease of my locker, turning it over to inspect it. Say what you want about Brooks, that his pompadour hair, penny loafers, and black-rimmed glasses make him look like a young Morrissey, which he vehemently denies, but he's a fiercely loyal friend.

Ivy pokes Brooks with her black lace parasol, reaches her laced-glove fingers out, and snatches the invite from his hands. The parasol was something she picked up at an antique shop during a weekend trip to London with her mom about a year ago and she's carried it with her ever since. Out of our group, Ivy is my best friend.

"Damn, Bean, this happened fast," Ivy says. "You bonded with Julia Patterson over Charlotte Brontë, and now you've got a Femme invite."

"Hand it over," Nico says, and inspects the invitation with her antique gold magnifying pendant, an artifact she wears around her neck. "Embossed lettering? One-hundred-and-twenty-pound card stock? Jesus, this is wedding-invite quality."

"Might as well be an invite to a coronation, with the massive social currency it carries, at least to the people in this school," Brooks says.

He's not wrong. Talentum is an elite private school twelve miles outside Manhattan. Countless articles have been written about the student body, how rich they are, how they skip out on required community service, how the antiracist missions have largely gone ignored. Talentum may come with a high price tag, but it's got a glare of privilege shining on it.

While the kids at Talentum are the power elite of the world, my friends and I, in our Victorian goth attire, are most certainly the outcasts.

My stream of anxiety comes to a halt when Brian-Michael Tenny and Steph Markowitz, in matching pink button-downs, make a beeline to Steph's locker, which is next to mine.

"Oh goodie, here comes the pink-shirts regime," Brooks says under his breath.

Brian-Michael pulls out his phone and starts taking photos. He's so embarrassing.

"Who are you taking pictures of?" I say.

Brian-Michael glares at us. "It's not Halloween. *Fucking goths,*" he says like it's a bad thing.

"Actually," Ivy says pointedly, "I'm afro-goth."

"You're what?" Brian-Michael says, chomping on gum.

"*Afro*-goth. Get the terminology right."

"There's no such thing as afro-goth," he says. "Goth is a derivative of white punk."

"Let me school you, Brian-Michael, a boy so important that your parents thought you needed two first names," Ivy says, and twirls her parasol at him. "A) Goth subculture doesn't exclude people based on race. B) Bauhaus, the pioneers of goth, admitted that they were basically influenced by reggae."

Steph and Brian-Michael stare at her blankly.

The outcast thing wasn't something that ever bothered Ivy. To her, Steph and Brian-Michael were just part of a handful of kids who made fun of us. I think she found arguing with them entertaining. She's the editor in chief of the school paper, part of Model UN and the International Girls Club. Last year she even joined the tennis team for a hot second. I don't have any of those fancy hobbies or extracurriculars that get you into college. I'm nothing like Ivy in that way.

"You're quite imaginative," I say to them. "Are you going to ask us next if we're going to a funeral?"

They roll their eyes and walk away.

Harassment is an unofficial pastime for these Talentum guys. They'd make the OG preppy '80s bullies proud. I've come to accept their secret clubs, their cliques, their Ivy League legacy sweatshirts, and their judgmental looks. Brian-Michael is not special in this way. He's from a long line of assholes who get off on power trips.

The only reason I go to Talentum is because my mother is a teacher here. The only other school I've gone to was a neighborhood public school in the West Village, where my mom and I lived in a studio apartment. My bedroom was a walk-in closet. Ivy always tells me that I have the right to be here more than anyone because my mom has influenced over a decade's worth of students with her feminist-focused history lessons. Yet *I don't belong here* is always in the back of my mind.

Which is why this invite makes little sense. Why would Julia Patterson invite me?

"Can we get back to this invitation?" Brooks says.

"Yeah, I thought you two were just friendly in class?" Ivy says. "Is this, like, a full-blown thing?"

"Calm down, it's just an invite," I say. "There is nothing full blown about it."

But I don't feel calm at all, and I'm starting to wonder if it was accidentally put in my locker. Though, how can it be accidental? It has my name in it. Maybe, just maybe, Julia knows about my crush and has one on me too.

No, that's impossible.

I tell my friends I'll meet them in the newsroom after class and give them updates with details. Always with details. And I'm reminded of the invitation again, all those details . . . *on the fall equinox, when the sun shines directly on the equator,* and an excitement creeps up my spine, to my shoulders, through my ears, and I shiver as I walk into class.

2

It's been four days or 180 minutes since Julia and I started working together as partners in Nineteenth-Century Lit, and during those hours I've suffered like a tortured lover, watching the door, longing for Julia to make her entrance, because when I see Julia Patterson, the world stops.

At least it stops for me.

She walks in a minute after the bell rings, coasting between the desks, her copy of *Jane Eyre* tight against her chest and her eyes on me. Even under the fluorescent lights, she's beautiful. I awkwardly wave because I don't know what to do with myself. A rush of red smacks my cheeks. My body warm. My hands sweaty as I fold the invitation in half. God, I feel so dumb.

"Ms. Patterson, you have to work on your punctuality," Ms. Taylor, our teacher, says. She says this to Julia every day. But Julia is like a like a unicorn coasting in on glitter clouds. The concept of time doesn't exist in Julia Patterson's world. Her lacy white top flutters as she slides into the seat across from me. She's wearing a short white ruffled skirt so I can see the light brown heart-shaped mole on her knee. I'm not being creepy about it. She pointed out the mole to me yesterday.

Julia's face melts into an easy, natural smile. Her complexion is dewy and smooth, just like you'd think it would be if your mother was a wellness and beauty guru.

"Hey, Frances," Julia says sweetly. She bites her lip as she unpacks her backpack.

"Hey," I say, my face still warm, the downside of pale skin. My embarrassment can never be hidden. I lower my head to shield myself, lightly pull my bangs in front of my eyes.

"Sorry that I'm late. I think I have undiagnosed executive functioning issues."

"Ah," I say. "I didn't have that on my *Why is Julia Patterson late?* bingo card."

She laughs. I want to melt.

"My mother thinks it has something to do with overcommitting to other people. She said if I had less on my plate, then I wouldn't be late all the time."

"If it makes you feel any better, the only reason I'm on time is because my locker is across the hall. I promise next time to wait a minute after the bell rings so we can be late in solidarity."

"You're so funny, Frances," she says. "By the way, can I call you Bean? I know your friends call you that."

"Of course," I say. "Call me anything you want."

Call me anything you want. Oh god. Was that too much? I can feel myself blush because even though I'm clearly flirting with Julia, I didn't expect myself to. I quickly riffle through the book.

"So, Jane Eyre, Victorian heroine. I was kind of thinking about free will." I open the book to a page that I've tagged with those little pastel-colored stickers, my face in between chapters as I try to muffle the way I'm practically unraveling in front of her. "Can I read this to you?"

"Sure, but you should know I'm completely against free will," she says, and smirks. "Kidding. Go ahead, read it."

"'I am no bird; and no net ensnares me; I am a free human being with an independent will,'" I say, quietly reading the quote.

"I love that," she says, and strokes the page with her tanned fingers. Her little pink nails. "So, Jane Eyre is saying that she's evolved away from what people expect from her. She's her own strong person who wants to make her own choices," Julia says. "Society put so many expectations on women back then. It must have been so hard for her. Something about it still feels current, you know?"

I think of the Deep Instagram page, the women and girls with their perfect hair. Their freckled faces. Their plump lips. Clear skin. Stress-free smiles. Everyone strives to look like them. I guess she doesn't see the irony, and I'm certainly not going to point it out.

"I wish there were more people in the world like Jane Eyre, being true to themselves," she says, and looks at me sweetly, an awkward grin on her face. "Kind of like you are."

"Like me?" I laugh. "How am I true to myself?"

"So many people at Talentum pretend to be weird and different. And you're actually . . ."

"What? I'm *actually* weird and different?" I laugh uncomfortably. "Because of the way my friends and I dress?"

"No, no, that's not what I meant," she says, lowering her voice.

She twists her body toward mine so she's facing me, real close. "I love the way you dress. The way you and your friends dress." Her knee touches my knee, and I know this sounds cliché, but it's an electric shock between us. I read somewhere that if one person feels this kind of intense connection that the other person has to feel it too.

"I mean, you're the coolest person I know, Bean. You don't act fake or anything. You're you. You act like yourself. You're beautiful."

It crosses my mind that I might pass out right here in Nineteenth-Century Lit, which would be appropriate. Women in the late 1800s were fainting all over the place because they were being practically suffocated by their tightly laced corsets.

"The girls in Femme are beautiful," I say. "That's not me."

"Yes, there're a lot of beautiful girls who are part of Femme. But you have a different kind of beauty. You have a unique beauty. Anyway, I've been pushing my mom to mix it up. The Deep Instagram account should represent a variety of all kinds of people and bodies and styles."

I pause because I want to bring up the invitation. Even if I'm so embarrassed and scared that my whole body is tingling, I have to say something.

"Are we just going to pretend like I didn't get that invitation?" I say.

She smirks. "I was waiting for you to say something."

"So it's real?"

"Of course it's real," she says, staring at me blankly.

"But why would you want me to come?" I look down at my black velvet skirt. "I'm not exactly 'dress white' material."

"Do you always sell yourself short like this, Bean?"

I love the way she says my name.

"I'm not selling myself short. I'm truthfully saying I won't fit in."

"Think about coming, Bean. You might like it. Everyone's really connected. There's inspiring talks. We hang out, sometimes braid hair . . ."

"Wait, that's what you do there? Braid hair?" I say, laughing. "I imagined these wild parties with everyone on mushrooms."

"Those are just stupid rumors," she says. "Yes, there's a lot of celebrating nature and ourselves. It feels good to belong to something, to be part of something that's not school, that's not so competitive. That was really important to my mom. You know, to be inclusive."

That surprised me because Femme seemed very *exclusive*. There's a viral Instagram video of a woman trying to sneak into Julia's house while her daughter was inside at a Femme party. After getting caught by security, the woman stomped down the gravel path, ranting, "I dropped my daughter off at Deena Patterson's house, and all I got was a fucking Deep swag bag."

Yet here was sunny, optimistic Julia, who seemed to believe that wasn't true. Sometimes all you needed was to believe something to be true and then it was.

"You should meet my mom one day," Julia says. "She's probably a lot like your mom."

I highly doubt this. My mother worries about things like how to get the moldy smell out of the washing machine. Her nail polish is always chipping. She's had the same blush for ten years.

Take a look at one picture of Deena Patterson on her Instagram page, her eyes perfectly relaxed, a white sweater slung over her shoulders, her skin sparkling like she's been drinking youth potion like snail mucin, that knowing smile as if she holds the secret to eternal life. It's why millions of people buy her products, why millions of people want to follow her—because they want her secrets too.

And I am absolutely sure that Deena Patterson never has to worry about things like a moldy washing machine.

Julia and I go back to working on the essay, sharing the passages from the book that stand out. Julia's pink nails drift along sentences. Would it be so bad to go? Or to at least say yes and think about it?

"Would I have to wear white?" I say, and I can feel a chill run through my spine. I can't believe she thinks I should meet her mom. I can't believe she said I have a unique beauty. No one has ever been this direct with me before.

She looks up at me, and I tingle everywhere, down my arms, my stomach.

"Frances Bean, you would have to wear white. But you can borrow something from me," she says, and bites her lip. "You know, if you want to go."

I nod slightly. "I want to go."

My face burns, and I turn away, barely catching my breath. Then the bell rings.

3

I sprint to the pressroom, where Ivy, Brooks, and Nico are hovering over a massive wooden desk, something from the 1920s, staring into the computer monitor.

"Bean!" Ivy squeals. "Come and look at what Brooksie made us."

On the monitor, there's a collage of celebrities wearing pink suits and pink button-down shirts.

"What am I looking at?" I say.

"The graphic that's going to go with our new story on pink clothing for men."

"Wait, what?" I say. "You're going to write about Steph and Brian-Michael and all of them, just to, what . . . retraumatize us?"

"Seriously, the whole pink-shirts thing could be a good deep dive for the paper," Ivy says. "Is there an underlying reason for the color? Some historical reference?"

Nico reads an article from her phone. "'Royals in the 1700s wore pink to distinguish themselves from the peasants below them.' There were sumptuary laws restricting purple and pink to royals. Bananas. Historically, pink gave them better standing in the rest of the world. Lower-class people wore brown, earthy colors."

"Makes sense," Brooks says. "Peasants dyed their clothes from vegetables in the garden. They didn't have silks like the monarchs did. The Fashion Police for the Age of Enlightenment."

"Hmmm, I'm liking this," Ivy says.

As the editor in chief of the *Talentum Free Press*, Ivy thinks only about the paper. I can see that itch inside her when she's eager about a story, and she'll scratch at it, peel it back, and make it bleed until she discovers an answer. It's a craving for her, which is why she's recruited us to work on the paper with her. I made this pledge to her to work by her side at the paper in the seventh grade—even though I had no interest whatsoever.

Last year, after our big investigative story on how the South Brent Historical Society siphoned fundraising money from the public library, the New Jersey High School Press Association awarded us with Best School Paper. They even had a ceremony at a tacky catering hall in South Jersey. Ivy got a plaque for writing, Nico for photojournalism, Brooks for an op-ed on how the historical district had gained too much power because of the real estate prices in South Brent. I got a plaque that read STAFF.

"I don't even deserve to be here," I told them.

"Not true," Nico said. "You give us moral support."

"Bean," Ivy would say, "you're the chief brainstormer in charge."

But that's what best friends do—they lift you up.

At the awards ceremony I stood there like a log. The audience clapped while they handed us little plaques for Best School Paper, and I felt a giant echo—all of it, empty noise. Now Ivy was look- ing for a new story, a story that could fulfill her. Because every- thing for Ivy was irrelevant unless she was uncovering a secret behind it. But Ivy was special like that. Ivy skipped admissions at Talentum because they approached *her*. Her father is Diego Smith, the award-winning journalist. Her mother, Amanda Cohen, is a classical pianist. The moment Ivy plucked me out of obscurity, making me her best friend, was the moment I stopped just being the teacher's daughter.

I don't know how I'm going to tell them that I agreed to go to this Femme gathering. Because in making that decision without discussing it with them, without agonizing over every detail, something already felt different. It happened in the ten minutes since I'd said yes to Julia in class and walked over here to the newsroom. And it happened without my friends.

"Maybe we do something on how pink was a sign of wealth and power until companies assigned a gender to it for marketing purposes," Ivy says.

"I can do a photo essay on it," Brooks says, and pulls out his Canon, his dad's old camera from the 1980s that makes a clicking sound when you press the button.

"Bean?" Ivy says. "What do you think?"

"Um, I spoke to Julia," I say.

The three of them stare at me, mouths wide open.

"Oh my god, Bean!" Nico squeals, and runs from behind the desk. "What did she say?"

"Well, she wants me to come."

"Holy shit," Ivy says. "And you're going to go?"

"I think so. What's the worst that can happen? I'll get free Deep Glow out of it."

"Don't they all wear white?" Nico says. "What are you gonna wear?"

"I know no one wants to hear my opinion—"

"Like we have a choice," Nico mutters.

"—but it's very weird that they wear all white," Brooks says.

"What's wrong with that?" I say. "We wear all black."

"*Everyone* wears black," Ivy says. "Except the guys who wear pink."

"Call me paranoid, but an all-white dress code makes it seem like they're sacrificing virgins," Brooks says.

"Okay, Brooksie," I say. "If there's a ritual sacrifice, I'll make sure to text you immediately to let you know you were right."

"Don't listen to him, Bean," Nico says. "I could knit you a white halter top and have it finished by tomorrow. The kind that ties around the back. Or I have this really romantic puff sleeve. Or, wait, my sister has an amazing white flouncy skirt. You're going to be fine. We've got plenty of pieces to work with."

"I'm sorry, guys, this is still feeling like *The Little Mermaid* to me. Why does she have to wear white just so she can make out with a hot girl?" Brooks says.

"She's not giving up her voice," Nico says. "The dress code is more like a costume party. Or Truman Capote's black-and-white ball . . . obviously not the black part."

"Fine, I can get behind an all-white debutante-ish vibe," he says. "As long as Bean is *choosing* to do it."

Here's what I know about my friends: They would never pressure me to do anything I didn't want to. They would never tell me that they loved something if they didn't. They're real, sometimes too real, sometimes too blunt, but with them, I know exactly where I stand. And I like that they want to protect me.

Ivy wrinkles her nose excitedly at me and squeezes my hand. I breathe her in, a mix of sandalwood and cinnamon. "I wonder if Harmony will be there?"

I knew this was coming.

Harmony Williams was Ivy's former peer leader. Everyone gets a peer leader at Talentum. Mine was Jacobson Delmar, who just kept telling me how Harvard was a lifelong dream as he slicked back his long red hair into a ponytail, and that I shouldn't be anxious about college. I wasn't anxious about college until Jacobson made me anxious.

I thought I was going to have a cool peer leader I connected to, the way Ivy and Harmony did. Someone who would take me under their wing and make me feel less like I was an outsider. Someone whose eyes I could follow through the sea of kids if I felt lost. But Jacobson was Harvard legacy. He didn't know anything about what it was like to be a teacher's kid.

As one of the few Black girls at Talentum, Ivy was disappointed when she first got placed with Harmony. "There's other Black girls at Talentum," she first said. "Why aren't they pairing me with them?" But those girls were like the other socialites at Talentum, imbedded in our school's storied traditions, like homecoming. They talked about wanting a big Greek life in college. They couldn't have been more different than Ivy. Despite Ivy being at Talentum her whole life, a prized student as they always told her, her parents, famous intellectuals. But because she was one of the only Black girls, she didn't always feel like she fit in. Harmony made Ivy feel seen. For one, Harmony's mom was a professional musician, just like Ivy's mom. Harmony's mom was a singer-songwriter living off residuals because one of her songs was the theme of an iconic teen show back in the '90s. They both identified as outsiders, and in a weird way, that's how they connected.

I was a little jealous, to be honest. But anyone would have been better than Jacobson Delmar. Harmony and Ivy bonded over everything, over their musically talented mothers, over their clothes, how Harmony would wear all those long colorful skirts like she lived on a hippie commune, and how Ivy would wear her afro-goth black smock. Harmony was unapologetically ambitious: she was the class president, head of Girls Learn International, director of the school play, president of the Women in Film club. Ivy idolized her.

Then, after Harmony graduated, about two and a half years ago, she started working for Deep, and basically disappeared. She never spoke to Ivy again. No explanation. The friendship was just over.

It's still a wound for Ivy. We try not to drive past the Deep flagship store on Chestnut Street, because Ivy didn't want Harmony thinking that she was stalking her or something. I thought it was more about Ivy not wanting to be reminded of what she'd lost if she got a glimpse of her, a big sister, a role model.

Nico and Brooks go back to playing with the collage at the desk.

No one wants to talk about Harmony, or remind Ivy about that hurtful part of her life. My mom told me once that when a friend breaks up with you, you never forget it. That it's worse than a romantic breakup. You expect to be dumped by a lover, but not a friend, my mom told me.

"I'm not sure if she'll be there," I say. "I can ask Julia."

Ivy shrugs. "Nah, don't worry." But I know she's feeling dejected about it. I can see it in her face. We've been best friends long enough.

"I'm guessing she will be," I say.

"It's fine," Ivy says.

"Don't say *fine*, Ivy. Come on. *Fine* is not a descriptor," I say.

"How else should I respond?" she shrugs. "I'm over it. It was two years ago, that whole thing with Harmony. This isn't about her. It's about you and Julia."

If it's not about Harmony, then why does this already feel like I've committed some kind of betrayal?

4

Saturday night, just before dusk. I'm in the white knit halter that Nico whipped up for me and her loopy sister's surfer-chick white gauzy skirt that we hiked up with safety pins in the front and back to make a balloon-like structure. I pull on a pair of black boy shorts underneath so it looks purposeful and my black combat boots to give it an edge. Yes, I draw on my thick black eyeliner because I'm not about to let this become a *Breakfast Club* moment where I'm the Ally Sheedy character who goes from goth to Laura Ashley.

I'll subject myself to white clothes, but I'll never give up my cat eye.

I can hear my mom talking on the phone, her pacing back and forth in front of the dining room table, where her books and papers are piled in high stacks. It's more like a library than a dining room. The brown chairs are from a flea market in South Jersey, and our cat, Mookie, uses the back side as a scratching post, loose threads spilling off the fabric. I don't think we've had a proper meal at that table for at least a decade.

"You have to be there for her, Shira," my mom is saying to her friend. I can hear her crying through the speakerphone. "But you also can't let her walk all over you."

My mom has always collected friends who needed help. She's a fixer. Everyone's therapist. It's the reason she got into teaching. She felt like she had a calling to help kids.

There's always someone at the door or on the phone who needs advice or an ear. Women from the neighborhood. A friend she has to run over to check on or, like now, Shira, whose twenty-something-year-old daughter is back in rehab.

She looks up at me, and takes her friend off speaker, her phone now balancing between her ear and her shoulder. I can see from her expression she's confused, pointing dramatically at my outfit.

"Shira, listen," she says; then suddenly her cheeks redden from a hot flash and she fans herself with someone's hard-worked essay. As my mom always reminds me, she's perimenopausal, her body temperature is constantly changing, and I should be empathetic because one day my feminine body will betray me too. "Bean just walked in, and I'm having a hot flash. I'll call you back in fifteen minutes," she says, and hangs up.

"You didn't need to hang up."

"My daughter is running off to Vegas to get married, and you don't want me to hang up?" she says, staring at me up and down. "Who's the lucky girl?"

"Mom," I say, and shoot her a look. "Stop. I'm just going out."

In the past, I've declared white to be a patriarchal color. The color society deemed appropriate for daughters to wear when their fathers give them away to undeserving men. A religious symbol for virgins. Now, here I am. *Blanco. Blanche. Lavan.*

"Frances Bean. You look very pretty. But you can't do some

teenage magic on me and expect me not to notice that you're wearing all white. Where are you going?"

"Teenage *magic*?"

"I don't think I've seen you wear white since they wrapped you up in one of those hospital blankets the day you were born."

"I'm sure I had something white since then."

"Okay, Bean. I have work to do. I have to call Shira back. Also, is it hot in here?" she says, and strips off her sweatshirt. "Please tell me where you're off to."

I typically can tell my mom anything. It's been me and my mom for most of my life. She and my dad got divorced about ten years ago, and he died last year. He wasn't exactly father of the year while he was alive. But telling my mom that I'm going to a Deep party is going to be like telling her I'm getting Botox injections in my forehead.

Unlike the rest of South Brent moms, and really, women across the country, my mom doesn't subscribe to Deep's miracle cures, their eye masks, their antiaging creams, and their clean mascara. She sees it as overpriced bullshit. My mom is the antithesis of Deena Patterson. To her, Deep is another elitist corporation trying to make money off the masses.

"I'm going to a Deep party. They have a thing for girls my age."

"I'm aware of the thing they have for young girls. I've seen them walking around school in white, Bean," she says, her eyes hard on me. "Is this a joke?"

"It is not a joke. It is a wellness company, Mom."

"I'm sorry, *wellness* is not a marketing tool," she says.

"What's the problem, Mom? You get acupuncture, you eat

organic foods. You use wild yam cream or whatever for perimeno-pause. You even went to a stand-up paddleboarding sound bath," I say. "You of all people should be more open to Deep."

Theoretically, Deep should be without controversy for my mom. What could be wrong with wellness for the masses? But my mom doesn't understand Deep and what it means to people. Their advertisements alone are so aspirational, with Deena and Julia Patterson in their white flowing outfits, a natural sheen glistening their skin, shilling for Deep Glow, their cheeks raised to the sun. They both looked so content.

I never admitted this to my friends, or my mom, and I probably never will, but when I'd look at those ads, I'd recoil, thinking of my own life, my skin, hiding my zits under cakey makeup, tired of our dark furniture and the pillows covered in cat hair. I know I should be kinder to myself. I know I should have more self-compassion. My mom says I should love myself for who I am. But didn't everyone want to repair their skin? Didn't everyone want to glow like Deena and Julia Patterson?

I am ashamed to tell anyone, but those advertisements inspire hope that you, too, could be like Deena Patterson one day. You, too, could get rid of your hot flashes or your acne or your anxiety! You, too, could have a perfect skin barrier! You, too, could have what they have!

My mom hardly wears makeup, except for a little blush. Her cheeks are plump, her skin's taut, and her cleansing routine consists of water and Vaseline if she's "in the mood." She might look tired—the dark circles don't help—yet, still, she is always beautiful.

"Bean," she says, and takes a deep breath. "What's going on here? Why are you going to this?"

"Because Julia Patterson invited me. And maybe I have a crush on her. *Maybe*."

"Julia Patterson? Oh, okay," she says. She looks at me wide-eyed, interested now.

But it's not over. I can see it in her face, an uncomfortable shift. There are more questions.

"Listen, there's going to be a lot of alcohol at this party. I've heard all about it. Wellness Moscow mules. Vodka infused with acai. I don't like it. I really don't like it."

"First of all, there is no such thing as a *wellness* Moscow mule."

"You know what I mean."

In the world according to my mother, alcohol is not an option. She's convinced I am going to die of alcohol poisoning, or I'm going to become an alcoholic and ruin my life like my dad. Her sister, my aunt, is a recovering alcoholic, too, so I've got the gene on both sides, as she has never failed to remind me.

Last year my dad died of "alcohol-related" diseases. Enlarged liver. Pancreatitis. Sepsis. It's an ugly disease. The few years before he died, he was living in a small house with broken peach-colored shutters near the train tracks. The house was tiny, almost too tiny for his tall frame, and I wondered if he was constantly hitting his head on the doorway. But he seemed to like it. He said it was like living in a storybook house. He was very much in a fantasy world like that, telling me how one day the floods would come and we'd live in that little house with the peach-colored shutters, sailing the world together.

24

My mom kept me away from my dad when he was drunk. But a few times, I visited him in the midst of a bender. He'd come out of the house, hunched over and smelling like a sour ashtray. He slurred his words, and he couldn't stand up straight. He told me that his bones ached. He was always wildly apologetic. *I'm sorry for being like this, Frances Bean. I'm sorry for who I am.* She'd whisk me off.

"We can support him in his disease from afar," she said after that because my mom, being the way she is, always wants everyone to feel good all the time. So she pushed me to let him know I was *at least* thinking of him.

I brought him matzo ball soup during Passover and brownies every once in a while. We'd leave containers on the front porch. I left a book about sailing in his mailbox. The front lawn filled with leaves. During the few stretches when he was sober—the longest time was for a year and a half—he really seemed like he'd make it. He came to my school play in middle school. We'd play three-hour sessions of Monopoly at the diner. Just as I trusted him, he'd relapse and start drinking again. He'd cancel plans or stop calling.

By the time he died, at the beginning of sophomore year, it was almost a relief. I couldn't stop thinking about him, that he was gone, but at the same time, I couldn't stop thinking about him when he was alive, suffering in that little house.

"Listen to me, Mom," I say, taking her hand, reassuring her. "It's a party. I'm going there because Julia invited me. I'm not gonna get hooked on Deep products or their whole wellness life or drinking or whatever. I'm going because I want to check it out. That's all."

"Oh, Bean," she sighs, those beautiful blue eyes of hers. "What am I going to do with you?"

"Think about all the Deep Glow samples I'll bring home."

"You know I only use Vaseline," she says. "And please remember, no one is perfect, honey, no matter how much Deep Glow they use."

5

Outside, in the windy autumn night, I stare up at the crescent moon, my hands shaking. I imagine the shorter days, in a month or two it'll get dark just before five o'clock, and somewhere I can hear Ivy's voice telling me to be careful. But the night, the windy sky, Nico's sister's white skirt blowing around my thighs, all of it moves me like it never has before, a golden light turning on inside me.

Julia's neighborhood is nothing like mine. Here, there are enormous houses, electronic gates, and lawns that seem to stretch forever. On my street, the houses are on top of each other. Once I saw Mrs. Hara, my completely harmless next-door neighbor who's always pulling weeds in her garden, staring from her yard, watching me in my bedroom. We met eyes, and she quickly turned away, but Julia would never experience that kind of feeling, like your neighbors are encroaching on you, in this section of town.

When I reach the large iron arched door, I check in with a blond woman in a white suit, a tag around her neck that reads DEEP. She leads me into a hallway with high ceilings, an extremely tall vintage-looking mirror on the wall and a white round marble table in the center with a vase filled with white hydrangeas. I can see a tennis court through back windows. Farther inside, past the winding staircase, there's a wide-open room where girls are animatedly chatting, all in white ruffled dresses like angelic soldiers.

Suddenly, I feel incredibly lonely, and utterly out of place, watching these girls giggle and hold hands like they've been doing it forever.

I see Kenny Khatri, Harlow Kennedy, and Grace Champlain, swinging on a large white leather hammock that hangs from thick silver mesh ropes, the whole thing covered in a cozy shearling blanket. The three of them, all Talentum girls, have become like social media stars because of the attention they get on Deep's Instagram page. Their empty faces and their bare toes skimming the floor, lifeless. They're at one of the most elite parties, yet it's almost as if they're bored.

Ivy deemed Kenny, Harlow, and Grace the "Manson Sisters" after seeing a picture of the original Manson family girls, three of them holding hands at their trial in 1970, laughing. Three cold-blooded killers and their stringy long hair, their jail uniforms, blue apron dresses and dark cardigans.

Nico called Ivy out for being mean. But Ivy told her: "It's not mean if it's historic."

Kenny, Harlow, and Grace snap out of their hypnotic stares and turn to me with big smiles, their faces flushed and their skin radiant, translucent.

"Hiii, Frances," they say, the three of them with the same sweet, sugary voices.

"It's *so* good to see you here, Frances," Kenny says, and hops off the hammock, oddly eager to talk to me. Kenny Khatri has never spoken to me once, but she embraces me, the sleeves of her white lace top roughly brushing my cheek.

"Julia is so excited that you're coming," Harlow says. I stare at her for a second, not knowing what to say. I knew that Kenny, Harlow, and Grace were part of Femme, but it was hard to tell if Julia was friends with them outside school. They crowded around me, so eager and earnest seeming. Their eyes wide and curious.

"Well, I'm here," I say awkwardly.

Kenny shakes a basket filled with little white packets, blinking her eyes cheerfully.

"We're giving out free samples of Deep Glow. Would you like one?" I pocket a few because maybe it'll help dry up some pimples—plus, it would cost sixty dollars for a tiny jar if I bought it at the store.

"Did you try the Reiki treatment?" Harlow coos. "I could actually feel the energy flowing through my body. We're so blocked all the time, you know?"

"So blocked," Kenny echoes.

I feel self-conscious with my heavy black eyeliner. Everyone here, all the girls are pink-cheeked and healthy-looking, their skin translucent, a whole no-makeup vibe. Why use makeup when their skin is so perfect from all the Deep products? But me, my skin is flaky from the aftereffects of an acne breakout, concealer covering my spots.

"Yeah. Maybe I'll do that," I say, rolling my neck from side to side. "My neck is in knots."

"Did you meet Kai yet?" Harlow says. "Kai is a healer. He does this no-touch massage, and it releases all the tension."

"He's a genius," Kenny says.

Kenny and Harlow start talking about Reiki and what it does for you. *Helps you sleep. Blah, blah. Gentle touch. Blah, blah. Life force energy.*

That's when I see Julia. She weaves through the white couches, past the DJ, who's playing some kind of electronic chanting music, past the crowd, toward me.

"Bean! You're here!" Julia says, her eyes glowing. Her cheeks shimmering.

A yearning shoots through me, and I want to squeeze her, curl up into her, hide in a corner with her.

"Your nickname is Bean?" Kenny says, lightly squeezing my arm. "I love that. I'm not sure if you know this, but my real name is Kamakshi. It means 'love and desire' in Hindi."

"Your mom calls you that," Grace says with a crooked smile.

"Yeah, she says *Kenny* is too Americanized. She hates it." Kenny rolls her eyes.

"We were just telling Bean about Kai, that he's a healer," Harlow says.

"We told Bean she was going to love him," Kenny says.

It throws me a bit that they start calling me Bean so quickly. I don't have anything against it. Hardly anyone calls me Frances, but it feels very intimate, and I think about how Ivy's going to react. *What, are you best friends with them now?* But I shake her out of my mind.

"Do you know Kai?" Julia says to me.

"Kai Edwards?" I say. "I think my mom was his history teacher, but it's been a while since I've seen him."

Kai Edwards was an enigma at Talentum. I was in the seventh grade when he was a senior, so there wasn't much I knew about Kai, except he was extremely good-looking, like, freakishly beautiful, a super creative who hooked up with a lot of people. I heard Deena Patterson was essentially his guardian after his mother died and that he skipped college to work full time for Deep.

"We've known Kai forever," Julia says. "Deena and his dad were lifelong friends. They went to boarding school in France together. So Kai is like an older brother to me. He's the one who helped form Femme. Well, he and my mom."

"*Such* a visionary," Grace says.

"Yeah, well, they thought it was important for girls our age to have the same experiences as the adult women did. He really felt like my mom gave him so much empathy, compassion, and a sense of belonging when he was younger, that he wanted her to share it with others too. Soon they'll move into boy world. But these things take time."

Someone walks around passing dried strawberries grown by a small family in Montecito, California. Each strawberry is squeezed with lime, and all the girls take one.

"They're a little spicy," Julia says, and her eyes twinkle. "They're dusted with spice from a woman-owned pepper collective."

"I never had strawberries with lime and pepper," I say. The strawberries look like dried candy, covered in a sugary red glaze. "Are they good?"

"In the store, we sell them for eighty dollars a jar," Harlow says, and pops one in her mouth.

"Eighty dollars for strawberries?" I say.

"Deena's favorite," Julia says, holding one between two fingers. "Open your mouth, Bean."

I release my jaw, and she drops the strawberry on my tongue, the tartness of the lime and the spice from the pepper mixing with the sweetness of the berry. Julia locks her eyes with mine as I chew the berry and swallow it.

"Wow, that was hot," Grace says.

Harlow smacks her arm. "We should go, you know, help set up the barn for Deena's talk."

They each kiss Julia on the cheek, and the three of them lock hands, snaking through the crowd. Their lithe bodies disappear between the sea of white.

"Do they always do everything together?" I say to Julia.

"Everything," Julia says. "They're like family. They're *my* family."

"I've never spoken to them before today," I say. "I didn't know how . . ."

"What?"

"I didn't know how nice they were."

Julia smiles.

Another waiter approaches us with tiny orange drinks. "Turmeric shots," Julia says, and hands one to me. "It's a great anti-inflammatory."

"Nothing alcoholic?"

She gives me a look. "No, what? I would tell you if that's the case. You think my mom is going to serve alcoholic drinks to minors?"

I feel stupid for saying it, buying into all the rumors I heard, like the one about the girl who was brought to the hospital not too long ago to get her stomach pumped.

"I'm sorry. I feel like a jerk."

"No, I know the rumors. I know people think things about what we do here. But it's a positive gathering. I mean, we can certainly raid Deena's liquor cabinet later . . ." she says slyly. "But she isn't serving it. No."

Julia lightly knocks her turmeric-drink-filled glass against mine.

"Here's to everything," she says, and downs it.

I put the glass to my lips and drink. It's tangy and sharp. And quickly my chest feels warm. "Here's to everything."

6

"Sister," someone says. It's Kai Edwards. He's standing there confidently, wearing a white linen shirt unbuttoned to the waist and rust-colored beads hanging on his bare chest. His thick brown hair is cut in wisps down to his shoulders, gleaming. His eyebrows are contoured like he was a model.

I'm not usually attracted to guys, but Kai is unusually beautiful.

"Brother," Julia says with a huge smile, and hugs him. "I have someone I want you to meet. This is Bean."

"Ah, Frances Bean. So nice to meet you," he says, his eyes fixed on me. "Tell me, what brought you to a Femme gathering?"

"I'm not a party crasher," I say, laughing uncomfortably. "I swear Julia invited me."

"Yes, I'm aware," he says, and stares directly at me, unbothered. "Were you interested in Deep before Julia invited you?"

"I guess I was curious about it," I say. But I don't really want to answer. What could I tell him? That my mom thinks Deep products are snake oil and my friends, well, just Brooks, thinks there's going to be a human sacrifice? Julia stands there quietly, waiting for me to answer. "I like your facial products," I say, and I feel like the zit that I popped this morning is screaming at them from my chin.

"A lot of people first come to Deep for the facial products. But then women, and girls, especially the ones who are part of Femme, they see that Deep offers a light in all the darkness. These are people who feel dismissed by their communities, or their doctors, or their friends. Deep is a collective. Because we all want to feel like we're a part of something, like we're being heard, like we belong."

What would it feel like to belong at Deep? Would you have to buy something? Would you have to wear white? In all serious-ness, I wonder if Kai really meant what he said. That people want to be part of Deep because they feel lost, because they want to be heard. It's like I've spent my whole life, certainly all my time at Talentum, feeling detached from the rest of the student body. It became my mantra: *Look at me, how different I am!*

I wonder how I'd feel if I opened myself up to more people than just Ivy, Brooks, and Nico. Would being understood by a larger group feel like freedom?

"There's a reason you're here, Frances. Something that's be-yond Julia. I suggest you listen to your curiosity. That's your inner voice."

He reaches his hand out, palm up, and motions for me to take it. He places his hand over the outside of my hand and guides it to my chest. "This is your instinct, Frances. It will never lead you to the wrong place." He smiles at me, holding my hand there still, and it feels genuine and calm, like I've pleased him. It's as if he can see through me.

"Harmony's about to talk in the barn, then your mom's going

to go on," he says to Julia, then looks at me. "So nice to meet you, Frances."

"You can call me Bean," I say. "It's my middle name."

He smiles politely. "I prefer Frances, is that okay?"

"Sure," I say, my hands beginning to tremble. Maybe it was time for someone in my life to call me Frances who wasn't my mother. Maybe Bean is a baby name.

He clasps his hands together and bows to us, then slips away.

Julia turns to me, beaming like a proud parent.

"So what do you think of this whole thing?" she says, motioning her hands in a circle, looking out at the room of girls. "I know it can be a little out there. A little *woo-woo*."

"I think it's interesting," I say.

She cocks her head. "What do you *really* think?"

I hesitate for a second. "Why does everyone have to wear white?"

She throws her head back, laughing, like I said the funniest thing.

"Phew, that's such an easy question. I thought you were going to tell me you wanted to leave. Please tell me you don't want to leave."

My heart swells. *Julia Patterson wants me to stay here.* It's hard for me to believe.

"I don't want to leave," I say.

"So, the white thing. A vibrational element happens when everyone wears the same color. In the spiritual world, white represents wholeness," Julia says. "But the truth is, the world is filled with such chaos. Deena wants everyone to feel protected and insulated. It's not just a color for her. It's not just a fashion state-ment. That's why Deena decorated our house in white. She wants it to feel like a refuge."

"Can I ask you a totally off-topic question?" I say.

"Sure?" she says, and raises her eyebrows.

"Why do you call your mom *Deena*?"

She laughs. "My mother transcends Mommy or Mom. She wanted me to call her *Mama* when Deep really blew up a few years ago. She liked how earthy it sounded. I was thirteen and was kind of a know-it-all. Like, years of calling you Mom and now, you want me to call you Mama because it sounds *earthy*? I started calling her Deena to piss her off."

"I guess mindfulness and compassion goes out the window when you're in middle school."

"Exactly," she says. "It's not entirely a secret. I told this story to *Vogue* when they interviewed us. But she still hates it when I bring it up. It's not my best moment."

I told this story to Vogue. Imagine if that's your life? You just breezily name-check *Vogue*? Still, I choke with laughter knowing that Julia Patterson intentionally irritates her mother like the rest of us.

Across the room the girls, about twenty of them, file out the sliding glass doors at the back of the house, a trail of them in the yard, through the meadow.

"What's back there?" I say.

But Julia doesn't answer, because in the distance, a gong rings out three times, echoing through the house.

"It's Deena. She's calling for us," Julia says.

She takes my hand and leads me through the living room to the glass doors. The girls notice us behind them, their eyes fixed on us. Julia's a superstar here, but me, I'm just Frances Bean. I was invisible to them before. Now here I am, the hair on my arms standing up because I know what they're seeing: Julia and me, latched together. I hear their whispers, "Who is she?" My heart throbs, and it takes every part of me to play it cool.

7

The wide meadow behind Julia's house is filled with white caps of Queen Anne's lace down a stone path that leads us to the barn. It's one of those barns you find on Pinterest, with white flowers wrapped around old beams, lit candles hanging from metal candelabras, and shiny wood floors.

Inside, the girls form a half circle, their bodies stretched languidly over white cushions and lace blankets, their wide eyes forward, their faces enraptured. In the center of the circle, Harmony Williams lights a sage stick and places it in a bed of flower petals, crystals, and candles. Her long dark curls frame her face, and with her white embroidered dress and ruffled shoulders, she seems like she's from another era, a French bohemian fairy tale.

I would never admit this to Ivy, Brooks, and Nico, but I love the lightness of it all, the candles, the white linen, the ruffled dresses.

Julia and I sit on a soft blanket as Harmony begins to speak.

"My mother didn't protect me as a child. I saw too much. My mother was a singer, and she'd perform her music across the country. For years, my sister and I would have to follow her around, staying in hotel rooms late at night by ourselves when we were little or sitting backstage at seedy clubs while my mother sang. We kept late hours. I had insomnia when I was only twelve years old. Isn't that awful? I had spent so many years at road-side hotels that I was terrified someone was going to come in the room. I never slept. By the time I was a teenager, I was exhausted. We ate crappy food, whatever was in the motel vending machine was dinner. My mother didn't mother us. I spent my childhood like an unhealthy adult, a little out-of-control girl."

I knew Harmony had her problems with her mom, but I didn't know they were this bad. When you have a dad who struggled like mine did, you're supposed to be compassionate, my mom always told me. But Harmony was such a model of perfection at Talentum. I could never imagine her in seedy roadside motels eating chips from the vending machine for dinner. Of all people, I should have known better what it looks like when someone puts on a front.

"Then I went to a school where everyone was supposed to feel like they belonged. But I didn't," Harmony says. "No one could understand what I went through as a kid. They talked about the importance of community. Everyone kept telling me over and over again, *this is the greatest school. This is how you'll find success. This is where you'll find stability.* Except I didn't feel connected or stable or happy. In a weird way, I felt like I was chasing acceptance like my mom was. I didn't know what my purpose was there."

I didn't know what my purpose was there.

Everyone was supposed to feel like they belonged. But I didn't.

It startled me how much I related to what she was saying. Almost like she was reading my mind. Harmony was right. Every Talentum student strived to be the best artist, or the best journalist, or the best school president, the best debater. They worried about whether or not they'd get into the honors track at BU or the drama program at Yale. They worried if their legacy status at Columbia would even matter anymore.

Ivy's mother went to Stanford. Brooks's parents both went to Columbia. Nico's dad went to Dartmouth. My mom went to a state school in New York.

Harmony's eyes well up, the sadness reeking. In a split second, she catches her breath and an air of calm comes over her. "Then I met Deena and Kai and started working at Deep. I told them how lost I felt. How empty I felt. That I didn't really feel like I belonged anywhere. And they said, *You don't have to be lost anymore, because we're here for you. We have a place for you here.*"

Kenny, Harlow, and Grace sit shoulder to shoulder, softly crying, tears streaming down their cheeks.

"Deena and Kai encouraged me to look at my bad habits, establish a good sleep-hygiene routine, treat my skin with great care, journal about what I put in my body. Most importantly, Deena asked me what *I* wanted. *Me.* I know many of you feel that way, under your parents' spell, people pleasing, trying to make your parents happy, everyone but yourself. You can stop doing that right now. Because I'm here to help you understand what *you* want."

Everyone claps for Harmony, wiping their tears away, rushing toward her and thanking her for telling "her truth."

"That was amazing," I say to Julia. "I had no idea about how Harmony grew up. I knew about her mom, but I didn't know how alone she felt."

"It's a real community here, Bean. We're not just selling products."

There's a rustle in the back of the barn, and Deena Patterson emerges in her signature floor-length white linen kaftan. Layered gold chains drape across her chest. Her glossy nude lip, like someone just painted it on her.

Julia turns to me and whispers, "Later, once she's done, I'll introduce you to her."

"I get it. She's like a guru. Everyone wants to be around her."

"She's not *like* a guru, Bean. She *is* a guru," Julia says.

Harmony presses her hands together in prayer and bends down in front of Deena. Everyone else follows Harmony's lead, bowing down to Deena. So do I.

"Hello," Deena says.

"Hello, Deena," everyone says back to her, in gentle, mantra-like voices. She tells us about the equinox, how the earth's axis stands perfectly balanced. She speaks about her journey: Born in Brooklyn. Beauty school. Had Julia when she was only twenty-five. Single mom. Importance of belonging.

"It's a time to center ourselves like the earth's axis. We deserve to restore our bodies," she says. "Because if one person has a spiritual revelation, then . . ."

"Then we all have a spiritual revelation," the group says together.

"If one person is triggered . . ." she says.

"We're all triggered," everyone answers, their voices following her rhythm.

"Spiritual emanation," Deena says, and pauses. "Spiritual emanation is when your spiritual connection trickles out to all of us, it emanates to others, it passes through you like sun rays, like streaks of light. And on the equinox, that's even more powerful."

Julia places her palm to her chest, then closes her eyes. The way everyone finishes Deena's sentences, knowing what to say, reminds me of going to temple with my nana. I felt so awkward as everyone in the rest of the congregation, person after person, repeated the prayers, except for me because I didn't know them. But here, something about it feels different. Deena Patterson's words feel welcoming. Julia takes my hand and squeezes it. It's a signal: It's okay that I don't know what to say in return. It's okay that I'm new.

"You are in charge of your life. You define yourself. You're in charge of yourself," Deena says. She coasts between us. "Say it with me. I'm in charge of myself."

Everyone repeats, "I'm in charge of myself."

"I'm in charge of my mind," Deena says.

I turn to look at Julia; her eyes are closed. "I'm in charge of my mind," she's saying.

I've never heard anyone speak like this before. There've been motivational speakers at school, and sure, I've seen people online preaching on how to live a clean life. But Deena's so passionate, so understanding. If one person is triggered . . . then we're all triggered. And of course, she's right. *I'm in charge of myself.* That's what I want. To be in charge of myself.

There's an originality to this whole thing, the girls in the barn, the white, Deena standing up there talking about independence, that kind of dazzles me. Where's my mother's originality? Even my name isn't original. Frances Bean. She always made it seem like she was so cool for being different. But what's so different about being named after a rock star's kid?

Julia goes to get us probiotic matcha drinks when Deena is finished. Harmony waves at me through the crowd of girls, and crawls toward me, her long white dress dragging behind her.

"Bean," she says serenely. She hugs me as if we were best friends, as if I saw her yesterday. "It's amazing to see you here. You always had such a special air about you."

She takes my hands and looks me in the eye, her face serious. "What do you think of all this? It's amazing, isn't it?"

I run my fingers across the soft blanket. "Everything is beautiful."

"Isn't the fabric so soft?"

"It's incredible," I say.

"We researched for months to get the right blend of lambswool and cashmere," Harmony says, stroking it. "It probably cost a fortune, but it's not just texture that's important to Deena. The pillows were made by a group of women in Vermont on their own looms."

Cashmere was a sweater I could never afford. I didn't know they made pillows out of it.

"So tell me, how is Ivy?" she says. "I was going through a really hard time senior year. I know I disappointed her. I know I disappeared on her. I've always felt bad about that."

You ghosted her, I want to say. *She never got over it*, I want to tell her.

"She's the editor of the school paper now," I say. "She's great."

"She was always so determined, so smart. Please tell her I think of her."

Harmony kisses me on both cheeks and stands up. "I'm so glad you got a chance to hear Deena speak," she says, and I nod my head.

"She's magical," Harmony says. Everything at Deep is magical.

Harmony blows kisses and floats away like a fairy.

Julia comes back with a huge smile on her face and hands me the probiotic matcha drink. I take a sip; it's disgusting, but I smile.

"This whole thing . . ." I say, and trail off. I don't have the words for it. The fuzziness inside me, like I'm in a dream. "Everyone is so nice, and your home, this space. It's so beautiful." I've said *beautiful* so many times that she must think there's something wrong with me.

"Oh, Bean," she says, "you haven't even seen my mom's spa yet. It's in the basement."

"Your mom has a spa? In her basement?"

"Deena's got robes and everything," she says with a sneaky look and scoots toward me. The candles flicker above us while hypnotic music pipes in from speakers. "Wanna take a tour?"

The way she stares at me makes me want to hold my breath. I want something to happen, for her to kiss me. My body tingles everywhere. A tour? She wants to give me a *tour*? That thrills me. "Hell yes."

8

I follow Julia downstairs into what looks like a Roman bathhouse, but it's the size of an entire living room. It's completely covered in tiny cream-colored tiles, with brass showerheads, a cold-plunge pool, and a hot tub. There's a sauna with glass windows and towels neatly rolled on wooden benches. Fluffy white robes hang on brass hooks. The air is humid. It feels like desire.

"Let's change into robes?" Julia says, as if it's the most natural thing in the world. As if it's normal to have a spa in your house.

"I don't have a bathing suit," I say, and I feel so puritanical because nudity is something that Julia Patterson probably doesn't even think about. But I'm not ready to get naked in front of her.

"We could do underwear and bra? Or I could run upstairs and get us bathing suits too. Whatever makes you more comfortable." She gives me a goofy smile.

"Bra and underwear is fine with me," I say, and we stare at each other for a second, our eyes meeting until we both laugh and turn around to take off our clothes. "It's so beautiful down here," I say a few times. I can't stop saying it. I sound like one of those girls at the Femme meeting already. *It's so magical. So beautiful.* I wonder if she's watching me, and I quickly turn around and see her long blond hair traveling down the middle of her tanned back, her strong shoulders. She's not watching me, yet I'm watching her.

Most people at school see Julia Patterson as unattainable. They talk about her in her full name, that's how you know. There's no other Julia in our school that I know of, but it doesn't matter. She's *Julia Patterson*. Someone out of reach, worldly, well traveled, chic.

I slip on the robe, and it's the softest, lightest material I've ever felt. Did I expect it to be any other way? I walk toward the fountain in the corner, the water trickling down into a stone pool.

"What made your mom want to make a spa down here?" I say.

"Her design inspiration came from an old spa in Paris. You should see that place, it looks like the walls alone should be in a museum," she says.

"Do you go to Paris a lot?"

"At least once a year. We have a feast at the Ritz every Thanksgiving."

"We add two card tables to our little dining room table, and my nana makes a disgusting green bean casserole with cream of mushroom soup," I say.

"Bean, you're so funny."

"What? It's true," I say. "Our moms are very different. Your mom is so . . . sophisticated. I mean, Thanksgiving in Paris? My mom's family from Long Island comes out. That's about it."

"Well, her close friends live there. My mom summered in France as a kid and went to boarding school there." The way she says it. How it so casually rolls off the tongue. *Summered in France.* "That's how she knew Kai's dad."

"Did Kai grow up in Paris too?"

"Kai grew up in different townhouses in Manhattan but sort of lonely with nannies in and out."

"How did your mom become so close with him?"

"My mom saw herself in Kai. They both had dads who were tough, not really compassionate, wealthy."

"I thought you said Kai's dad and your mom were friends?"

"*Were* friends. Not anymore."

"Oh," I say. "So what's the story with Kai's dad?"

"Let's just say he wasn't a good person. Kai connected to my mom because she's so motherly, so caring, you know? Kai's mom died when Kai was about twelve. When he needed someone to lean on, Deena was there for him. She used to say, 'He's a child without a mother.' Then at a certain point, Kai wanted to leave his boarding school. He was so unhappy there. So he moved in with us soon after that."

"It sounds complicated."

"It is complicated," she says, and shrugs. "I haven't seen my father since I was little, and I always wanted a bigger family. It's been nice to have Kai around. He's always been like a brother. The only simple thing about it is that Kai and I both have shitty fathers. Both were nonexistent. Sorry I'm being so blunt about it."

"It's okay. My father isn't around either," I say.

A common thread between us. Two girls without fathers.

She scoots over to the mini fridge and shows me a glass bottle without a label. "My mom's friend makes this small-batch vodka. It's really good." She takes a swig and hands it to me.

I think of what my mom said before I left, how she worried about me drinking. I've spent so much of my life avoiding anything that remotely had to do with alcohol that I feel tired from so much resistance. But I need to lighten up. I'm not my dad. I want to be the kind of girl who walks into a spa and drinks handmade vodka with Julia Patterson.

I sip from it, the vodka burning my lips, and quickly I feel a buzz through my belly. Ivy's dad keeps a small bottle of bourbon in their kitchen. We've had a couple of tastes of that, the intense smoky aftertaste. This is nothing like that.

Julia has a little bead of sweat above her lip from the humidity, and I almost want to reach forward and kiss it off her. She takes off her robe and steps into the hot tub, immersing herself. "Aren't you coming in?"

I take off my robe, a thrill tussling inside me, my shoulders bare, dangling my feet in the warm water. Our eyes float toward each other, and she takes my hand, leading me in. Our faces almost touching. My body tingling from the vodka, from the warmth, from being so close to her.

"Can I tell you something?" she says.

"Of course." I wonder if she's going to tell me that she wants to kiss me. My heart is racing like crazy.

"Do you know why we're partners for the *Jane Eyre* project?"

"No, why?"

"Because I asked if we could be paired together."

I've never had anyone tell me that they purposely wanted to be paired with me for anything.

"Really?" My hand trembles under the water. I wonder if she notices. "Why?"

"You come up with so many cool ideas in that class. When we were first assigned *Jane Eyre*, I was dreading it. But you were the only person who wasn't embarrassed by any of the questions Ms. Taylor asked."

"Teacher's kid," I say. "I don't mind raising my hand."

"Well, it inspired me. I wanted to work with someone who had real ideas. So I asked her. And she said yes, but then I got worried you would think I wasn't smart enough. Or that I couldn't be analytical enough. I was intimidated by you, Bean."

"Me? Are you kidding? I was intimidated by *you*. With your mom's company. All of the attention she gets. The magazine articles. The famous people."

"That's her, Bean. That's not me," she says. "And my mom's wheelhouse is *not* Nineteenth-Century Lit."

"True, but your mom is so, I don't know, elevated," I say. "I hope you don't think it's weird that I'm saying that."

"A lot of people feel that way. You're not alone in that."

Her blue eyes sparkle. I don't know if it's the water, or the soft lighting in here, but Julia Patterson glistens. Music streams in from somewhere, and it's a song by the girl with the baby voice. "*Say yes to me,*" she's singing.

Ivy, Brooks, and Nico would say it's corny, like a teen movie from the '90s—the music, the hot tub, the robes. But they're not here. I don't want to think about them. I want to be goofy and sink into this water with Julia.

She bites her lip and wraps her finger around my pinkie toe.

"What are you doing?" I say. "Trying to crack my toes?"

"Come here, Bean," she says softly.

I scoot over, and I wonder if I'll ever feel anything more clearly than I do now, my chest aching to kiss her. The heat rising up to my brain, and I feel dizzy almost, so I get out of the tub and sit on the edge. Julia hops up next to me, and our thighs touch. We both start giggling even though nothing is funny, but everything is funny. My breath is so loud it knocks against my ears.

"Can I kiss you?" I say, then lean forward so close to her, my hand on her elbow. If I don't touch her, kiss her lips, I'm going to pass out.

"You better," she says.

I lean forward and close my eyes, and our mouths touch, and it's like my whole body lights on fire, between my thighs, in my chest, in my feet even. I want to do something like place my hand in her hair or somewhere like on her hip, the way you see people kissing each other in movies and on television. The way I've seen people in school in the hallway making out, but I can't move anything, except for my head. I can hardly breathe.

I kiss her soft lips, sweet as candy. I think of a Tootsie Pop. I want to laugh, and I know I shouldn't laugh, but I can't hold it back.

"What? What is it?" she says.

"I had a funny thought."

"Now you have to tell me. You can't just kiss someone, exclaim that you have a funny thought, and not share."

"When I was kissing you, I thought of a Tootsie Pop."

We burst out laughing, our bodies still clinging to each other.

"At least tell me the flavor that I am. And don't you dare say cherry," she says.

"Never cherry," I say in almost a whisper. "Grape. Chocolate on the inside."

I blush saying that to her. It sounds so sexual.

"I've been wanting you to do that for a long time," she says. "Did you know that?"

"Me? You've been wanting *me* to do that?"

"Well, truth be told, I've been wanting to kiss you for a while, but you beat me to it," she says, her face pink and flushed. "I feel like I'm going to pass out. Let's go in the cold plunge."

We hop into a small but deep pool that's freezing cold. "Two minutes, Bean. You can do it. It'll give you the best serotonin rush. It's amazing for your immune system." It actually feels refreshing, jarring me back to reality. Isn't it funny—it doesn't even feel that cold? We jump out of the pool and wrap the robes around us. Julia lightly tugs at my robe tie. The only kisses I've ever had before were Margo Schultz at camp on the boat dock and Zoe Peluso in the bathroom at the eighth-grade dance because of a dare. No tongue.

"I've never done this before," I tell her, though it's so embarrassing to admit it.

"Your lips are shivering," she says, and runs her finger on them.

"It's from the cold pool," I say. But it's not.

It's her. It's all her.

9

In the morning, just as I'm opening my eyes, my mom is on the edge of my bed, rubbing my calves. "Sorry to wake you up, but I'm off to a meeting."

She's a board member for the Homeless Children's Education Fund because it's not enough for her to teach kids all day and grade papers and listen to her friends' problems. She's got to solve the problems of homeless kids too. I'm kidding, of course. My mother is amazing, but lately she hasn't been home a lot. Also, she just started dating Doug, and they are going out to lunch after the meeting. Doug is sober and has a five-year-old daughter who lives with him.

I want to tell her about the cold plunge last night, about the barn, how romantic it was, but then I'd have to tell her about everything else. About Julia. About the spa in the basement. About how much I liked Deep. Too many questions for this morning, and I'm a little hungover from the vodka and the oxytocin burst in my brain.

"Was it fun?" she says.

I'm still trying to hold on to those feelings I had last night, that rush pulsing through my chest. I glance down at my phone. Endless texts from Ivy, Brooks, and Nico.

Brooks: Did it get deep?

Ivy: How deep is your love?

Nico: Bean, we're going to torture you with Deep puns until you tell us about the party.

Ivy: Meet at my house at 5

"It was fine," I say to my mom. "People were really nice." I suddenly realize that I didn't even meet Deena Patterson. At least, not a formal introduction.

"How was it spending time with Julia?" she says.

"Mom, stop fishing."

"Okay . . . but just so you know, I'm open to listening to any details you want to share with me," she says playfully, and kisses me on the knee. "I won't be home until six."

"I might be at Ivy's later," I say. "I guess I'll see you when I see you."

She gets up and slowly walks to my bedroom door. "Maybe you could babysit for Doug's daughter one night? So he and I can go out to dinner instead of just lunch dates? He'd pay you well," she says.

"Doesn't the little girl have a mother?" I say, and roll my eyes.

"Bean, that's not nice," she says. "His daughter's name is Caroline. She lives with Doug, and you know that."

"Mom, I'm exhausted. I was up late. Can I think about this another time?"

I'm not used to my mom being so busy and not being around. When my father was sick, and years before that, my mom was home all the time. Too much. She was always talking on the phone to his sister, his cousin, my grandparents, giving them all updates. As if updates would make the situation better, giving us some control over a man who'd decided to remove himself from everyone he knew. My parents hadn't been married all that long, but she was still the conduit to his family. She was the mother of his child.

Theoretically, it had been *my* idea that my mom started dating. Maybe I'm taking too much credit, which is entirely possible. But one night the two of us were in her bed eating Chinese food, and I turned to her and asked her if she thought she'd ever fall in love again. My dad was still alive. She didn't want to put me through the agony of dating, she told me. She felt like she had put me through enough.

"It's me and you now, kid," she said in that kind of cheesy, but comforting way.

But I dreaded her saying that. I listened to my mom for years talking to her friends and helping them through their problems, telling them that they're not alone. Couldn't they do the same for her? Why did it have to be *me and her*?

"You should find someone you can hang out with, Mom," I said to her. "Like a man. You should have a boyfriend."

Now she has a boyfriend, and he has a daughter.

"You're not going to expect us to be like one of those blended families you see on TV, are you?"

"Bean, I would never make you do anything as normal seeming as that."

"Thank god," I say. "Okay, fine. I'll babysit her sometime."

10

I sleep for a few more hours, dreams of white sheets floating in the wind. Julia and I running through the grass, a white wreath in my hair. Except it's not my hair. My hair is white. I stop running and touch it, staring at Julia in complete bewilderment. It wakes me up, startling me. The back of my neck damp. I shuffle through a book on dreams my mom has on her shelf. Hair in dreams can symbolize a transformation: *You're in the process of becoming your own person.*

That can't be right. I can't be becoming my own person if I've never felt so confused in my life. Femme isn't my thing. Right? *Right?* I'm not one of those girls. How could I have possibly fit in there last night? With Harmony floating around like a fairy. Me and Julia making out in her mom's basement spa. Was any of it even real?

I don't know if I can do another one of those. Sensory overload.

Around five o'clock, I walk over to Ivy's. Nico and Brooks are already in her room, and they're standing in front of some large object that's about three feet tall, hiding it behind them. "We've got a surprise for you," Nico says.

"Where's Ivy?" I say, looking around the room.

"Don't worry. She's in the bathroom," he says. "Come on, try to guess what we have."

"A dead body?" I say.

"Guess again," Nico says.

"A third grader? Honestly, I don't know."

Nico and Brooks hop in the opposite direction to reveal a vintage-looking trunk. Brooks makes a big deal waving his hands around like it's some magic trick and opens it up.

"What do you have here?" I say. "And what are we doing?"

"It's time for a little dress-up. You've been kissed, and we're going to celebrate," Nico says.

"I got some stuff from the Renaissance Faire a few weeks ago. Plus, I did some secret thrifting and picked up lace shirts, see-through slips, and a bunch of stud belts. It'll be decadent. We'll do a photo shoot."

Ivy shuffles into the room and collapses on her bed.

"Ivy, we're playing dress-up," Brooks says. But it sounds more like a command.

She shrugs. "Have fun last night?" she says coldly.

In an instant, the whole mood shifts. I straighten my back.

"What's your problem?"

"Not everyone can be twirling in a cloud of love like you, Bean." It stings.

"Are we really doing this?" I say. "I just hung out with her one night."

She holds up her phone, and there's a screenshot of an Instagram post. It's a photo of me and Harmony talking, the two of us holding hands after she spoke.

"I didn't realize they were going to post that," I say. I'm

intrigued, because I know Julia said that she helps approve the photos on that account. I don't want to show my friends that I'm pleased. Clearly Ivy's not.

"Would you have just left this little conversation with Harmony out of the details completely?" Ivy says. "Pretended like it didn't happen?"

"I don't have to pretend anything. Harmony and I spoke. It's not a secret. They caught a moment, that's all." That seems to satisfy her.

"What did she say?"

"Not much. She's at a very different place in her life now that she's with Deep. She's happy. I spent all of five minutes with her."

Ivy picks at her nails. She won't look at me.

I remember the first day of school. They told me to sit on the "buddy bench." Sit there and you'll make friends in no time, the dean said. But the kids either strolled by like I was invisible or snickered as they passed. A school failure, this buddy bench, propelling kids into being social pariahs. *She's been there for twenty minutes*, I heard one girl say to another.

Seconds later Ivy was standing in front of me. Her hair not as long as it is now, her curls soft around her face.

"That's a pretty intense quote for the first day of school," Ivy said, and pointed at my T-shirt.

I looked down at my shirt, adorned with a Sylvia Plath quote: *I desire things which will destroy me in the end.*

In retrospect, not the best choice. I was only in the seventh grade.

"I thought I was playing it safe with Sylvia Plath," I joked.

"Not at Talentum," she said. "They only know Emily Dickinson."

"Well, I impressed *you*, didn't I?" I said. And that's when Ivy Cohen-Smith rescued me from the buddy bench, sweeping me under her brilliant and protective wing.

"It's going to be so different for us, you know, going forward," she says now, her face framed with disappointment.

"Why is it going to be so different?" I say to her. "Because I kissed a girl?"

"Because of Julia, Bean. Because of who she is. Because of who her mother is. They take over people's lives. I'm afraid she's going to take over your life."

This is not just about what happened with Harmony. I can see right through it—the jealousy. It happened years ago when I first met Nico in the ninth grade, and she invited me for a sleepover. *What, are you going to start sleeping at Nico's every weekend now?* I remember Ivy saying. Her staring at me like I had dropped her from a twenty-foot cliff. I quickly remedied it, making sure Ivy and Nico met at the little coffee shop where Ivy and I used to go before it closed. *This is my best friend, Ivy,* I said when I introduced her to Nico, emphasizing *best* so there was no confusion.

"Listen, Ivy," I say, and crawl on the bed next to her. I rub her ankle, rolling it back and forth between my palms. "The only thing that'll change is that I'm going to have better skin."

Ivy falls back on the bed laughing, then nudges me with her foot.

"What? It's true!" I laugh. "They gave out Deep Glow packets last night," I say, and take a handful from my bag and toss them on the bed.

"Make it rain Deep Glow," Nico says, and grabs a few packets, chucking them up in the air.

"Speaking of people we like to kiss," Brooks says, and hops up, holding his phone. "I just got another text from Sal."

"*Oooh,*" we shout as he scurries out of the bedroom to call Sal, the boy from Bloomington whose father makes high-end Italian suits. Our reaction is so cheerful, so supportive. I wish they had the same casual reaction about me hanging out with Julia.

"So tell us something cool about last night," Nico says.

"Last night I ate strawberries that cost eighty dollars."

"How did they taste?" she says.

"How do you think eighty-dollar strawberries tasted?" I say. "Amazing."

Soon everything calms down and I'm describing the all-white wardrobes and the inspirational talks and how beautiful Kai Edwards is. We split up a cannabis gummy Brooks gleaned from his dad's stash. Once it kicks in, we dance around in our costumes for a while, our bodies buzzing like this is the only place we should be, ever. Except my mind is with Julia, and how the two of us were together last night. Our hands floating back and forth in the water, making ripples.

Soon, we collapse onto Ivy's bed and Ivy rants about this new story on the pink shirts for the paper, how good it'll feel to piss off Brian-Michael and his friends, and how it'll shock the Talentum staff. After the whole historical-society scandal, I remember overhearing one of the school secretaries say, *I hope I never do anything to make Ivy Cohen-Smith want to come after me.*

Within an hour, Nico is lightly snoring, her big red hair down, spread out at the bottom of the bed. Brooks is on the phone again with Sal in the other room. Ivy plays with my hair, pulling it apart piece by piece, massaging my scalp the way I like it.

"Pull harder," I say.

"So demanding, Bean," she says, and tugs a little tighter. I think of Julia, how soft her lips were. The moist air. I squeeze my eyes and open them quickly. I want to be present here with Ivy, but it feels impossible. I inhale; I think of Julia. I move; I think of Julia. I open a book; I think of Julia. It feels physically painful knowing I have to wait an entire day to see her. I want to make myself small so Julia can carry me around in her pocket with her.

"You joke about strawberries and skin serums," Ivy says. "But it's true. It's going to be all different now. Not bad, but just different."

I stare back at her, and there are tears in her eyes. Ivy has always been the girl I've happily followed, and she's never led me astray. But this is new territory for us. I've never had a girlfriend. She's never had a boyfriend, or anyone else, for that matter. Since we've been best friends, we've made all our changes together, every step of the way. And now I'm doing something on my own, with Julia.

"Ivy, come on. Give Julia a chance. You'd really like her."

"I might like Julia," she says, tugging on my hair, "but I'll never like *them*."

I don't respond to her because I don't need to. I don't tell her that I've been waiting for this feeling for so long. That feeling of warmth when you love someone.

Like I do.

11

Monday morning, Julia, who is always late, is sitting at the desk in our lit class. Her hands folded. Her copy of *Jane Eyre* wide open. A pen wobbling in her mouth.

I've been partners with Julia for eight days, and I've never seen her on time.

I slide in next to her. My face burns from the heat of being close to her again. I haven't seen her since Saturday.

"You're here before me. Did the world explode? Are we living in a different universe?"

"I was excited to see you," she says, blushing.

I don't know what to say. I can barely catch my breath.

"Julia, I'm glad to see you on time," Ms. Taylor says, and approaches our shared desk. "I think Frances's punctuality is rubbing off on you."

"Frances is definitely rubbing off on me," she says, and I crack a smile so big that I might almost explode with nervous laughter. Instead, I bury my face in my hands.

"Okay, ladies, I want a topic for your *Jane Eyre* project by the end of the period," she says, and walks away.

Julia's eyes twinkle when she looks at me. "What do you think our topic should be? Are we going with free will like you said last week?"

I shuffle through the book, pushing the pages left and right. My mind scrambles. "I like the free will idea, but I also love that Jane Eyre's not subservient to anyone," I say. "How about we do a paper on that? It's not terribly original, but we can make it work."

"What do you mean *subservient*?"

I open a page that I've bookmarked with a rectangular pink sticker and read it out loud to her. "'Women feel just as men feel . . . it is narrow-minded in their more privileged fellow-creatures to say that they ought to confine themselves to making puddings and knitting stockings.' That's written in 1847, when women barely had any rights."

"I didn't even read it that closely," Julia says. "Some of the text, I'm not going to lie, just sounds like gibberish."

I hear Scotch Steiner coughing behind us. Julia doesn't seem to notice. She skirts toward me like she's going to kiss me. "How are you even concentrating right now?" she says.

But I don't respond because I can feel Scotch staring. His beady little eyes. I whip my head around to him.

"Are you two going to, like, hump each other right here?" he whispers, and grins.

"Shut up, Scotch. You're disgusting," I say. He sulks in his chair.

"I'm glad you did that," she whispers. "Because of Deep, I usually avoid conflict. I can't just tell people to shut up."

"I don't understand."

"Deep. Our reputation. I can't give anyone something to talk about. My mom's been very explicit about that."

"So you can't defend yourself from guys like him?"

"It would be *promoting reactivity*, as Deena calls it. She doesn't want anyone to go after us. You know like, 'Deena Patterson's bitchy daughter mouths off in school' or something. I always have to play it cool."

Appearances, I think. I see how that must be a constant struggle, to not express how you really feel.

That whole week, Julia and I get hall passes to see each other. I sit there restless in my classes waiting for her to appear in the door-way, signaling me to come out. We scatter down the hall, giggling, our hands intertwined. For years, I've seen so many other couples doing this, heart-eyed, crashing into each other. I never thought it would be me.

Kenny, Harlow, and Grace, in their long lace skirts and their tight white crop tops, even though the dress code clearly states you're not supposed to wear crop tops, saunter down the hallway, calling my name when they see me, no matter how many people are between us. "Hiiii, Beaannn." I blush as they wave their fingers at me.

Thursday, Julia takes me to Talentum's old creepy basement, where they keep the art supplies. They changed the locks after Jory Matson got caught giving a blow job to Brian Kaplan last year.

"I thought they locked this place up?" I say, looking around the hallway as she jiggles the lock.

"I have a key," she says, laughing, as if it's the dumbest question I've ever asked.

"How?"

"Um . . . I asked for it."

This tracks. What Julia Patterson wants, she gets.

Downstairs, Julia rubs her palm against my hip and kisses me hard as the old boiler clanks away. I want to fry inside it.

I'm flustered when we walk out, I fix my hair, straighten my clothes. I've seen people walk through that basement door before, their hair a mess, their clothes untucked. People look at me in school, but usually not because I'm coming up from the basement. Now it's me and Julia, giving that air of desire like something happened down there. And it did.

I go to bed wanting to text Julia, tell her that I'm thinking about her, but it feels like too much, like I don't want to scare her off. I stalk the Deep Instagram page to see what they've posted this week. A picture of Deena holding a green drink. A four-day detox. Their new Deep Face Oil. Kenny, Harlow, Grace, and a few other girls dancing in a circle.

I dream of holding hands with Julia, in the spa, in her barn, in the meadow behind her house. I imagine myself in a white slip dress, something with a lace trim. My body exposed to her, all of me. Who are she and I together? Are we *anyone* together? I feel so unsure of myself.

Are you my girlfriend? I text her. It feels like an anvil drops on my stomach, and right as I send it, I regret it. I look so desperate.

I press that little unsend button, but it doesn't work. I've never done anything like this before, longed for someone so badly that it hurts, like my chest bone is going to pop out of my skin.

Those three dots appear. She's writing something. Then nothing.

Finally her words come back: **Yes Bean you're my girlfriend. Your heart is mine.**

12

One day after school that next week, Julia takes me back to her house because her mom is trying out a new lymphatic-drainage facial.

"Frances, I'm so glad you're here," Deena says from a table, her hair wrapped up in a towel, the smell of lavender lingering in the air. A woman in white stands behind the table, stroking Deena's collarbone.

"Deena gets to try out the new facials down here," Julia says. "Don't you, Mom?"

"Well, you know our bodies can't work properly until all the toxins are pushed out," Deena says, and laughs heartily as the woman smothers her cheeks with a milky substance. "So, do you girls want to try this new lymphatic-drainage facial too? It's like getting rid of all the bad energy you've collected throughout the week."

"Wanna get a facial?" Julia says to me.

"Like, right now?" I say.

Suddenly, two other women in white appear, bright skin, big smiles on their faces. They bow to us in prayer position.

Ten minutes later, I'm on a heated table, under a silk sheet with a fluffy blanket, getting my face depuffed. Julia reaches over and scratches her nail softly on my hand. Expelling bad energy.

———

The next day, at the caf with Ivy, Brooks, and Nico, the four of us pick at greasy Tater Tots. I wonder what Julia eats for lunch. Probably wild grilled salmon. A cleansing green drink. Salad dressing with nutritional yeast.

"You're barely eating," Ivy says.

"Everyone loses their appetite when they're in love," Nico says.

"And it makes you dress like the other person too, I see," Brooks says, pointedly looking at my white shirt. I'm wearing Julia's white lace top under my black leather jacket. I give him the finger.

"Did you hear about their new lawsuit?" Ivy says, slipping a Tater Tot in her mouth, seeming pleased with herself.

"Some woman did this beesting therapy that Deena Patterson recommended and almost died."

"I don't believe you," I say.

"Fine, don't believe me. But it was in the *Science Journal*, Bean. Look it up."

I try to ignore her because I know what tactic this is. It's Ivy throwing Deep under the bus because she's worried about our friendship. I nod, like it's the most fascinating thing I've ever heard.

"Okay, okay, enough bullshit about beestings. We want details about the royal couple," Brooks says. "Come on, you've been making out with her all over school. You're wearing her white lace top like a varsity jacket. Tell us how you feel about her. Tell us what it's like being Julia Patterson's girlfriend."

"She's a good kisser," I say. "We're kissing. I can't deny that."

"You're glowing," Nico says. "You look like you're in love."

"I just went for a facial yesterday at her mom's house. It was pretty amazing."

"What about your mom?" Ivy says, and shoves another Tater Tot in her mouth. "Has your mom hung out with her, like outside of school?"

"You're going to make fun of me," I say.

"What?" Nico says. "Tell us."

"I'm embarrassed to take her to my house."

Julia practically lives in a castle, enormous and mystifying. The barn in the back. The white halls. The staff cleaning up after her. The spa in the basement.

"You should never be embarrassed about who you are," Ivy says. "Don't let them put their shallow wellness fantasies in your head, Bean."

"I'm not embarrassed about who I am," I say, and hike my back up straight, confident. "This is why I don't want to tell you anything. You're so judgmental."

"*I'm* judgmental? You're talking about being embarrassed of your house, Bean. Your cozy place with all of your mom's books? Anyone you fall in love with should love you for who you are, where you live, how you dress."

Ivy's waiting for my response, but I can't meet her eyes. She's got all the answers, doesn't she? Sometimes she's just impossible to talk to.

"You don't think I know that, Ivy? Really?"

She sinks into the hard orange cafeteria chair, saying nothing.

But she doesn't have to say anything. I know what she's thinking. There's that heavy feeling between us. She just doesn't get it.

"You won't have to worry about inviting her over, Bean, because next thing you know, you'll be living together," Brooks says, his tone light and wry. "What's that joke about lesbians? They bring a U-Haul to the first date. Gets serious *real* quick."

Ivy's gazing down at the pile of greasy Tater Tots, swirling one of them in a mound of ketchup.

"I thought you were trying not to be a jealous bitch," I say. It comes out harsher than I want it to.

"I'm sorry. But I'm not ready to be a maid of honor. Knowing Julia, she would make me dress up in a white lacy dress and run through a field with a crown of crystals," Ivy says. "Forgive me if I miss you."

My heart breaks a little hearing her say that.

"I'm not going anywhere, Ives."

Ivy and I were connected long before the Victorian wardrobe. Long before I dyed my hair. Long before the parasol. I guess we evolved this way together. I went along with it because I liked the idea of following in the footsteps of my beatnik, nonconformist grandmother. And I watched Ivy blossom into this world, her showing me pictures of black women in studded collars, black lace gloves, and draped pearls. She read me essays about the connection between goth and blackness.

"If you think about it, Bean, goth is all about pain and trauma and horror, which matches Black history. Enslavement. Violence against Black people. It's so clearly right there in front of me."

Then the T-shirt with the saying SO GOTH I WAS BORN BLACK. That's when she stopped straightening her hair, too, letting it go natural. We'd pass all the girls in our school with their long hair, their curling-iron beach waves.

"I have to be the opposite of those girls, Bean. I can't pretend to have long wavy hair like them, that's not what I look like. I have to look like me."

That's when I cut my hair, too, bought one of those Japanese razors and started slicing off pieces. Ivy dyed my hair platinum blond, the two of us in the drugstore with boxes of bleach and hair color. We both found new identities. I pushed away from my father and his sickness, my mother and her presence at this school. I turned myself into someone else. Then it became the four of us, me, Ivy, Nico, and Brooks, the outcasts at the school of East Coast elitist spawn.

Now I know she sees me as someone else. Someone who fits in with other people, girls who are very different than what I used to be. Very different than her.

13

I've gotten into a habit of doing a Deep Glow mask in the morning for the past two weeks, and even *my* skin is clearing up, those crusty zits disappearing more and more each day. I'm getting used to being this person, the kind of person who's in love with Julia Patterson. The kind of person who wakes up fifteen minutes earlier for school just to put a face mask on. I spritz my neck with a spirit mist Julia gave me. It's called Allow, and it's a mix of patchouli and lemon, which, according to the little raw-hemp paper it came with, "encourages us to become connected to our spirit." I've never felt more myself. It's like it's going to be this way forever.

My mom walks in my room on her way out the door and scrunches her nose. "Do I smell patchouli?"

"It's a spirit mist, and yes, it has patchouli in it."

"I thought only hippies from the nineties used patchouli. It reminds me of when I lived in San Francisco—" she says, then stops, noticing the mask on my face. "Wait. You're doing all of this now? You're going to be late for school."

"My face needs to breathe."

"Your face needs to breathe?"

"You don't understand anything," I say. "You don't have to work at your skin like I do." I go to close the door, but she stops me.

"Bean, you're perfect the way you are."

"You're my mom. Of course you would say that." I wash the mask off my face and stare at myself in the mirror. One of the vanity lights is out above the sink, and it gives off a hazy sheen. My translucent skin, so heavenly. My white peasant top and the way it gathers around my shoulders so it shows off my collarbones. Even my straw hair looks angelic around my face. I like this girl. I like who I see. Doesn't my mom see how much I've changed for the better?

"I don't think I'm going to wear any makeup to school today. I think I'm going to go natural."

She stands there staring at me, her face in a muddled confusion.

"Who are you? And what did you do with my daughter?"

In the bathroom, fixing lips, a new glossy sample from the Deep store. Kenny, Harlow, and Grace saunter in, lean themselves in a line against the row of sinks.

"Bean, we've been looking for you," Kenny says.

"You have?" I say, stunned. These are girls who never spoke to me before the Femme gathering.

"Why are you looking for me?" I say carefully. My mind starts racing. Are they going to tell me that I should stay away from Julia? That I'm not good enough for her?

"Why?" Harlow giggles. "Because we want to hang out with you, you silly Bean."

"You're so funny, Bean," Grace says.

The three of them pepper me with a rash of questions. *Where do you get your clothes? Who cuts your hair in those layers like that? Do you think you'll come to another Femme gathering?*

"I'm not sure. When's the next one?" I say.

"About two weeks," Kenny says. "Ask Julia about it. I know she'd want you to go again."

I smile, not knowing what to say. "She has so many people in her life, why does she need me to go?" I say, and it comes out sounding so insecure. But even though I barely know Kenny, she has that kind of open face where you can almost feel compelled to tell her anything.

"She doesn't need you to go, she wants you to go. There's a big difference. Me and Harlow and Grace, we have each other, but Julia, she's more of the type who flies solo."

"It's different for her, since she's Deena's daughter," Harlow says.

"She's not like us," Grace says. She's right. They all have the same look as Julia, the same hair, the same skin, the same clothes, but she's different than them.

Kenny lifts the lid off a small bottle with a Deep label and mists her face, then pats it into her cheeks gently. She sprays Harlow and then sprays Grace. Watching them, how in sync they are, how Harlow and Grace lift their heads up just the right way, close their eyes with such trust, I feel myself thinking about Julia again.

I want them to drench me in that Deep mist. I want to be consumed by it.

"Want me to spray you too?" Kenny says. "The air is so dry in school, especially because this is such an old building. It's good to hydrate your face."

I nod my head yes, and I close my eyes, letting the mist rest on my skin.

14

"Why are we together?" I ask Julia.

It seems like an out-of-the-blue question, but after about three weeks together, or twenty-one days since the first time we kissed, I'm starting to feel insecure about our relationship.

It's not exactly the right time to feel insecure because she and I are making out under the full moon behind the trampoline while Caroline, my mom's boyfriend's daughter, who I got suckered into babysitting for, sleeps upstairs. There, with Julia in the grass, I feel free, wanting to touch her in places I've never touched anyone before, between the legs, down her pants, inside her thighs. I want her to explore me, and know me, understand me too. I want to tell her everything.

But if I'm going to tell her everything, I have to be truthful about my insecurity. We've been inseparable for a month since we started dating, but I don't understand why we're a couple. I don't understand why she likes me.

I have questions for Julia, and I hold my breath, fingering my sweatshirt until I get up the courage to ask her.

"Why are we together? Let's see . . . because you're amazing," she says.

"Too vague."

"Okay, because I gave you my orange the other day, and you peeled it?"

"It was a mandarin," I say.

"Bean, why are you doing this?"

I think about the next Femme gathering, which is a week from today. I think about how Julia is so involved in Deep. How her life is like clouds above mine. I don't know how we can possibly make this work. I take a few deep breaths because I know I'm making her so nervous.

"Are you literally asking me why I like you? Why I can't keep my hands off of you? Why I think about you all the time?" She pulls me into a hug, and I rest my head on her shoulder as she strokes my hair. "What's going on? Seriously?"

We are so close—so connected, the two of us—but I feel so intimidated by her still. Like I can't tell her the truth. I don't want to withdraw from her, though, so I have to spit it out.

"You haven't invited me to the next Femme gathering. And I wasn't sure if that meant something. I wasn't sure if you were going to phase me out."

"Phase you out like you're one of my mom's products? Are you kidding me?"

"I feel so silly. All of this is so new. And I've never been in a relationship before, and sometimes when I'm around Kenny, Harlow, and Grace, I feel like the resident vampire."

This she laughs at. Then she takes my hands in hers.

"I love the way you dress, Bean. It's one of the reasons I've fallen for you. Because of your individuality," she says. "And I'm sorry I didn't bring it up sooner. I thought you wouldn't want to come."

"What? Why would you think that?

"I didn't want to make you dress in all white. I didn't want to push all those girls on you who weren't your friends. Just because they're important to me, I didn't want to make it your thing too."

"You're not pushing anyone on me."

She bends down on one knee.

"Are you proposing to me?" I tease. "Because Brooks already thinks you're going to show up to my house one day with a U-Haul."

"Do you *want* to be part of Femme, Bean?" She strokes my arm slowly, looking up at me. "We can be part of something together, something bigger. You saw how much we do. You saw how all those girls responded. Teary-eyed, got excited for their future. I think you see that we've evolved way past Deep Glow. We're so much more than that." I love how talking about Deep makes her seem so energized.

I nod my head yes because I can hardly speak; my brain, buzzing like an instrument, I can feel it clicking inside me, growing louder and louder. Do I want to be part of Femme, part of Deep? I don't even know what that completely means. I know I have a sharp ache to sink into Julia, to do anything for her. But here is the truth: I also crave to be part of that elusive world, with the candles and the soft chanting and the healthy drinks and the words that are so free of anger. I couldn't turn back if I told her yes. And that's what I want. To say yes.

15

Glistening white. Calming white. Billowing white. Like a cloud, cloud upon clouds. "So pretty, so pretty," I keep saying, pointing at the linens draped from the ceiling. We're at the Deep shop on Main Street, a standalone building with gigantic loftlike windows, and I'm uncontrollably gawking.

Julia points up to the linens. "All of them are woven by a fair trade organization in Bangladesh so women can make living wages."

Ivy would probably question if the "fair trade" thing was even real.

"Beautiful," I say.

A girl I sort of recognize from the Femme gathering, her brown hair long in a soft tangle down her back, her glowy brown skin, a pink hue seeping through her cheeks, walks over to us. She has the gait of a dancer, so elegant.

"Bean, this is Katrina, our tech wiz," Julia says. "She'll probably be in charge of Google one day and leave us all behind."

"Julia, stop! Like I would ever leave Deep," Katrina says, laughing. "Bean, it's so nice to meet you." She shakes my hand. Her skin, so soft. Probably because she rubs some magical Deep oil into her skin daily.

Then Julia introduces me to Imani, who has a baby voice and

is wearing a white off-the-shoulder peasant shirt. "Imani is from LA," Julia says.

"Oh, why did you move to New Jersey?" I ask her.

"For Deep," she says with a tone like she's surprised that I would even ask such a question. "I came to one Femme gathering, then I stayed. Now I share everything with the girls. And Kai. They're my family."

My family. It's the third time, maybe fourth, that I've heard people say that. Julia about Kenny, Harlow, and Grace. Then Harmony in the barn when she was speaking at the meeting. Now Imani. I'm not sure what to make of it, if it's their language, or if they genuinely feel that way. Imani looks about my age. I wonder what made her decide to leave home at sixteen and just stay here.

"Give me everything you've got to make me look twenty years younger," a woman with a pink polo shirt and a white visor announces as she boldly walks in the store. "I don't care how much it costs. I want to look like Deena Patterson."

"Let's start with a hormone test," Julia says cheerfully, and leads the woman into a separate room.

"Why a hormone test?" I say to Katrina.

"Because it's all connected," Katrina says. "You can get all the filler and Botox you want, but if you want to see what's happening inside of you, we have to come up with a holistic plan that targets the whole body."

"You know a lot about this," I say.

"I've been working at Deep for over a year. Once you start working here, you get committed pretty quickly."

"What made you start working here if you're a tech person?" I say.

"It's a long story," Katrina says. "I was starting to age out of the foster system when I met Deena and Kai. Kai did a hypnosis technique on me, and he really helped me through my trauma. He still is."

"I didn't know hypnosis worked for trauma," I say.

Katrina looks at Imani, and they exchange a smile.

"Most people think hypnosis is a magic trick," Imani says. "But it's so much more."

"Yeah, they've been treating soldiers who have PTSD with hypnosis since the nineties," Katrina says. "Kai calls it a portal to the unconscious. It sort of takes the bad memories you have and restructures them in a positive way so we're in charge of our thoughts, which is pretty incredible. Because trust me, I was a mess when I first got here."

Imani lightly rubs Katrina's shoulders. "She's been through a lot."

"I'm sorry I'm asking you so many questions. I hope I'm not being intrusive," I say.

"No, I know most people in this town haven't encountered someone in the foster system. I get it."

Suddenly, I feel like an asshole thinking that my life is so bad. A sheltered asshole who lives in South Brent. Who attends Talentum. There are people who have much less. Maybe that's what Imani meant. It's possible she didn't have a home or a family to go back to.

"You look stunned," Katrina says, kind of laughing. "It wasn't a complete horror story. My foster parents sent me to after-school coding programs, which is why Julia said that before. But it is *my* story, if that makes sense. Anyway, growing up in the foster system, it's hard to feel like you're part of something," she says. "But Deep made me feel like I found my people."

"Same," Imani says. "I know I should have been living a healthy lifestyle being that I'm from LA, but believe me, I wasn't. It was all fast food. My parents constantly working and living in chaos. Now with all the meditation, eating clean, organic products in my body, I feel like a different person."

Three other women walk through the door, all of them with similar outfits, those six-hundred-dollar sneakers that are meant to look roughed up, with diamond tennis bracelets jingling from their wrists.

Katrina stiffens, lets out a long exhale. "Healing is multi-dimensional. Everyone is looking for different solutions," she says. "Even them." Katrina lifts her chin, motioning to the women. Shoulders back, a pageant girl's smile. "Hiiii, ladies." Her energy completely shifting.

"Is Deena in the store today?" They all want to know, with their puffy, Botoxed faces, their loud voices.

"Bean, so glad you're here." I turn around, and there's Harmony, her hair in a messy knot, wearing a white lace skirt and V-neck sheer cotton top. "You're like a breath of fresh air," she says. "Come with me. Julia's in the back waiting for you."

16

"Sorry for disappearing," Julia says. We're in the back offices. A row of glass windows. The smell of patchouli. Five women are gathered at a long table, all of them in white linen, working on laptops.

"I heard those women come in asking for my mom, so I had to make a quick exit," Julia says. "My mom has to hide back here from women like that. Otherwise they'll come in all day and ask to take selfies with her."

"Julia, don't say it like it's a bad thing," Harmony says. "They're not bad. They just—"

"They just want a piece of my mom," Julia says flatly.

"No, they feel inspired by her," Harmony says, and then looks at me. "They're not just customers. They're people whose lives have changed because of Deep. Whether it's one product or multiple products, or maybe a meditation class, or one of our wellness workshops, they feel heard. They feel like they belong. So we have to be kind to all of them."

At the end of the hall is Deena's office. It's decorated simply, with a white desk in the center, a wall of floor-to-ceiling bookshelves with magazines, crystals, books, and clear perfume bottles stylishly arranged. Light blazes through windows onto her perfectly uncluttered desk.

I think of my mom, with all her notebooks and the endless papers she's grading sprawled across the dining room table, the dining room chairs with cat scratches all over them. The messiness of her life.

Deena and Kai lean against her desk like they're having a serious conversation.

"Knock, knock," Julia says. "Is this a good time?"

Deena swoops around her desk. "Oh, yes, my darling," and she collects Julia into a hug, kissing her on both cheeks.

Then she reaches out to shake my hand, at least I thought that was what she was doing, until she takes my hands in hers, cupping them like she's holding a firefly.

"Frances Bean, it is so lovely to see you again. I didn't have nearly enough time to get to know you when we were trying out the lymphatic-drainage facials."

I don't know what to say, I don't want to embarrass myself or say the wrong thing, and I can feel my skin heating up. So I turn to face this massive clear crystal—like, it's about fifty pounds, sitting on a coffee table in front of a white couch. It takes up the whole table. I can't even imagine how much something like that costs. Thousands?

"I've never seen a crystal that big before," I say.

"Isn't it incredible?" Deena says, strolling over and stroking one of the large clear points. "It's quartz, which filters negative energy. I got it from a miner in New Mexico. The mineralogist called me from the desert and said, 'Deena, I have something special for you.' And oh, is it special."

"The only problem is how heavy it is when we have to take it outside for the monthly moon bath to get recharged," Julia says, and everyone laughs. I don't know what a moon bath is, but I go along with it.

"So Julia tells me you've been working as a babysitter?" Deena says.

"Yeah. I've been babysitting this kid down the street for the past year."

"Ah, so you're a caretaker," Kai says, tossing his long, silky hair away from his face. "Hi again, Frances. We met at the gathering."

I think of the little boy and how I let him throw M&M's in the backyard and run wild until it's time for bed. I'm not exactly a caretaker.

"I guess you could say that," I say.

"That's what we do here too," Kai says. "We take care of people. That's what you would be doing here at Deep if you worked for us. If you were part of Femme."

"See, Frances, I started Deep when my father got sick," Deena says. "I felt like the doctors weren't listening to my suggestions about alternative treatments. Then I started talking to other people, mostly women, who also felt abandoned by their doctors. If you're anxious or depressed or you gained weight, or you felt tired, or had acne, doctors will often tell you the same thing: get more rest, take this pill, or there's nothing wrong with you. I wanted other options. Because if you don't feel good, that's not in your head. That's *actually* how you feel."

"People come here, and we help them," Deena says. "Because

Western medicine failed them. Even if it's something small, like wanting their skin to glow again. Because how you feel on the inside reflects the outside."

"Deena always says that wellness should be for the masses. That's what we're doing here at Deep," Kai says.

Deena asks everyone to give her and me some time to speak alone. Julia tells me she'll see me out front, and she, Kai, and Harmony all walk out of the office.

"I sense you're nervous, Frances." She sits on the couch in front of the massive crystal and pats the spot next to her. "Come, sit. I just want to know more about you."

I fight not to pick my cuticles. I'm sure Deena would see that as a weakness.

"Julia is a special girl, isn't she?"

"Yes," I say. *I've never felt this way before about someone,* I want to tell her.

"She tells me that you have an independent spirit. And I can see that in you, Frances. But I also see a darkness in you. You remind me of me when I was young," she says. "I grew up without a mother. Just a father. He was the president of an enormous publishing company in France. The tabloids called him the 'Parisian press baron.'"

"What's a press baron?" I say.

"A press baron? It means he owned a lot of newspapers, and while none of those papers exist now, it made him a very rich man back in the 1970s and 1980s. I came to the States for college and never looked back. But when I was growing up, we lived in a huge house with fifty-one rooms. Who needs fifty-one rooms? As I mentioned, he got sick. The doctors wouldn't listen to different ideas about treatment. Plus, my father was stoic. He'd say he didn't need my help. It left me feeling powerless. Do you know that feeling, Frances?"

Yes, I know it well, I wanted to tell her. It was like she could see through me.

"Has there been anyone in your life like that?"

"My dad," I say.

It's not your job to take care of me, Bean, my dad would say. Or *It's not your fault, Bean*. But I wanted to take care of him. There were times when he was sober. They were short lived, sometimes three months, sometimes six months. Couldn't I help stretch that? Make it go longer? Stop him from getting "sick" again.

There was so much shame in having a dad who died practically on purpose. If dads die it's because of a car accident, or a heart attack or cancer. They don't die by choice. They don't die because they chose to drink themselves to death. And, yes, I know that's harsh and I know that being an alcoholic isn't a choice. I've been told this so many times at Alateen meetings that I could practically regurgitate the twelve steps on command. So many nights spent in the basement of a church, right down the hallway from the AA meetings, where all the alcoholics stood in the hallway and smoked cigarettes in the parking lot and drank coffee. I hated every second of it. Listening to kids' stories about how their parents made them stock beers in the fridge. How their dads would come home wasted. How their moms would scream.

For a split second I think about what my father would have been like if he had met Deena Patterson. Could she have changed his life?

"Tell me about him," Deena says.

"He was an alcoholic," I say quietly.

"Ah, I know that well," she says.

She takes my hands in hers. Almost whispering to me. Her thick voice, wrapping around me, motherly.

"You're here with us now," she says. "I think you'd be an excellent fit at Deep, Frances. I hope you take the time to think about it."

17

Just as I exit Deena's office, I hear a sound coming from an open door with a sign on it that reads MEDITATION ROOM. Is someone chanting in there? I slowly, so slowly, peer into the room.

Then I see legs.

They're unmistakably Harmony's legs, because I notice her delicate gold ankle bracelet.

As I peek in further, I see Kai's body on top of her.

They're passionately kissing, her hand in his long hair, their mouths connected, their bodies intertwined. I didn't expect to see them, the table beneath them squeaking back and forth. I can hear Kai moaning, and I have to stop myself from gasping.

One of Harmony's legs is wrapped tightly around Kai's hips. Their half-naked bodies shuddering against each other, his face now buried in her neck, his pants down, and her lace skirt hiked up. Harmony's head arches back.

I trip backward into the doorway, making a sound, and Harmony opens her eyes, filled with shock. I gain my balance and run down the corridor. I've definitely seen something I'm not supposed to.

———

Julia and I go back to her house afterward, and the smell of luxury in here is inescapable. She has a whole vanity (white of course) filled with Deep skin care, a set of crystals on a mirrored tray, white fuzzy carpeting, white linen sheets like butter, and a velvet headboard that matches the white walls. It's a cloud upon a cloud. The only pop of color in her room is a pink neon sign in script that says her name: *Julia*.

Her bed is the softest bed I've ever been in, and we sink into each other. I roll down her white jeans and watch her face light up in surprise. I kiss her down her thighs in between her legs, her long tanned legs, and I've never felt like this before, like I want to bury myself inside her and never look back. I want to tell her I love her, that she and I are the center of everything.

A flash in my mind of Harmony and Kai, and I want to move like that with Julia, reach down into her and hear her moan. And the more she feels, the more she loosens her hips, the more I crawl into her. The weight of her pressed up against me, until I feel her turn inside out.

I spent so many years wondering what it was like to have a girlfriend. Someone who wanted to kiss me and touch me. Someone who wanted to run her fingers through my hair and hold my hand at the movie theater. I place my hands on her soft, soft skin and kiss her tightly. Everything I imagined is just like this.

This is all I want.

———

"So . . ." Julia says. "What do you think?" Her head rests gently in the crook of her arm. "Do you think you'll want to work at Deep?"

"I guess I'd want to know more about what I'd be doing," I say. "And you know, what the dynamic is there. Who's in charge."

"Well, my mom, of course," she says. "But also Kai sometimes. I guess he's like a manager."

I think about Harmony and Kai again, the way their eyes were connected. Like he had a spell over her. The way her fingers were planted on his cheek, as if he was breathing life into her.

"I saw him and Harmony having sex," I say.

She sits up, startled. "Oh, that."

"*Oh that?* What, is the meditation room like their hookup spot, and I accidently stumbled upon it? I thought you do sound baths in there."

She grasps for the right words. "Let's put it this way. Kai . . . falls in love harder than most people."

"What does that mean?" I say.

"It means he's a really intense person. He's also a spiritual person. The two of them have something very special," she says. "But Kai is everyone's emotional-support person. Because he lost his mom at a young age, he wants to spread love that he missed out on. You know how Wendy was to the Lost Boys in *Peter Pan*?"

"Yeah, sure."

"Well, they're the Lost Girls."

Julia kisses my neck and my shoulder. "Trust me, both Kai and Harmony are emotionally disciplined people. If you saw that in there, then it means there was a reason for it."

"Yeah, because they were horny," I say, and laugh.

"No, Bean. Because they want to express their love."

Later that night, Harmony calls me. "Bean, I wanted to talk to you about what you saw earlier," she says. I thought she would sound shaky, embarrassed. But she sounds confident, like she needs to console me.

"Oh, it's no big deal," I say. "I shouldn't have poked my head into that room."

"It is a big deal," she says. "We believe in meeting love where it finds you at Deep."

I'm not sure what that means, but I'm tempted to call bullshit.

"Okay."

"Sometimes love finds you in the meditation room, and you have to express that love," she says. Weird. It sounds a lot like what Julia said to me about them. "When you come from a home with a single mom, like you and I did, you don't get to see the full expression of love. You don't see parents kissing and devoting themselves to each other. But that's what Kai and I were doing in that moment. I hope you understand that it's an important part of growth as a loving human who wants healthy relationships."

I don't expect to be so taken by what she says, but now I get it. I get that there had been something missing in me for so long and I feel like I found it with Julia. Of course if Harmony and I are anything alike, and I know we are, then she's doing the same thing with Kai. She's desperate to connect. She's desperate to love. How can I judge that?

18

Ivy, Brooks, and Nico are waiting for me at the park about a half mile from my house. I've hardly seen them outside school in the past few weeks because I've been spending so much time with Julia. I know they're going to give me shit about it. About not showing up to the newspaper meetings. Plus, I'm wearing a white crushed-taffeta dress with tiny flowers and my cropped black velvet jacket. That will most likely be the thing that irritates them. That I'm trying to *hide* my true self or something.

I watch Brooks and Nico swinging, the two of them both dressed in black, like flying crows in the wind. Ivy leans against the gazebo with her parasol wide open, and I give her a big hug and we rock back and forth together, doing a little dance.

"*Bean, Bean, Bean,*" Brooks says, and sings that song to me about the sunny day and the cemetery gates.

"So what's new, lover girl?" Ivy says. "We've hardly seen you."

"I saw you yesterday at school. What are you talking about?"

"Feels like centuries," she says.

"We just miss you is all," Nico says, slowing down her swing. "Maybe we can hang out tonight? We can do a little sleepover at my house. Watch *Heathers*?"

"Our love is God. Let's go get a slushie," Brooks says, and hops off his swing.

"I can't tonight. There's a Femme gathering. I have to go to it," I say. A look of judgment passes across their faces, and I nod, taking it in, attempting to banish whatever thoughts they're pushing. I can tell them now about meeting with Deena Patterson, or I can hold it in. But it's better to be honest with them now. Let the repercussions come as they may.

"Speaking of commitment, they asked me to work there."

The three of them stare at me, their mouths dropped open like I told them the sky is falling. I pull my velvet jacket tight across my chest. Not that it's going to hide my dress. Not that it'll hide anything.

"Who asked you to work there?" Ivy says.

"Deena Patterson."

"*The* Deena Patterson? You actually met her?" Ivy says.

"It's not like that's some anomaly. She's her girlfriend's mother," Brooks says.

"What does she look like in person, like she drank from the fountain of youth?" Nico says.

"She's really nice, actually. And more beautiful in person."

"So you're going to quit your job and work for them? Are you serious?" Ivy says.

"Um, I think working at Deep would be much better than babysitting, don't you? Anyway, Brooks, you would die if you had to put little kids to sleep."

"Children. Yuck," he says.

"I'll get a thirty percent discount. I thought everyone would be excited about that."

"I'm already making my Deep-holiday-product list, don't you worry," Brooks says, and pretends to jot down notes. "We'll have Deep Glow and matcha lattes coming out of our ears."

"We're excited if you're excited," Nico says, except she doesn't seem remotely excited.

I glance over at Ivy, waiting for her approval, waiting for something. Anything.

"I'm happy for you, Bean," Ivy says as she twists her parasol tip in the dust, like she's crushing an ant. "So many people want that job."

"So then, why is your face like that?"

"Like what?" she says, but her face is classic Ivy. She makes a slight snarl; her mouth goes a little crooked. "Truth? It's moving fast. You have a girlfriend, and now you want to work for her mother. I'm just trying to catch up."

"That doesn't mean it's bad," Nico says, interrupting.

"I never said it was bad. I said *fast*," Ivy says. "It just might not be a bad idea for you to take a pause."

Ivy has always been protective of me since my dad died. She watched me speak at his graveside. Before Nico and Brooks, Ivy was the only real friend I had in life. She held my hand while I spoke at his graveside, not my mom, as the tears poured down my face, as I took those sobbing gasps. *I love you, Dad, I know you tried, I know you wanted to be healthier, I know you wanted to be well.*

"What could happen?" I say. "Seriously, what bad thing could happen?"

"You and Julia could break up," she says. "And I'm not trying to wish that upon you, I'm really not. I'm just seriously asking. What if you break up? Do you get fired from the store?"

"I don't know. I didn't really think about it. I guess we'll get there if we get there."

"You know I'm just looking out for you," Ivy says.

"I know."

Nico gently squishes herself between me and Ivy and wraps her arms around each of us. "Come on. We have to let our Bean spread her wings and fly."

Our. This is how my best friends speak about me. *Our Bean.* There was a time when I loved it, when I thought I wanted that kind of ownership from them. Now it makes me feel icky, like I've given them too much power. Did they always see me as such a lost soul, someone they had to claim?

"I personally think Bean should make her own decision about this, if anyone cares," Brooks says. "I'm more interested in the gossip. Is there fighting between the Femme girls? Do they give out free lace dresses? Who's the biggest bitch?"

I grunt out a laugh, grateful for the topic change.

"I know this is going to sound very boring, but everyone's really nice," I say. A flash of Harmony and Kai having sex at the office comes back to me. How she opened her eyes and saw me. I haven't seen her since, and that was a few days ago. "Except something weird happened. I saw something."

"Uh-oh," Brooks says dramatically.

Ivy laser focuses on me. "Tell us what you saw."

I pause for a second, take a long exhale. Why do I need to share

97

this? Why? Especially after Harmony and I spoke about it. We understood each other. We are alike, she and I. So what compels me? What?

Don't say it. Don't say it. Don't say it.

"Kai and Harmony. I saw them having sex."

"Wait," Nico says. "Where did you see them? In his car or something?"

"No, at the Deep offices," I say, their gasps practically in unison. I can feel my words speeding up. "Do. Not. Say. Anything."

"Who are we going to tell?" Nico says. She shoves a piece of gum in her mouth and chews fervently. A huge smile comes over her face. "That's crazy!"

"They're in love," I say. "They seemed like they were in another world."

"Pretty kinky that they were having sex at work, though," Brooks says. "I'm not against it, trust me. But that's bold."

"It was a private moment," I say. "I shouldn't have blabbed."

Ivy shakes her head and shrugs.

"What? What's the headshake for?" I say.

"Don't take this the wrong way, Bean. But I looked up to Harmony when I was a kid. How smart she was. She seemed to have such a huge future ahead of her. And now she's fucking some guy in a conference room at work. It just seems so sleezy."

"Meditation room. Not conference room."

"Whatever, Bean. You know what I'm talking about." She clicks her tongue in disgust. "Having sex in a meditation room. Like that's her full potential in life? *That?*"

"That's cruel, Ivy. Harmony's highly regarded at Deep. She's an inspiring person."

"How do you know, Bean? Because you saw her speak at a party once? Anyway, it sounds like a great trajectory for you," she says with that snarky tone. "Start working there instead of going to college, have sex in a meditation room. Perfect. Super ambitious."

I regret meeting them at the park. I am regretting giving them any personal details.

"That's mean, Ivy," I say. "I'm supposed to just sit here while you degrade my relationship with Julia?"

"This isn't about Julia. This is about all of them. That whole place."

"Really? Because it doesn't sound like it. And you don't know how I feel about her. You've never felt things like this. I want to be around her all the time."

"I'd like to know how you feel about her. I'd like for you to share *something* with me. But it's hard to talk to you. You're holding hands with Julia every day. Now you're going to work at Deep. You never come by the pressroom. You're going to Femme parties," she says. "It's like your whole life has been taken over by them already."

"It's not my whole life. I'm at school all day, what are you talking about?"

There's pain in her face that I can't name. A divide between us that I don't know how to fix. "I promise you, Ivy, she's not replacing you. She can never replace you."

"I'm not jealous, Bean. That's not what this is about."

But I see it all now. She doesn't understand Deep. She never did. She didn't see how beautiful it was, so bright and airy, a million miles away from the dark-paneled, church-like building that was Talentum. How different it was from my mom's own cave-like house.

Ivy can't fathom this because Ivy Cohen-Smith knows *exactly* who she is. She's the girl who last year told me she wanted to win a Pulitzer Prize for journalism. I teased her for being so type A, calling her a nepo baby.

Maybe it was because I didn't know what I wanted at that point and I didn't understand or relate to her wanting so much more.

Now here I am, the one with the specific desire.

"Come on, let's do a Don's run," I say. "McDonald's fries fix everything."

"You think that's going to go over well at Deep? It's not exactly healthy food."

"It'll be our secret," I say, and I take her pinkie like we used to when we first became best friends. Her warm pinkie curled around mine.

Ten minutes later, we're in the McDonald's drive-through, ordering large fries and Diet Cokes. Ivy and me in the front. Nico and Brooks in the back. Ivy pulls over in the parking lot, and we swirl ketchup from those tiny packs on top of the fries and wash them down with the fizzy, cold soda.

Ivy eats her fries differently than me. She inspects each first, nibbles at it like a little rabbit, then crumples the whole thing into her mouth until it disappears.

It's like how she is in life, so careful, then all at once, taking over.

"Bean?" she says, and wipes the ketchup off the corner of her mouth. "I'm sorry about before."

"You mean when you told me not to work for Deep?"

"I didn't say that. I said it was moving fast."

"But that's what you meant. So it's the same thing," I say. "Listen to me. *I'm fine.*"

I'm fine. Part of me learned from my dad how to pretend like everything was fine. The way he would come over with his little basket of chocolates on Valentine's Day during one of his short-lived moments of sobriety and smile so sweetly. My dad reassuring me with all his lies while my mom looked on from inside the house. *Everything is good, Bean. I didn't just lose my job because I was drunk, Bean. I didn't just come from a bar before I came to your house, Bean. I haven't been tormented by my past, my crazy parents and my crazy sibling. Everything's fine.*

But now I really am fine.

"This is very beautiful," Ivy says, leaning over the center console, and touches my white lace dress. "I like how it's paired with the black jacket."

"It's sort of like the ying and the yang," I say. "I'm a blend now. A little bit of Julia. A little bit of you, Nico, and Brooks."

"I heard my name," Brooks says.

I look down at the carton of fries, and they're almost gone. "Maybe I can bring you to a Femme gathering. You and Nico would love it. The house is so beautiful."

"I would totally go," Nico says. "It would satisfy all my cottage-core fantasies."

"What cottage-core fantasies?" Ivy says, whipping her head around.

"Uh, hello? What about me, bitches?" Brooks says.

"It's only for girls," Nico says.

"Yeah, except for Kai," Brooks says, and snorts.

"No sanctimonious comments in front of the fries, please," I say, and hold the last fry out for Ivy. "Take it," I say, my fingers covered in traces of ketchup.

"Split it," she says, and so I break it in half, each of us taking a piece.

19

"Oh my god, look at this house," a girl says. She's very loud. "I saw that hammock in a magazine for sixty-five thousand dollars," she squeals, and circles the hammock like it's prey.

I understand how distracted she is by the grandness of Deena Patterson's house, entering with the same amazed looks I did when I first came.

But now it's my second Femme gathering, and by your second one, you're expected to be nonchalant. That's why I'm here at the door, greeting a group of girls who have been flown in from LA. There are about five of them, all in white flowing dresses, their lithe bodies, their glowing skin. Instagram friendly, which I have learned is important, even though we don't discuss how important it actually is.

"You want to make them feel welcome, just like you felt welcome," Harmony told me earlier. "You're a special person, Bean, because you have that inviting energy."

I'm trying, but this is challenging.

"Hi, I'm Bean. What's your name?" I say.

"I'm Sunny," she says, and stares at the hammock. "I thought that was just for pictures. I saw that hammock in the magazine where they had the home spread."

"Not just for pictures, it's her furniture."

"Can you imagine spending sixty-five thousand dollars on a hammock?" she says.

Could she be right about the hammock? Sixty-five thousand dollars? I knew Deep was a very successful company. I knew Deena Patterson was super wealthy, but I can't believe the amount of money that's spent on nice things. I guess that's what rich people do. They surround themselves with pretty objects, pretty people.

I give Sunny, along with the other girls from LA, name tags, press the tags up against their white lace dresses, and usher them into the house for turmeric shots. The music echoes as if you're in a tunnel, a constant reverberation like a heartbeat. Or is it my own heart? I press my hand against my chest, and I scan the room looking for Julia among all the girls in white. I recognize some of them from the last Femme gathering. They buzz around Harmony, gushing to her like groupies as she hands each of them daisies, all picked from the meadow out back, I presume. *Do you like my dress, Harmony? Feel how soft my skin is, Harmony. I've been doing the Deep Cleanse, and I feel so good, Harmony.* Each of them longing for her approval.

Just then, Harmony turns to me, sees me watching her. She flits through the group of girls, holding the big bunch of white daisies.

"Bean, it's so nice to see you. I was going to hand one out to everyone else, but how about you do it?" she says, and smiles. Her mouth glistening with some kind of gloss. Her eyes sparkling.

"Sure," I say. I know my voice is too flat, so I act more cheerful, but the talk of the sixty-five-thousand-dollar hammock isn't sitting right with me.

"What's wrong?"

"One of the LA girls was going on and on about that hammock and how expensive it is. I'm not sure what to say."

"What do you think you should say?"

"That they shouldn't be so focused on money?"

She laughs lightly. "No one is making it about money except for you, Bean."

"I don't know what you mean," I say uncomfortably.

"The hammock isn't just a luxury item. Do you know why it costs so much?"

I shake my head no. "No one told me." She smiles and continues.

"It was hand made by an artist in New Mexico who spent a year making this one object. She tanned the leather herself. She makes the wool felt from her own loom. The steel rods are American. It's not just a hammock, and it's not just a work of art. It's a masterpiece in sustainability."

I'm not sure she was entirely right. Did you really need to spend sixty-five thousand dollars on a hammock to prove a point about sustainability? Deena could have given that money to a homeless shelter. But who am I to say? Maybe she had. Harmony was so confident about her answers that it was hard to doubt her.

For a moment neither of us speak. The room is getting louder with all the girls dancing around. Everyone so carefree, so healthy-looking, the daisies in their hair.

"Look, Bean, it's okay. We help so many girls, girls like me and you. Girls who need us because most people don't live like this. So we want to make them feel welcome."

I didn't know they thought of me as someone who *needed help*.

"If someone is stunned by something like the hammock, they're trying to process all the beauty, which can be uncomfortable. Because they might feel like an outsider here."

"Wow, I didn't know that."

"Yeah, it was supposed to be like in the MoMA, but here's the deal, Bean. That hammock signifies the ability to soar, which is why Deena hung it. She wanted to make it accessible. Because Deep, and the Deep lifestyle, should be accessible to everyone, right?"

Harmony gives me a big smile and squeezes my hand. I nod my head like I agree with her.

"I'm so proud of you. I know it's hard to be friends with someone like Ivy and date someone like Julia. They have a lot of privilege. But Julia's nothing like Ivy."

"Wait, what do you mean *it's hard*?" I say. "And what do you mean she's nothing like Ivy?"

Harmony closes her eyes for a second, lets out a deep sigh.

"Ivy is a sheltered girl. She lives in this massive house with people working for her. A house manager. A gardener. Her parents came from wealth. They're both famous. I'm embarrassed to admit it, but I was angry back then. I had jealousy in my heart. I constantly compared Ivy and her mother to my own mom. Granted, I have issues with my mom, but I felt sorry for her. My mom was this struggling singer, barely selling out the local bar, and Ivy's mom is selling out Carnegie Hall."

Harmony's mom wasn't exactly struggling, I think. I still hear her song on TikTok. But I know what she means. Just because her mom was this one-hit wonder doesn't mean she has the recognition that Ivy's mom has.

"I hope you can hear my truth without judgment."

"You can talk to me," I say.

"I know Ivy struggled trying to fit into Talentum. Part of me wanted to take her under my wing. The other part of me resented her. She had everything, yet there was always a complaint. And I'd say to her: *Why can't you just be in the present, in the moment, Ivy? See all of the goodness that you have right in front of you.* But she couldn't. It triggered me. I was dying inside. I had to let go of toxic people who were bringing me down. I've tried to come to terms with it, I really have. But I had to take care of myself."

I remember when Ivy would meet with Harmony, giddy like a little kid before she was supposed to sit down with her. She'd gush about Harmony as if she were a crush. But Harmony isn't wrong about Ivy. I don't feel disloyal hearing this.

"She loved you, Harmony."

"I know," she says, breathing hard, twisting her hands.

"Is that why you stopped speaking to her?"

"One of the reasons," she says. "Also, I got caught up with Deep. Deena and Kai, they've given me so much. And I fell in love."

As if he can sense she's talking about him, Kai appears across the room, reaching his hand up wide in the air, signaling to Harmony.

She hands me the bouquet of daisies. "Do you mind passing the rest of these out?"

"Of course not."

"I'll check in later," she says, and blows a kiss, running toward him.

I'm circling the room, handing out daisies to the girls, but also to a few men. I have no idea who they are.

Kenny, Harlow, and Grace wiggle through the crowd and slide up to me. I hand each of them a flower, and Kenny snaps hers off at the bottom and tucks it behind her ear.

"I saw that girl on Instagram years ago," Kenny says in a forced whisper, and points to one of the LA girls. A blond wispy girl with a white lace parasol. The irony. Ivy would laugh.

"Years ago?" I say. The girl looks a little younger than us, about fifteen. "When she was, like, a baby?"

"Her mom used to follow her around with a camera. Saying all of the pictures she took of her daughter were"—and she does finger quotes—"*organic.*"

"Nothing about following your kid around with a camera is organic," Harlow says.

"Meanwhile the mom had an outfit and looks planned out every day," Kenny says. "I'm sorry to be negative, but when I saw her, I had a trauma response."

"What do you mean?" I say.

"Kenny's mom used to exploit her with photos when she was little," Harlow says. "She said she was a photographer, she'd take weird pictures of Kenny, like, pretending to smoke cigarettes. She showed her work at a gallery. People bought photos of Kenny, one of her naked in a tub of milk hangs in someone's house."

"Deena and Kai were the first ones to take my protests about those pictures seriously," Kenny says. "Everyone in my mom's circle called it art."

"You're really trying to heal your heart," Grace says, and strokes Kenny's long hair, from her forehead to her shoulder. "Aren't you, Kenny?"

"I'm always trying to heal," Kenny says, and smiles.

I start to feel uncomfortable. I worry that they will start asking me about my dad and his problems. I'm not ready to divulge that.

"Well, I should probably hand out more flowers," I say.

"Who told you to do that, by the way? With the flowers?" Harlow asks.

"Harmony," I say.

Harlow and Grace look at each other and roll their eyes. Worse, Kenny snarls.

"What?" I say.

"Do it if you want, but don't do it because Harmony told you to," Harlow says. "She thinks she's in charge."

"Isn't she?" I say.

"No," Kenny says in a husky voice. "No, she's not."

20

About a half an hour later, when I'm done handing out the daisies, Kenny takes my hand in hers and pulls me into a corner,
then materializes a small flask out of her white linen pouch. Silver with pink floral etchings, something a Russian princess from
the 1800s would carry.

"I added a little rum to the turmeric shots. Mixed it all up in
here. Isn't that brilliant?" she says. She takes a long sip, then
hands the silver flask to me. I think of my dad, sitting there in
that sad, sad house with that heavy stink of failure all over him,
the stench of Coors Light.

Then I look at Kenny. Fresh-faced. Pink-cheeked. Her little silver flask with pink engraved flowers, drinking away her thoughts
about her shitty mom, who had no boundaries and took disturb-
ing pictures of her.

I take a small glug. The taste numbs my mouth as it hits, and
it goes down easily.

"I can trust you, right, Bean? You're not going to say a word to
anyone about this," she says.

"No, of course not," I say, and cough. The mixture of rum and
turmeric is, like, buttery but spicy.

I scan the room, my body buzzing already, watching. There's a
group of four men who look like they're in their thirties or forties,

slick, all of them wearing what looks like the same white pressed button-down shirt. They're drinking something that looks like bourbon on the rocks and hover around Katrina and Imani, their arms around them, taking selfies. I can't tell if the girls are happy with it or not.

"Who are they?" I say to Kenny.

"They're businessmen. They're investors. They're here to observe how Femme works because they're thinking of expanding to other cities," she says, her voice starting to slur. "But this is very hush-hush, Bean. Two of them are from Antoine Gagnon's company. They like to keep that under the radar. They're rebranding or whatever." Kenny takes another slug.

All I know about Antoine Gagnon is from what I saw on social media. This rich French guy who lives in NYC. There was video of him surrounded by young women on his yacht. Then I saw he was arrested for sex trafficking. I saw images of him walking in and out of the courthouse in New York, the press after him, his shiny gray hair, slipping into a black car.

"Gagnon, the businessman who's been in the news? The one who's in jail?"

"Gagnon the *billionaire* businessman. We don't say *jail*," she whispers. "Kai's brilliant like that. Getting these kinds of guys with shitloads of money to invest in new projects."

Two of the men motion to us and stroll over. White stiff-collared shirts, light blue jeans, and suede loafers with a gold bar across the top. Cologne like cheap perfume, the kind that wafts around the mall, seeps off them.

"Enjoying your drink, ladies?" one of them says. "I'm sure it's tasty." He introduces himself as Sebastian and the other one as James.

"How do you know what we're drinking?" Kenny smirks.

"I used to bring flasks to parties too," the other one says, and calls one of the waiters who has a drink tray over, then takes two glasses and hands them to us.

"It's Deep Beauty Powder and a turmeric shot, what *ever* could you be talking about?" Kenny says, and winks.

"You don't have to hide here. Everyone's out for a good time, right?" Sebastian says. "I remember what it was like to be your age."

Kenny smiles and leans close to me, whispers in my ear so it almost tickles.

"Don't worry, we only have to stand here for a couple of more seconds," she says.

It's a joke, but I do worry. I feel weird, the way they're staring, and I don't know where Julia is.

"Oh, come on," Sebastian says. "Don't tell secrets, now."

"Yeah," James says, and puts his hand on Kenny's waist. "What could girls like you, so sweet and innocent, be scheming up, huh?"

Kenny lets out an awkward giggle. But I don't like it. The music pulses even faster now; a couple of the girls dance in the center of the living room, their dresses in a white blur. I'm buzzed from the drink, and Sebastian places his hand on my hip. I step back to get away from him, but he leans in closer. "Aw, don't be shy. We're just talking."

I want to tell him to fuck off, to use less hair gel, to not wear his shirt unbuttoned down to his stomach, that any man named

Sebastian is a creep, but I also understand that this is very much a work event and I don't want to insult Deena's investors.

"I think I need to use the bathroom," I say.

"Oh? Okay," he says. "I can take you there." He's sloppy and tries to put his big sweaty hand on my back. I shake him off.

"I think I got it covered," I say firmly. His heavy breath of alcohol so sour. It's so familiar. The blood fills up in my ears. I start to feel dizzy.

"Hey," a voice says, and it's Kai. *Kai.* He stretches out his hand so he's between me and Sebastian. I stumble a bit and hold Kenny's hand for balance.

"Kai to the rescue," Kenny says in a slurry laugh.

"What can I help you with?" Kai says to them, his voice deep and commanding.

"Oh, we were just talking to the girls," James says. "You know, casual conversation."

"I don't think you have much in common with them. They're a little young for you, don't you think?"

Sebastian takes a step back.

"We're just talking, man," Sebastian says. He throws his drink back; an ice cube drops on the floor. Drunk. "Whoops," he says, and laughs uncomfortably, then stumbles off.

I cover my face with my hands. I'm so embarrassed; a sick feeling comes over me. I feel lightheaded, and I get that heat up my throat like I'm going to vomit. Kenny and Kai lead me over to a seat and have one of the waiters get me a fresh ginger tonic.

"Sip it slowly," Kai says. "Ginger helps settle the stomach." I look up and see Julia walking toward me with concern.

"What's wrong?" she says, and crouches on the floor in front of me.

"Some of the guests got a little handsy," Kenny says, and rolls her eyes. "It wasn't a big deal. They were harmless." But I don't know why she's minimizing it. They were creepy. They're grown men hitting on girls like us.

"Are you kidding?" Julia says. "Did they touch you? Who? Tell me which one."

"I'm sorry. I don't want to cause any trouble."

Kai stares at me closely. "Bean, look at me. You did nothing wrong."

"I don't want to upset anyone," I say. I think of his sour breath again. Sebastian. How it reminded me of my dad. I don't really understand why it's bothering me so much. I just had a sip from Kenny's flask. I shake it out of my head.

Julia wraps her arms around my knees and rests her head on my thighs. "I'm so sorry, Bean," she keeps saying.

"Deena and I are going to have to be more exclusive about the guest list going forward," Kai says to Julia. "This can't happen again." He leans over and looks at me, making eye contact, and says firmly: "This won't happen again." I believe him.

It's about an hour later, and Deena has wrapped up her inspirational speech. Julia and I pull some cushions into the grass so that we're staring up at the sky.

"It's a canopy of stars," I say.

Julia rolls over and kisses me. It's so nice, the two of us together like this. Those men were a blip. I think of how Kai was so protective, and how it made me feel even closer to the group.

"I'm sorry about what happened earlier," she says, and strokes my arm.

"I'm going to tell you something weird," I say, and turn over to face her. "They reminded me of my father." I explain how their breath reeked of alcohol. I tell her about all the times I wished my father looked like a responsible businessman and how disappointed I was that those businessmen were so vile.

We shove our cushions so they're touching, almost overlapping, and Julia and I curl up together.

"That behavior didn't belong at a Femme party. We're here celebrating girls," Julia says. "It's supposed to be a protected space. But Deena, she wants to make everything so transparent. She wants the world to see how we've inspired so many young women."

"It would have gotten weirder if Kai hadn't come over," I say.

"Kai takes care of us." Julia beams.

There's a sound bath happening in the barn right now, and the vibrations travel through the air, draping over my skin, through my ears, relaxing me. It almost doesn't seem real.

"So, I've made up my mind about something. I want to work at Deep," I say, and the relief on her face makes me want to melt.

Later that night, when I'm home in bed, I call Ivy.

"There were these weird older men," I say. "Kai had to help us out of this prickly situation."

"What do you mean by *prickly*?"

I use Kenny's word. "They were getting handsy."

"Wait, grown men were at a party for teenage girls, and they put their hands on you? Like, where?"

"On my hip," I say. "But Kai handled them. He always knows what to do."

"Always?" she says.

I want to ask what she means, but I don't say a word.

When I fall asleep that night, I quickly dream about me and Julia cuddled under a blanket. *Look at me, Julia. Look at me*, I'm saying. But she's already got her eyes locked on me.

21

At the Deep shop on Monday, my first day, the nap dresses arrive.

"Nap dresses!" Julia squeals. Kenny, Harlow, and Grace come running over. Everyone's excited about the nap dresses because Kai wants to do a photo shoot, with all of us modeling them.

After the Femme party, Deena had a little talk with Kenny and me, about Sebastian and James and the way they acted. She told us that she would never jeopardize our safety, that she's sorry anyone was made to feel uncomfortable, and that there should always be open communication if anyone feels unprotected.

"Do you believe her?" I said to Kenny when Deena walked away.

She looked at me, surprised. "Why shouldn't I?"

Julia throws the boxes onto a large worktable and gently opens up the first one, picking apart the layers of white tissue paper and throwing them to the ground. "Do you know what this means, Bean? How important these are?" she says.

"Pajamas are important?" I say. I don't mean to sound rude, but I don't know what a nap dress is.

She carefully unfolds one of the dresses from the box. A simple white A-line dress with ruffled shoulders. She places it up to her body and stands in the mirror, staring at her reflection.

"Here's the thing, Bean. People don't sleep. They're up all night tossing and turning. But imagine if we get the National Sleep Foundation behind us. And then when people see photos of us in this dress, they'll want to make time for sleep. *I need that dress,* they'll tell themselves. It won't matter that it's three hundred dollars or five dollars, because this dress is going to change their life."

She inhales the fabric of the dress, a smile on her face like she's been blessed by a thousand angels.

"This nap dress, Bean, it'll trickle down into society. And it'll be because of us. Because these nap dresses were selected by the people in this room."

"Cerulean blue?" I say.

"Exactly," she says, and winks.

Harlow takes one and rubs the fabric against her cheek. "Handmade by the cutest queer couple in Brooklyn. And they're so soft."

"Crushed fucking taffeta!" Grace says, swooning.

"Naps as resistance," Julia says, her voice filled with adrenaline. "Someone write that down!"

Grace grabs a pen and a pad and takes notes.

"Nap *dresses* as resistance," Kenny says.

Julia begins tossing the nap dresses one by one up in the air. White dresses, dresses with tiny lavender and pink flowers, dresses with ruffles and lace bodices.

"We have to use that as a tagline," Julia says.

"Julia, those are three-hundred-dollar dresses. You can't use that as a tagline," I say, slightly horrified, but also incredibly entertained. I've never seen someone be so careless with something so beautiful. Imagine selling resistance for three hundred dollars?

"Oh, but Bean, can't you picture how it will change people's lives?" she says.

She buries her face into a light blue checked one, breathes into it like she's inhaling a drug, and lifts her chin, stares at me with tears in her eyes.

"Julia, are you crying?" I say. I reach over to her, stroke her shoulder.

"I've never seen such beautiful dresses before. All the potential in them, they're so beautiful."

"Oh my god," I say, and it comes to me so quickly. "You're Daisy Buchanan flipping through Gatsby's pink shirts."

"Oh, I am, aren't I?" she says, and throws another one up in the air. "I can't help myself. They're so beautiful."

Just then, Kai walks in with a bottle of kombucha and sees the dresses all over the floor. "What's going on here? A nap-dress explosion?" He laughs, looking pleased.

Kenny, Harlow, and Grace prance out of the dressing room, all three of them in the A-line dress, ruffled shoulders, tight smocking across the chest, and covered in a soft floral print. They fervently twirl in circles, dancing around each other, gushing over how much they love it.

"I got a little excited," Julia said. "Bean thinks I've turned into Daisy Buchanan."

"Tell me," Kai says to me, his tone more concerned. "Do you like being called Bean?"

"Yeah. It's my middle name. Everyone calls me that. My mom. My family. My friends."

"Do you *like* being called Bean, or is it something you've accepted because that's what people have decided to call you?"

Kenny, Grace, and Harlow stop spinning to watch him speak to me. Julia too. All their eyes on me.

"Oh, I like it. I like Frances too. I'll go by either."

"I'd like to know what *you* prefer to be called. Because I've been calling you Frances. When we first met, I told you that I prefer Frances. But it's not what *I* prefer. It's what *you* prefer."

Bean is fine, I want to tell him. But I can tell that answer would be too wishy-washy for Kai. He'd encourage me to be more concrete.

"I like Bean."

"There we have it," Kai says, and claps his hands together once like a gong.

"Beannnnn," the girls squeal. Julia wraps her arms around me, then kisses me on the cheek. I feel like I've been anointed or something, but I'm not sure for what.

"What's the plan for the photo shoot, Kai?" Kenny says. "Where would you like us?" She stands there so willing. Her face so cheerful.

"Actually, I think I've changed my mind," Kai says. "I think I'm just going to work with Bean," he says.

I can see Kenny's face drop. The palpable disappointment.

Kai hikes himself up so that he's sitting on the desk and plays with his crystal necklace.

"Your look," he says to me, and then glances at the three girls, "and *their* look . . . no. We can't have you all together. Too much competition. We need a singular focus for this, don't you think, Kenny?"

He looks to her, the cheerfulness gone.

"Oh, yes, absolutely, Kai," she says, a disappointed grimace.

Kai takes a sip of his kombucha, wipes the fuzz away from his mouth, and then stares at me with those eyes, like he knows something's wrong.

"Does that make you uncomfortable, Bean? To be photographed?"

"I don't know why anyone would want to take pictures of me," I say shyly.

"So there's a critical voice in your head. We all have it." He looks at the girls. "Right?"

"Yes," they say in unison.

"Think about what you just said, Bean. 'I don't know why anyone would want to take pictures of me.'"

"Okay," I say uncomfortably.

"Why *wouldn't* someone want to take pictures of you, is the question," he says. "We talk about this a lot. How can you awaken into a new mentality so that voice stops mattering? You'll never be free unless you listen to your own voice. Are you ready to stop the voices and become nobody?"

"Nobody? What does that mean, becoming *nobody*?" I say.

"It's actually a Ram Dass concept," Kai says. "He was a spiritual teacher who died in 2019. The idea of becoming nobody is about letting go of the ego. The ego is the voice in your head. If you can become nobody, then you lose the ego."

Of course I have that voice. I never noticed it was a problem. I always just accepted it.

"So how do you just ignore it?" I say.

"Ah, that's the question, isn't it?" he says.

"I always have that voice," Grace says. "But Kai's helped me tamp it down. Now it's a murmur."

The girls nod. They've been around long enough to know the answer. He motions Julia to put on music—light drums and chanting sounds. He tells us to sit on the floor in a circle. Our legs crossed. It excites me to sit here like this, the six of us in a circle, so intimate.

"When you first came to us, Bean, you were immersed in the darkness," Kai says.

"I was?" I say. The idea of it makes me worry. I've already forgotten what I was like when I first met them, what they must have thought of me. It's so different now with me holding this white nap dress in my hands like it's some kind of sacred object.

"Your energy was murky, like there was darkness in your past," he says, and pauses, rooting his gaze into me. "Was there?"

Julia holds my hand. "Kai, maybe we should stop."

"I think Bean is strong enough for this," he says. "What do you think, Bean?"

Julia holds my hand. "Kai, maybe we should stop," she says again.

"You have the power to control your own life, Bean."

"I don't even have my own car," I say.

They all laugh, except for Kai, who doesn't think it's funny.

"See, this is what I mean," he says gently. "You have to accept your self-worth. You have to allow yourself to shine. Taking photos of you in the nap dress is just an example." He leans closer to me. "Bean, are you worried about what people might say if they see you in a white nap dress?"

I think of the way Ivy, Brooks, and Nico would react seeing me like that. What they would say. I think of my mom's reaction and how shocked she was just seeing me in white. People have been used to me looking like a blackbird on a wire.

Kai nods his head slowly. "If people can't accept that you want more out of your life, then they might not have a place in your life."

"It's not about them," I tell him. "It's about me." This is about the way I see myself.

Kai goes to gather his equipment while Julia goes to help Katrina in the store. There's a swarm of customers clamoring over the new Deep Cleanse Kit. It comes with an oil and a dry brush to promote circulation and drain your lymph nodes. When I tried the dry brush, my skin turned bright red and rashy. When I mentioned the skin irritation to Katrina, she told me it was the toxins working their way out.

Kenny, Harlow, and Grace stay behind cleaning up Julia's nap-dress explosion. There's an awkward silence between us.

"I just want to make sure," I say, stumbling over words, "that

I'm not stepping on anyone's toes. You know, since we're not doing this photo shoot as a group."

"Bean," Kenny says very seriously. "If one person feels good, then we all feel good. Spiritual emanation, as Deena says. There's no upset here. Just joy."

"Kai taught me to trust people again. Let's just say things aren't great at home. And I needed someone to understand me," Harlow says. "So if Kai thinks that the right move is to photograph you alone for this, then it's for a very good reason. And we're behind him."

"There's no one like him. If you let him in, he'll change your life," Kenny says.

22

Outside, the light is a crisp yellow, hitting the leaves like a wall of gold. I follow Kai into the freezing-cold air, barefoot in the parking lot. Nothing about this nap dress, with its tiny ruffled shoulders exposing my chest and arms, protects me from the elements.

"Everyone's going to want to sleep in these after they see you in them. Like a little garden fairy in her luxurious nap dress," he says, laughing to himself.

He's got a big fluffy brush and dips it in a jar of powder that has an iridescent sheen to it.

"I should probably get our makeup team in here, but fuck it. I want to catch the light," he says. "Come here. Stand close to me. I'm going to coat you in this." He dashes it across my neck and collarbone.

Kai tells me to place my hand just under my chin and look down at the ground. "Now, I want you to think about something, someone you love. I want you to feel like you're aching to find it. Show that to me in your eyes."

I thought this was about sleeping, not love, I want to say. I start to think about Julia, how I feel about her, but it's impossible to think of anything because I'm so uncomfortably cold. I bounce up and down on the freezing pavement.

"What's wrong?" he says.

"I'm freezing. My toes are, like, numb."

"Good, get on your toes. Dig them into the pavement. Find the discomfort. The only way you can find love is to push yourself through pain."

"The only way to find love is through pain?" I say. It stops me from bouncing. "Is that really true?"

He nods, dead serious. "Enlightenment exists on the other side of pain, Bean."

"Do you really believe that?"

"Of course I do," he says. "And I'm sure you do, too; you just don't realize it. How's this: Do you love your mom?"

"Yes."

"Has she also caused you great pain?" His voice is so calm as he talks.

I nod. I don't know if *great* pain is the truth, but I don't want him to think I'm being closed off.

"What about your dad, Bean?"

I nod, and my eyes well up. I don't know why. Usually I can talk about my dad so easily, disconnected like it didn't even happen. But for some reason, maybe it's the sharp, cold ground under my feet, maybe it's the nap dress, I'm emotional.

"I want you to think about that pain, Bean. Think about a specific moment, about how that pain hurt you."

The first thing that comes to my mind: It was the second night of Hanukkah, and I was about ten. My mom and I pulled up to his driveway. I had bought him a little medal that said NUMBER

ONE DAD at the school holiday market. Those were the options. Either an eraser or a NUMBER ONE DAD medal. They didn't have medals for mediocre, addicted dads. He stumbled into the driveway and called to my mom. She told me to wait in the car and got out to talk to him. Tears covering her cheeks when she got back in the car and pulled out of the driveway.

"Now, push your hair in front of one eye and bite your lips so that they get pink," Kai says. "Bite down hard." I do what he says and look up at him. "Don't look at the camera. Look down. Bite your lips again. Think about that moment of pain. Shove your feet into the pavement if you have to. Channel that pain, Bean. Don't look at me. I'm not even here."

I hear the camera shutter clicking away, and I want to cry thinking about my dad. Part of me wants to hit him for leaving me so confused and so scared. The other part of me wants to hug him because of how sad I feel that he was such a fucking mess.

"Where are you in the pain, Bean? Talk to me."

The dress flies in the wind, and my shoulders feel tight. I'm shivering from the cold.

"It's about my dad."

"Walk me through it."

"He was an alcoholic. It killed him," I say.

"My father had an addiction too," Kai says. "I had to remove myself from him to become who I am now. I had to become a new person and untangle those old connections from people who were bringing me down."

Kai steps close to me. "Look up at me, Bean." I'm shivering, but I look at him. His hair blowing in the wind. "Let go of those memories. Leave it all behind."

I want to lose myself, let go of that haunted girl trying to un-derstand who her father was. I shake it away, the light shining on my face.

"Think of the best moment that you've had recently," Kai says, and I go right to Julia and me making out in the hot tub. A warmth crosses over my face. The sun is down and the light is gone. I'm freezing, my teeth chattering, but I feel safe, at peace.

"That's the smile I want to see. That's the bliss." Kai looks at the photos in his camera. "Jesus, these pictures are going to be incredible. Deena is going to lose her shit."

I nod my head, wrapping my arms around myself, hopping up and down, my fingers tingling.

"I have so much energy," I say to him. "It's like I want to dance around out here. Why?"

"We did a little work on your way of thinking. It's an exercise, to trick your brain into making endorphins. You get really low and then force it into bliss."

He shows me the photos of me in the dress flowing and the sun hitting the wall of golden trees behind me. My cheeks full and my skin translucent.

"You were possessed while I took these, do you know that about yourself, Bean?"

"I think I was just cold." I laugh.

"I think you're very good at diverting your pain so that you don't have to feel. But here in that moment, in these photos, you channeled your pain. It's the purest form of love," he says. "I can see why Julia has a thing for you. I see why Deena wanted you to work here. You resonate."

Resonate? What do I resonate, I wonder. I don't ask him; instead, I watch him play with the large crystal around his neck. It's brown, almost muddy, yet translucent.

"Look, Bean, I know a lot of girls like you. You feel misunderstood by your mom. You feel disconnected from the parental figures in your life. You have deep concern about what your future is going to look like. I get it, Bean, I really do."

He lifts his hands, palms facing me.

I stare down at his palms.

"Is this a game where we slap each other's hands?"

"What?" He laughs hard. His green eyes gleaming. "I'm going to put the question back to you. What do *you* think we're supposed to do?"

"Play a trust game? Dance? Honestly, I don't know."

"Place your hands close to my hands. No touching, just hover them. Feel the energy between us." I hover my shivering hands over his and feel warmth.

"You're in charge of your own life. You get to make the choices. No one can do that for you," he says, and lowers his hands. "Go ahead, get inside. Wrap the sauna blanket around you. And, Bean, keep the dress."

"Keep it?" I have so many ways I want to respond to him. The way Frances Bean would respond. *It's a three-hundred-dollar dress. It's white. What will I do with it? Why do I deserve this?*

But I realize this is what he's been telling me all along. That I *do* deserve it. That I belong here.

"Okay," I say, my emotions swirling, I'm crying, and I don't even realize it until a tear drops on my chin. "I would love to keep it."

23

It's been about two weeks since I started working for Deep, when Ivy asks me to meet her at the pressroom one day before I head to the shop. I've been fully immersed in learning about clean beauty, supplements, and luxury face creams, so we haven't spent much time together. I don't know the last time I was in the pressroom. Ivy's sitting at her desk. Brooks and Nico are there too, lounging on the small Victorian couch, Nico busy with her knitting. Ivy grimaces as she glances up at me.

"What's going on?" I say, uneasy.

"What happened to your outfit you had on earlier?" Brooks says. He's talking about the black velvet dress I was wearing. I changed into white overalls in the bathroom, because I still feel weird about wearing all white to school.

"You were wearing a long velvet dress, or am I imagining things?" Brooks says. "What happened to that?"

"What is this, the fucking inquisition?"

"I'm sorry, Bean," he says. "You just . . . you look like one of them."

"Brooks," Nico says. "This is not right."

"Oh, so this is what we're doing now?" I say. "This is why you called me here, to make fun of what I have to wear to work?"

"We called you here because we want to talk to you about something serious," Ivy says.

"Bean," Nico says, her face slack and serious. "We love you. You know that, right?"

I stand there, in shock in the middle of the room. "Someone please tell me what's happening?"

"I've been thinking about what you told me about them," Ivy says. "I've tried to reconcile it in my mind. First it was about Harmony and Kai having sex in the middle of the office."

"It wasn't in the middle of the office."

"Close enough," she says.

"You don't have to be defensive," Brooks says.

"Don't I?"

But then you told me about those businessmen hitting on you," Ivy says. "What were businessmen doing there at a party for teenage girls? You know this has to be wrong, Bean, or you wouldn't have told me about it."

"Kai handled it. That's why I was telling you. It wasn't a big deal."

"How could it not be a big deal?" Ivy says. "How, Bean? Girls from our school are dying to be part of Femme. Their mothers are dying for *them* to be part of Femme. Do you really think that people would be so excited to be part of Femme if they knew grown men were going to hit on them? If they knew the boss, who is supposed to be some spiritual guru, is sleeping with one of his employees?"

I stand there quiet, looking back and forth between the three of them, their long, weary faces. And then it hits me.

"Are you writing about this for the paper?" I say, every part of my body from my arms to my chest filling up with rage. "Is that what you're doing?"

Ivy walks toward me with her laptop open, her face stony. "You're not going to like it. But it had to be written, Bean. Do you understand? It had to be."

I snatch the laptop out of her hands. The headline blares:

INAPPROPRIATE BEHAVIOR AT DEEP HEADQUARTERS

For years, Deep promoted itself as more than just a wellness company, but with its Femme offshoot for girls, it was a safe haven for young women looking for spirituality and empowerment. "I feel safe at Femme," one former Talentum student told the Talentum Free Press. "The Femme gatherings have helped me learn about myself."

Now, according to sources, multiple businessmen have been accused of groping a few of the partygoers at a recent Femme gathering and two senior Deep employees were recently found engaging in a sexual act in a public area.

"Inappropriate?" I say, holding on to the computer. I can barely read the second paragraph. My heart racing. "*Sources?* Are you fucking kidding me, Ivy?"

"Believe me, she wanted to write something else," Brooks says. "Like, 'Sexual Assault at Deep Headquarters,' but we convinced her not to."

"You can't write this," I say.

"I wanted you to see it before it was published, do you understand? I'm doing this out of respect for you. I'm trying to give you a heads-up here," Ivy says.

Nico's pacing back and forth, like she's going to dig a trench in the floor.

I slam the laptop shut, my stomach sinking.

"You can't do this, Ivy. I didn't agree to this. I told you this information in confidence. You can't use this."

"The more and more I thought about it—"

"If I don't say *this is on the record*, then it's not on the record. I didn't even *ask* to be anonymous. This is breaking all sorts of journalistic ethics. What do you not understand about this?"

"On or off the record isn't a legally binding agreement, Bean," she says.

"*Legally binding?* Oh my god, Ivy," Nico says, and stops pacing, then takes my arms. "I want you to know that I don't agree with this and I told her not to do it."

"Let me explain," Ivy says.

"Explain *what*? That you're going to run a story about my girlfriend's mother's company? Something that could ruin their business? Something damaging?" I say.

"If they act like this," Ivy says, "if they allow this kind of behavior, then what else are they capable of? What else are they doing? What's been happening at these parties that you haven't witnessed?"

I can't look at her anymore. I can't even breathe. I want to run out of the room, but I think about what Kai said. *The only way you can find love is to push yourself through pain.* Is it possible that Ivy loves me so much she's trying to make me feel pain first? Or do I love Julia so much that I have to feel pain to defend her?

"I understand you're in pain, Ivy. I know this is hard for you that I have a girlfriend. That I'm not here at the paper every day after school. I know it's hard for all of you to see me dressed like this. To see me changing," I say. "I know it's because you love me. I understand how rejected you must feel. But you know you can't write this. You know that would ethically be wrong."

"Pain?" Nico says. "What are you talking about . . . pain?"

"Whoa," Brooks says.

"Bean, this goes against everything they stand for, like wellness and safety and health," Ivy says. "Deena Patterson is practically a celebrity. Kai Edwards too. People, *people our age*, are buying shit-loads of their products. Millions of dollars in sales. Meanwhile, Kai, who is supposed to be like Harmony's boss, or have a superior role, could have sexual harassment charges against him."

"Well, that's not going to happen. They're in love," I say.

I have a flash of what Kai said to me that day when we were doing the photo shoot in the nap dress, me in the freezing cold.

You'll never be free unless you listen to your own voice.

What's my voice telling me now? It's telling me that Ivy has unresolved issues about Harmony. It tells me that my friends don't really understand Kai and how much he has to offer. That Kai protected us from those men that night. And they especially don't understand my relationship with Julia.

"I love Julia," I say. "And if you can't respect that love, then I'm not going to be able to be around you. You're going to have to work through your pain on your own."

"Bean, come on," Brooks says. "Let's talk about this."

"I think it would be a good idea for you to come to the store. Kai's doing a few meditations on living in the present, and another one on finding love through pain. It would be beneficial to you."

Ivy takes a step closer to me. Her face in a pinch. I can see the anger boiling up in her, the way her eyes are so bloodshot.

"They're using you, Bean. I don't know how exactly. Maybe it's to seem more legitimate. Maybe that's how they use all the girls, they bring them in all innocent, and then they take advantage of them somehow. I haven't figured it out yet, but I know it's not healthy. I know it's not right."

I smile at her brightly. Center myself. Feel my feet strong under me.

"Ivy, I know why Harmony dumped you," I say, the words tumbling out of me. I want to hurt her. I want to hurt her like she's hurting me with this article. I know this isn't part of the pain scenario Kai explained, but maybe by expressing this, it'll bring us to the other side together. Maybe it'll make us closer. "Harmony cut you off because you're toxic. Look at how you're acting now. You say you're going to be supportive of me, but you're trying to weaponize me against them."

Ivy's stunned. Shocked like the time we found out last year's valedictorian had paid someone else to write his senior thesis. Shocked like when I told her my dad died.

I can feel the tears filling up my eyes. "I don't want to be here anymore," I say because I can't look at her crushed face, so I bolt out the door, barely able to breathe.

Nico follows me down the hallway, calling after me. "Please wait, Bean. Please . . . let's talk."

"Everything's okay, Nico," I say, and stop. "Ivy's having her process. But she's going to have to do it alone. I can't be part of this negative loop."

"What if the negative loop is the truth?"

"It's not. I promise you that. This is the first time in my life I'm listening to my own voice. Isn't that great? It's not just Ivy's voice in my head. It's me, finally."

"You have your own voice, Bean. What are you talking about?"

"You might have thought so . . ."

Nico's black mascara runs down her face like caterpillars.

"It's like you're cutting us out of your life. Like Deep has taken over and there's not enough room for us," she says, and wipes her face, smearing her makeup even more.

"Nico," I say, and reach into my bag, handing her a small travel-size envelope of Deep makeup wipes. "Take these."

She looks down at them like I've given her the weirdest thing on the planet. And maybe I have.

24

"When did you start working at Deep?" my mom asks Julia. We're out to dinner at a vegan restaurant—my mom; Doug; his daughter, Caroline; Julia; and me. We're all picking at a smoked-beet-tartare dish.

"Oh, I've always worked with my mom. She and I used to put little crystal packages together when I was like ten years old."

"That's how old I am," Caroline says, very proud of herself. My mom gives her a sweet grin.

"I was kind of her helper. She would write these newsletters, and sometimes I would draw on them. We'd package vitamins and oils and like I said, crystals. Then everything changed once she started promoting some of the, let's say, more controversial treatments."

"Like the beesting-therapy thing?" my mom says. "I heard that woman almost died."

I want to kill my mother. I've only been at Deep for three weeks. Why does she have to insult the place right off the bat? I kick her under the table, and she gives me a side-eye.

"She almost died because she did it alone, because no one was there assisting her," Julia says. "And she went way overboard, allowing her own bees to sting her multiple times."

"Ouch, that sounds like it hurts," Doug's daughter says.

"When it's done the right way, it's sort of like acupuncture," Julia says, and smiles.

Doug picks at the basket of whole-wheat breadsticks uncomfortably.

"I've had acupuncture, and I've been stung by bees," my mom says. "And I can tell you that beestings hurt a lot."

"But did you ever try it in a controlled environment?" Julia says.

"Can't say I did," my mom says.

"Insect venom is really good for inflammation, for arthritis and for so many skin issues. It's like if you got honey through an IV. I heard a woman say that it got rid of some of her scars."

"Got rid of a scar?" my mom says.

"Obviously that's anecdotal evidence, but we have to believe women when they tell us their stories."

"We have to believe science too," Doug says, lightly drumming his breadstick on the table.

"Oh, one hundred percent," Julia says. "But is science without any error?"

"Of course not," Doug says.

"Here's the thing. My mom wants to see people feel well. There are so many women who come to her and feel like the medicine they've been given failed them."

I like Julia's answer, how confident and secure in it she is. Not defensive at all. Of course, Deena Patterson never said she was a healer. And of course, science can sometimes be wrong, or at least interpreted incorrectly.

"We didn't bring Julia to dinner to ask her about her mom's company," I say.

"I really don't mind answering," she says. "Questions are good. Questions are important."

"No, Bean is right," my mom says. "And Bean has been floating on air lately. It's so nice to see her so happy. Really, that's all that matters."

Julia and I place our heads together. I squeeze her thigh under the table. Breathe her in. Her soft hair next to my face.

"Sixteen years old," Doug says. "I don't think I was dating anyone at that age. I was kind of a late bloomer."

"You were waiting for me," my mom says, and strokes his face.

"Eww, are you two going to kiss?" Caroline says.

My mom and Doug laugh, but I'm with Caroline. Glad to see my mom happy, but entirely grossed out. I stand up and take Julia's hand. "We're going to the bathroom," I announce.

Julia and I stand in front of the bathroom mirror. She looks like a little girl, her eyes sad, her mouth downturned.

"What's wrong?" I say.

"Your mom thinks I'm a quack. She hates me."

"That's not true. She doesn't at all. Didn't you take her English class last year? She loves you."

"That whole thing about the beesting?" Julia says. "It was weird. I felt uncomfortable."

I don't know what to say, so I edge closer to her. "My mom

thinks you're amazing. She just likes to ask questions. I'm sorry if she was being insensitive."

A woman walks into the bathroom, and I can see right away, she recognizes Julia. "You're Deena Patterson's daughter. Deep. Right?"

Julia looks up from the sink and flashes her a big smile and nods.

"That energy drink I bought at the Deep store, it changed my life," she says, coming closer. "I thought it was too expensive, but I realized how well it worked after the second week, it was life changing."

"Oh, I'm so glad to hear that. Thank you so much."

The woman gives Julia a friendly grin and goes into a stall.

Julia smirks at me and shrugs. "Not everyone thinks we're terrible, I guess."

"Why did you have to say that to Julia?" I ask my mom the moment we walk back in our house.

"What are you talking about? Say what to Julia?"

"The beesting thing, Mom. Why did you have to bring that up?"

"It was in the news, Bean. A woman died. It wasn't exactly a secret."

My mom sits down at one of our dining room chairs and stares up at me.

"Why can't you fix these things?" I say, and tug at a long strand of fabric hanging off the back of the seat. "They look like you got them off the street."

"I think I did get them off the street," she says, and chuckles to herself.

"It's not funny, Mom," I say. But it's not about the chairs. This is about what happened at dinner. "Julia is sensitive about things that have to do with her mother's company. She takes pride in Deep. Why did you have to act so dismissive when we were talking?"

She takes a sip from the water bottle in front of her, nodding her head, very serious. "I'm sorry, Bean."

"That was so incredibly rude, Mom."

"What am I supposed to say if something concerning stands out? Should I say nothing?"

"Yes! Say *nothing*! Think about how it might affect your daughter."

I stalk to the kitchen, picking up cereal boxes, slamming them down on the counter. I don't know what I'm looking for or why I'm doing it. I can't stand still.

"When you're around her, you should respect her and her family. Just like you want me to respect Doug. Or any of your other friends."

She nods her head quietly. We're both silent for a moment.

"I'm sorry I brought up the bee thing."

"Fine," I say, and I stomp to my room and shut the door behind me, collapse on my bed. I think of Julia's face, how peaceful she is. The way she wants to embrace everything I do. The way she makes me feel. I've fallen in love with her, her whole world, her whole way of being. I've never felt more sure about anything.

25

There's going to be a "blood moon" lunar eclipse tonight, and of course Deena is going to have a party to celebrate. Hundreds of silver art deco moons hang from the ceiling, and there's a thick smell of roses and palo santo that wafts throughout Deena's house. Candles light up all the empty spaces. They're all from a local beekeeper who makes the candles from his hives and then sells some of the propolis to Deena to make her antiaging serum.

"You look beautiful," Julia says to me.

I'm wearing a soft linen midi dress from the store with intricate cutwork around the collar and lace-trim sleeves that hit at the elbows. Buttons up the back. A 458-dollar dress. I've never seen anything like it. Kai told me to pick out something to wear for the party, something that represents the blood moon.

Kenny, Harlow, and Grace clapped when I walked out of the room. "Twirl for us," Harlow said. So I twirled.

"It's yours, Bean," Kai said. "The dress was made for you."

"I can't take it," I told him. "It's so expensive. It'll be all of my paycheck."

"I'll get pictures of you at the party. After how many nap dresses we sold with you in it, it's yours," he said. "Consider it a bonus."

Someone is handing out the signature Deep turmeric shots along with little cards about the blood moon.

"Look, it's orange to celebrate the blood moon," Julia says. She clinks my glass, and we both down it.

"Not only that," someone says, "but it's a time of great upheaval."

We turn around, and it's Deena wearing a white silky metallic kaftan. She gives Julia a hug, then me.

"What are you doing down here?" Julia says. "I thought you were still getting ready."

"Oh, I just wanted to check and see how everything looked before people started pouring in." She looks at me. "Frances, you're glowing."

"Thank you," I say.

"Really, I wanted to make sure that the servers are talking about the importance of this blood moon. I wanted all you girls to know."

"I think everyone knows," Julia says.

"It's fair to say that I don't know," I tell them, and Deena's face brightens up. I've learned to be more honest with Julia and myself. I don't have to pretend to know something. I can learn from her, from Kai, or from the others.

"Frances, it's so important to take accountability for the truth during this blood moon. A lot of old wounds will be opened," she says. "You have to approach the past with compassion."

I can't help but think about Ivy. Should I have had more compassion when she told me about the article that she was planning to write? Even Deena Patterson wouldn't find compassion for someone who was trying to tear her business apart, right? Nico has been texting me for days about talking to Ivy, but it's just not something I want to think about. Not now when things are so good with Julia.

"You seem like you have something on your mind," Deena says.

"Me?" I say. "Oh, I'm having some issues with a friend. I thought of her when you mentioned the old-wounds thing."

"Upheaval in our lives can teach us incredible things about ourselves," she says. "Eclipses can sometimes be like a ravaging fire. Everything burns down so you can build it back up again."

Deena's attention flits away to something else. It's Harmony, slurring, stumbling toward us. Julia and I quickly go to help her, wrapping our arms underneath her so she can stand.

"I don't want to see her," Harmony says, slurring, and glares at Deena.

"Julia, I think you need to help our friend to another room where she can rest," Deena says, her tone irritated.

"I don't want to rest!" Harmony yells.

Deena clutches Harmony's arm and seethes. "I think you had too much to drink, dear. I think you have to recenter yourself. Give yourself some space."

Deena smooths out her kaftan and straightens up, smiling. "I'm going to finish getting ready and mingle with the guests." Then she slips away.

Harmony squiggles away from our grip.

"Maybe you need a Deep Calm drink?" Julia says. "That ashwagandha infusion for stress?"

"I don't need any fucking ashwagandha. Don't sell me,"

Harmony snaps. "I need to find Kai." Harmony stares at us in a heavy silence, and then she storms away. In the few weeks I've been at Deep, I haven't really seen anyone upset before, especially not Harmony.

"What was that about?" I say.

"Everyone struggles with their sense of self, you know? Harmony is complicated."

But I watch Harmony trail across the room searching for Kai, asking guests where he might be.

Meanwhile, Kai weaves his way through the party and makes a beeline for us. He doesn't have the centered, controlled appearance he always has when I've seen him. He's wearing a white linen shirt wide open, with a gold pendant around his neck that he's playing with.

"Where did Harmony go?" he says.

"She was looking for you," Julia says. "She was pretty unstable. Just warning you."

"She's been a little paranoid these days," he says, then looks at me. "You should know that, Bean. When Harmony feels threatened, when Harmony feels insecure, she spouts fear and paranoia. She often says things she doesn't mean."

"She didn't say anything to me," I say, but I don't understand why he's telling me this.

Just then, Harlow, Grace, and Kenny run over to us, flapping their hands and squealing. "We just took some Delta-8 drops, and it's freaking amazing. You have to try it." Kenny shakes a little brown tincture in Kai's face. I'm kind of surprised that she's doing that so blatantly, right in front of everyone.

146

"Not here," Kai says, and snatches it from her. She looks upset, but says nothing.

"What's Delta-8?" I say.

"It's a legal form of weed," Julia says. "All THC sourced from hemp."

"And superpowerful," Harlow says, "but also really good for you."

"Yeah, powerful at getting you fucked up," Grace says. Her lips are all cracked, and she looks wired. I can see it in her eyes.

"That's not true," Kenny says, and smacks Grace hard, so that I can hear the slap of her hand against Grace's thin white skin.

"You should do it, Bean. It's actually way more mild than regular weed," Kenny says, but her hands are jittering and she has a black-and-blue mark on her arm, which I stare at. "Oh, that? I bet it's from Harmony. She's been so unhinged tonight."

"I'm good," I say.

Then Grace starts laughing and can't stop. "You guys, I'm going to pee in my underwear. Literally."

I think about what Deena said minutes ago about the blood moon, how it reopened past wounds. I wonder if any of that is happening with Harmony. Maybe Kenny. Maybe all of them.

"Take her to one of the bedrooms," Kai says to Kenny.

Kenny stares off into space, her eyes blurred. She doesn't respond.

"*Now*, Kenny," he says.

Kenny looks weary, but she listens and slips her arm through Grace's. Harlow takes Grace's other arm. The three of them, a human daisy chain, walk out of the room.

"You really have to do something with them," Julia says to Kai.

"Harmony was supposed to do something with them," Kai says. "Navigating this eclipse is proving very challenging." Kai tells us he'll be back, that he needs to check on something.

"What the hell was that about?" I say to Julia.

"They have no center, that's what that was about."

Julia takes my hand, and we walk to the back of the house, passing by a lot of guests who are streaming in the front door, including three men who look like replicas of those slick-haired businessmen who harassed me and Kenny at the last Femme gathering.

"I thought these old men aren't coming to these parties anymore?" I whisper to Julia.

"Listen, Bean, Deena has to invite colleagues. Deep is a spiritual movement and a wellness company, yes, but it's also a business. I promise to keep you far away from them."

"Not just far away from me," I say. "From the other girls too."

"Of course," Julia says. "Look, right now my mom is fighting the good fight for all of us," Julia says. "Having to deal with all these guys, so that one day when we're running some big company, we won't have to."

In my head I hear my mother saying, *I'm sorry,* wellness *is not a marketing tool.*

"Let's go snack on the salmon tacos they're making in the kitchen. Ocean-farmed salmon. Brain food for clarity," she says, her eyes twinkling. "What is Deena always telling us? That you can't think unless you have clarity. You can't love unless you have clarity." I never heard Deena say that, but it sounds good to me.

26

I tell Julia I'll meet her in the kitchen, but that I have to use the bathroom first. That's when I see Harmony outside the door, wiping the tears from her eyes, the breezy demeanor I'm used to, gone. As I approach her, she places her index finger to her lips, mouthing *Shhh*. She tugs me quickly into the bathroom and locks the door behind her, then slides to the floor.

"Harmony, what's going on?" I say.

"Do you know what he promised me? A makeup line. My own makeup line. Can you believe I was that stupid?" she says, still slurring her words. "They pick people they want, and then they do what they want with them. And when they're done with them, they toss them to the side."

"Who's *they*? Kenny, Harlow, and Grace?"

"Them?" She laughs, but it's an unhinged laugh, too much. "Those girls? What kind of power do you think they have? Because I'll tell you: none."

It's weird, because Kenny said the same thing about Harmony. I wonder if she is paranoid like Kai said.

"Femme is a gateway, Bean. I'm sorry to break it to you like this because you're so sweet. But it's an epic fucking gateway."

"A gateway to what, Harmony?" I soak a washcloth with

lukewarm water the way my mom would when I ran a fever. Not too cold, you don't want to shock the system. I place the cloth on her forehead. Her eyelashes are in globs under her eyes. I want to wipe the darkness away from her face, but she jumps up quickly, then chucks the cloth at me so it hits my dress.

My white 458-dollar dress.

"What the fuck?" I gasp, and look down at the fabric, the soft linen, praying that her wet fake eyelashes didn't come off, caked in black mascara. Is that shallow? That it's the first thing I think of? "Why did you do that?"

"Because I wanted to ruin their dress, that's why. Because that dress symbolizes them, and I want to protect you from them."

"I was trying to help you," I say. "You knew they gave the dress to me for the party. You knew Kai was going to take photos of me in it. I'm going to have to fight to get this stain out."

She shrugs, her face hardened. "So sad, isn't it? All that white, spoiled. Rotten." She stares right at the black glob, like a caterpillar stuck to my dress, and says nothing.

"What if I paid for the dress? How do you know it wasn't mine?"

"I know you didn't pay for it because that's how they reel you in. All of these nice things, the *luxury*, they do it to control you," she says. "In the beginning, I loved all of the things too. Oh, they got me in the beginning. I stopped talking to my family, even." She goes off on a tangent, her face in her hands, crying now, harder than before. "I've destroyed so much, Bean. I don't know what to do."

I want to stay and help her, but she's scaring me.

"Look, Harmony, I need to get back to Julia," I say. "She's going to worry. Take a few deep breaths. Julia and I'll come back and check on you. Just stay here."

"Oh, you and Julia. The two of you, the perfect couple," she says, then stands up, wiping her eyes. "You don't think you'll be wanted to do more? You think they'll leave you alone because of Julia?"

Harmony shoves into my shoulder, then barricades the bathroom door with her arm.

"What are you doing?" I say.

"Stay away from them, Bean. Don't work for Deep. That's the best advice I can give to you," she says, sounding slurry and not lucid. I just want to get away from her.

"You have to let me out. Now." I don't want to push her, but I will if she tries to keep me in here.

Finally, she stumbles over to the cabinet, holding herself up.

"I thought I had a future," she says, and I'm afraid. The look on her face, those dead eyes, tears streaming down her cheeks.

"Harmony, you need help. I'm going to get help."

"Not them," she says, and slumps to the floor. "Not them."

"If not them, then who?"

She cradles her face in her hands, and I promise her I'm going to get help.

I quickly walk down into the living room, white flowers on every table, plus more flowers and ivy drape from the minimalist lights in the ceiling. Fairy lights and candles swing from the tables to the bar to the pendants.

Julia runs up to me, her hands quickly around my waist. "You look like you've seen a ghost, what's wrong?" Then she looks down and gasps. "Okay, that needs some seltzer," she says, and grabs a can of seltzer from the bar, dabs at the black stain. "Don't worry, Bean. You can change into something of mine."

"It's Harmony. She's not well," I say, dazed. "She needs help. She was having a total meltdown in the bathroom. She practically locked me in there. And then she threw a dirty cloth at me, and my dress—"

"What? Oh my god. I knew this was going to happen. I knew she was going to freak out," Julia says. "She and Deena have been having some disagreements lately. I didn't want you to hear much about it, but Harmony can get very messy. She can become paranoid. I'm used to dealing with this, sadly."

"What disagreements? I thought your mother practically saved her? She told me that she owed everything to your mom."

"My mom saves a lot of girls. Look at Katrina. Look at Kenny. They came here with so many problems, and Deena was always there for them. But for some reason, Harmony thinks that because she's been working for Deep for a long time that she can call the shots. She's irrational if she thinks that. That's not how it works. My mom calls the shots."

"They can't work it out?"

"I love how sweet and empathetic you are. God, I love that about you." She takes my chin gently in her hand, kisses my lips softly. "Sweet Bean. Sweet little Bean. I should explain to you, if you work for Deep, you don't just *work* for Deep. You're part of Deep. You can't just do it because you want power. Harmony's ego has taken over. It's very sad."

I think of Harmony's face and the way she tried to lock me into the bathroom. *You don't think you'll be wanted to do more? You think they'll leave you alone because of Julia?* What did she mean?

"I need to change into something else," I say. "But can we stop at the bathroom where Harmony is, to check on her?"

"Of course," Julia says.

We hustle toward the bathroom, through the party, through the smiling faces, the silver moons dangling above us, the light jazz seeping through, until we get back to the bathroom. I stare at the door, feeling funny about this whole thing.

"Hello?" a woman says when we knock. I don't recognize the voice, but it's not Harmony. "Be right out."

"Oh, sorry!" Julia says, and turns to me. "She's not even there."

"Let me text her," I say. "Check up to make sure she's all right."

H, looking for you, I text. Please come find me. We'll be out back.

"You're a queen in shining armor, do you know that?" Julia says. She's so cheery. I thought it would have bothered her more that Harmony was so disturbed. But maybe she's seen this behavior before, like she said, and she's used to compartmentalizing it. I know all about that.

27

I change into a low-cut, floor-length white satin dress that looks like a vintage nightgown. "You look like a Hollywood starlet," Julia says.

"My bra is showing," I say, looking in the mirror.

"Go without one," she says, and trails her finger down my chest between my breasts. "It's sexy."

"But all those businessmen. I don't want my nipples peeking through."

"Oh, please, those old guys? They're practically my uncles."

"Yeah, creepy uncles."

Julia digs through her drawers and finds a pair of pasties, and tosses them to me. "Problem solved."

Outside, we head to the garden, where dimly lit lanterns hang blithely in the trees, and white cushions rest on top of bamboo chairs and chaise longues. Harlow, Kenny, and Grace are practically attached to Kai when they slink over to us. Why isn't Kai checking on Harmony?

"You look radiant, Bean," he says. "Like a new moon."

Kenny, Harlow, and Grace shake to the music, barely able to separate themselves from each other. It's been about an hour since I've seen her, so I guess Grace is feeling better.

"Bean, you seem distracted," Kai says, waving his hand in front of me.

"She's worried about Harmony," Julia says.

"I saw her in the bathroom, and . . ." How do I tell him that she warned me about Deep? That she tried to barricade the door? That she purposely stained my dress? I can't.

"You look like you need grounding," he says, and hands me a bracelet with a black crystal on it. "It's black tourmaline."

"I don't need to be grounded," I say, and give the rock back to him. I know right away that rejecting his offer is a mistake because the girls look at me like I've chopped his hand off with an axe.

"I can feel some kind of resistance, Bean," Kai says. "This is all about Harmony? Or it's something else?"

"Well, she was upset. She was crying."

Harlow rolls her eyes. Not hiding any disdain. "Yawn, yawn, yawn," she says.

"Harlow, that's not how we talk about people who are struggling," Kai says. Harlow slinks into herself, looking down at the ground.

"Bean, I appreciate your concern. *We all* appreciate it. But Harmony's not allowing people to help her right now. That's her struggle," he says. "Did she seem like she wanted your help, Bean?"

Did she want my help? She wanted to destroy my dress—I know that. When we went back to the bathroom to help her, she wasn't there.

"No," I say.

He leans closer to me and speaks softly. "We have parents who were addicts, you and I. Your history is affecting the decisions you make in the present. Do you understand that?"

"Why did you change your clothes, Bean?" Julia says. But she knows why. She just wants me to say it to all of them. "Go ahead, Bean. Tell them why."

Julia watches me, her head slightly cocked to the side, putting me on the spot.

"Because Harmony stained my dress."

Kenny's, Harlow's, and Grace's mouths drop open in disbelief.

"Do you think that's acceptable behavior, Bean?" Kai says.

"No," I say.

Kai looks at me, his big green eyes shining. "Harmony doesn't need to be saved, Bean. I want you to understand this. No one needs to be saved. That's a patriarchal way of thinking. No one will save you except for yourself."

"I know I can't save her," I say, "but what about friendship? Can't you help someone?"

"You can't help someone who won't accept your help," he says. "That's the key to enlightenment. It's possible that Harmony wants to go through pain."

"Pain leads to love," Kenny says, and smiles brightly. I forgot that she is high.

Julia and the girls stare down at their drinks. Close their eyes. It's like Kai's giving a sermon. I don't know what to think. I've always been told to support people who are in trouble. I watched my mom act as therapist to her friends for years. Yes, that's been my mom's philosophy, but maybe it's not a healthy one. Maybe it's why she was with my dad, someone who was clearly such a mess. Because she wanted to *help* him too.

Kai poses with a turmeric shot in his hand, his back straight, then downs the shot in one gulp. Everyone's silent.

"Look, Bean, I can tell you this isn't healthy, but I want you to recognize it. Ask yourself: What do you think should happen?"

"I think we should find her and make sure she's safe. This isn't normal behavior for her. You know, figure out what's going on."

"Well," he says, and smirks. "How about asking your community. Like the women right here in front of you. Ask Julia. Ask Kenny, Harlow, and Grace. It's not *all* about you, Bean."

"Oh," I say. The four of them stare at me. My heart is beating. My lips begin to quiver. "I thought you were asking me."

Kai laughs, throwing his head back, pushes his hands through his hair, and lifts his chin so you can see all the angles of his perfect face. *"I thought you were asking me,"* he says, in a high-pitched voice, mocking me.

Kenny, Harlow, and Grace lightly giggle. Julia says nothing.

"I do know it's not all about me," I say uncomfortably. I want to get up and run away and hide. I want to defend myself, but I think the more I speak, the worse I'll sound.

"Do you, though? Do you really understand that?" He's still

laughing, but it's not real. "That would be a great poster for a narcissist, wouldn't it? *I thought you were asking me.*"

The girls laugh flippantly again, and I feel a stabbing through my heart, humiliated. *Am* I a narcissist? Is that why I'm barely talking to my friends right now? Have I been making it all about me and my wants?

Julia purses her lips, looking disappointed. I'm not sure what's happening right now. I feel so confused. Is it possible that I didn't have any of this right? I have to rethink this. I only got here a month ago. Now all of a sudden, I have the answers about how to help Harmony? It's very possible that I don't.

"Look, don't be upset," Kai says, and pats me on the shoulder paternally. "I think you *all* can figure this out together. Harmony is a Femme leader. She's integral to Deep. So you can all decide together what to do. I trust you."

He stands up and claps his hands together. "I've got to mingle. It's not just a party for me. It's business too. Plus, I've got to get behind that camera. Pictures don't take themselves," he says. "Bean, I want to get a shot of you in this dress. It's iconic."

I nod, still shaken.

"We love you, Kai," Kenny says, and I see him hand her a small metallic pouch.

"Yeah, Kai, we love you. Thanks for your guidance," Harlow says.

Julia blows a kiss to Kai, looking grateful.

I glance over at Julia. Then to Kenny, Harlow, and Grace. "I'm sorry," I say to all of them.

In seconds, we all huddle up together, hugging, the five of us in a bundle, our knees touching. "Kai's right," Julia says. "Let's talk about this as a group."

"I hate to say this," Harlow says. "But this is what happens when Harmony drinks too much. She gets angry and paranoid."

"Does that mean we should just leave her, though?" Julia says. "I remember last time I tried to pull her off the floor and then realized it was best to keep her there."

"We could put her in a bed," Harlow says. "Make her go to sleep."

"Shhh, Harlow, shut up," Kenny says.

"I thought we were supposed to discuss," Harlow says.

"How much can we discuss? Like Kai said, we don't want to be enablers."

I agree with Harlow; I think we should find her and bring her to a safe place. But I don't want to overstep again. I feel so lost.

I'm not sure how it happens. But a decision is made. Kenny, Harlow, and Grace are going to look for Harmony. If they can't find her, then Julia and I will look. If we find her, we'll help her calm down, get her coffee, water, and some ginger tea, which are Grace's suggestions.

"First, though, before we search for her, to clear our minds, to gain some clarity," Kenny says, and pulls out the metallic pouch Kai slipped her, "let's have a taste of that Blue Honey."

Kenny opens a little glass jar and hands it to Julia. She places a tiny bit on her pinkie and sucks on it. She dips it in the jar again and places it in front of my mouth.

"I thought you were doing that other stuff. The Delta-8," I say.

"Oh, that's nothing," Grace says. "That's just weed. This is mushrooms."

"Not mushrooms," Julia says, correcting her. "Psilocybin. It's just a tiny bit mixed in honey, and it alters you just a little. You'll feel so good, like all of the problems will just slide away."

"You've done it?" I say.

"I've done it a few times. It's a beautiful experience. A lot of doctors are using it for depression these days. Lots of write-ups in medical journals. Deena's excited about it," she says, and kisses me. "We could do it together. It'll just give you a little glimmer."

"A glimmer?"

"Yeah," she says, and trickles her fingers in the air like she's sprinkling fairy dust. "Glimmer."

Julia pulls me close with her other hand and nuzzles my neck. I think about Harmony crying in the bathroom, and I think about what Kai said, that you can't sit there worrying about addicts and worrying about emotional people. You can't enable them. I know he must be right. This whole night has felt like a whirlwind. I want Julia to see me free and confident. I don't want her thinking that this kind of thing makes me nervous.

I open my mouth to Julia, and she slides the dose onto my tongue. I swallow, and she kisses me, the honey melting, her sweet mouth on mine.

28

About a half hour later, Julia and I are dancing in the garden around a firepit. The beat of the music drumming in my heart. The hedonistic vibe isn't lost on me, all of us, bearing the spirit of Deep as we dance around the flames. It's way more than a glimmer.

Kenny, Harlow, and Grace circle Julia and me, the three of them, their hands fused together. Kai moves his way over to us and dances with Kenny, their bodies pressed against each other, an intimacy I haven't seen before. I know it's perfectly innocent. I know they've been partying, but I wonder what Harmony would think about this.

Harmony. Harmony in the bathroom. *Stay away from them, Bean. Don't work for Deep.* Make it go away. Wipe it away.

Harlow hip-shakes herself close to me. And there's Grace gyrating against Katrina too. Maybe Katrina took the Blue Honey also. Then Imani, dancing with her arms in the air, reaching for the sky. Kai slides up next to Julia, and all of us dance in a circle together.

"Let's play never have I ever," Kenny says, and pulls out her flask. Katrina has one too. The two of them take sips.

"Never have I ever gotten a speeding ticket," Katrina says. Kenny drinks, then passes her flask to Julia.

"Never have I ever done anything naughty," Grace says. Everyone laughs, our hands touching, reaching for the flask.

"Never have I ever lied to anyone here," Kai says, making eye contact with each and every one of us. No one drinks. Would they dare?

"Never have I ever sprinted through a meadow with my girlfriend," Julia says, then turns to me. "We should change that."

She takes my hand, and we race out the large glass doors, outside, across the lawn, her white dress dragging through the meadow grass.

"Never have I ever seen such joy in this space," she says, and collapses back into the meadow, the lace from her dress sprawling around her.

"So much beauty," I whisper, staring at her.

"So much beauty," she repeats back to me.

A man—slicked-back gray hair, sunglasses on even though it's night—passes about twenty feet from us. He's in the garden with a woman I don't recognize, calls out Julia's name and speaks to her in French. He blows a kiss to Julia. She blows one back.

"He looks familiar," I say.

"He's a banker. My mom's financial advisor. Really nice person. I promise, nothing weird."

"I didn't think it was anything weird." Except, of course I did. I still don't understand why any men are here at all.

Julia hops up, shaking the grass off her dress. Her freckles radiant under the twinkling lights. "It's time for the pool, Bean. Let's do a cleansing, all of it from the past, wash it away . . . Never have

I ever jumped in a pool with my girlfriend with all our clothes on!"

Then she races through the grass, back to the pool, and dives in, her dress floating around her like a crown when her head pops up.

"Come on!" she yells from the deep end. "Never have I ever!"

As I come closer, I gaze into the water, the black bottom, like there's no end.

"I changed into this dress because the other dress got stained, do you not remember?" I say.

"So what," she says. "It's all replaceable. We'll get it dry-cleaned. Get in!"

I plunge in, my feet first, the dress up around my waist, the pasties floating away, my nipples popping through the dress, and I don't care. It's just a body. We're all just bodies. I feel something shifting in me, and I think it's the Blue Honey. The water feels silky between my fingers. My hair feels so soft, not like damaged hay, the way it always does.

Suddenly, Kai dances over to us, poolside, barefoot, his linen shirt unbuttoned, all those beads, the crystal, too, his long hair just below his shoulders, and snaps a few pictures of us.

"With the light shining, there's a reflection of you both against the water. Your shadow twins."

Steam rises above us in the dim pool light. I feel so lightweight, so free in the water, in this dress, this satin dress rising around me like silk balloons.

Julia pulls me close to her, my hair wet, dripping around my face. Wraps her legs around my waist.

"You never looked at me before this year, Bean," she says.

"So tightly wound around Ivy, Brooks, and Nico and all their darkness."

"I was always there," I say, kissing her.

"I see a different side of you now," she says.

"A less antisocial side, you mean?"

"Yeah, I guess." She laughs. "I've told you this before, Bean. Before *Jane Eyre* I was a little intimidated by you. I didn't know what you were going to be like. I just knew you and your friends were in this antieverything clique. You all against the world. Now look at you."

"So because I microdosed and jumped in the water in an expensive dress, I've drastically changed?"

"No, because of the way you look at me. Because of the way you've embraced yourself. The way you've committed to Deep." She kisses me gently. Her wet lips on mine. "The way you've committed to me."

I want to ask her if I'm a narcissist. If she agrees with Kai. Wouldn't that sound narcissistic? It's like saying: *What about me?*

The two of us crawl up on top of a swan tube, resting our bodies on its soft, pillowy back.

Floating. Flowing. Floating. Flowing.

"How does it feel, Bean?"

"It feels like I'm free. Free. Floating. Flowing. Free. Falling."

It's the last thing I remember.

29

Blackness.

I hear screaming. A woman's voice. An echo of a woman's voice.

Someone crawls on the floor past me, her white dress in tatters. I can't see her face. Just that the lace is ripped, dragging across the floor like a disassembled wedding train.

I hear shushing. It's a man's voice. *Shhhh.* I see Julia sleeping next to me. Her dress blowing like there's a fan on us. Or is it wind? Are we outside or inside?

Blackness again.

I can open my eyes a sliver. I'm on the ground, and the carpet is white shag. This is not Julia's bedroom. Kai is smoking a cigarette. A white cloud surrounds him. Kai smokes?

I try to move, but I can't.

"She's awake," someone says; maybe it's Kai. Harlow and Kenny and Grace are spinning and spinning, dancing, their dresses see-through to their stomachs, the outlines of their belly buttons, sweaty from all that dancing. Their faces like rocks. Their eyes, not blinking. Are they the same person? Is this a dream, or is it real?

"What's happening?" I say, but no one hears me.

Kai leans down next to me; his eyes are bloodshot, like he's been crying.

Shhhh, someone is saying. *Shhhh*.

I black out again.

30

When I wake up, I'm in a bed. At least I believe it's a bed, because it's soft. I'm not on the hard floor like the dream I had. It was a dream, wasn't it? Everything is groggy; my eyes come slowly into focus, but the room is dark. I reach my arm out, and there's a body next to me, so I gasp, spinning over to see who it is; then the streaks of blond hair come into view. It's Julia.

"Wake up, Bean. You have to get up."

I look across the room at a digital clock. It reads 5:35.

"Did we pass out?" I say. I can't get any more words out. My lips aren't working. I feel . . . drugged. Not in a good way. Sluggish and not alert, like someone's sitting on my chest. Disoriented, like the way I do when my mom would give me Benadryl.

"Get up, Bean. You have to get up." Julia places her arm behind my back and lifts me to a sitting position, but I wobble with no control over my limbs. I can feel myself crying.

"I can barely move," I say, my mind everywhere. "What happened to me?"

"I don't know what happened," she says, her voice shaky, on the edge of tears. "But you have to come with me."

Julia helps me stand up, and I press my feet to the floor. "I feel like I'm going to puke, Julia. Where are we going?"

"Bean, something happened," she whispers, her voice breaking. She nuzzles her head in my neck. Her damp hair grazes against my cheek. "I'll show you. But we have to be quiet."

She takes my hand, and we walk through the house; it looks perfect, cleaned up, and so quiet. The white Moroccan shag carpets, fuzzy under my feet, and the linen couches, crisp. It's as if no one had been there. There's not one single remnant of the party. No bar, no smoke, no champagne flutes or wineglasses. The men. The DJ, the music. The girls. It's like someone came and erased the night. The silence is eerie.

"Where are you taking me?" I say.

"Into the spa," she says, and looks back at me, her eyes hollow and tired, her pupils dark. I'm scared to see her like this. "Julia, what's happening?"

She grasps tighter on to my hand, tighter, then walks me down the stairs and opens the spa doors. The radiant heat warms my cold feet but stings. Steam lingers as the blue dawn rises through the windows past the hot tub.

The hot tub.

The water.

Someone is in the water.

My head's in a tight vise from the night before, the Blue Honey, my brain feeling like someone is twisting the life out of it.

Julia falls to her knees about ten feet from the tub. A grunt out of her like the world has ended—and maybe it has.

"Julia, who is that?" I say, my hands trembling. "Julia?" But she won't look at me.

In the tub, I see the hair, the dark curly hair. The hair floats, bobbing up and down on the water like it has a life of its own. Pooling into hearts.

It's her. I can't swallow. I can't get the words into my head.

It's Harmony.

I creep closer toward the hot tub, see her arms floating out to the sides like an angel. Her body so still.

"She was in here when I came down." Julia's weeping now. I hear her, but I don't turn to face her. "I don't know how long she's been like this. Bean, what are we going to do?"

I kneel on the soft-white tile. I can barely see in front of myself, my body dizzy, my head feeling like it's detached. Harmony's hair, her beautiful curls, her white dress floating.

"Julia," I say, crying, my voice shaking. "Help me. We have to get her out of there."

I reach into the tub and pull Harmony's body closer to me, turning her over to see her ashen face. Her beautiful face, her eyes open. Her lips bloated and blue.

"I can't do it, Bean. I can't." She's hysterical now.

"We can't leave her like this. You have to call the police." I don't even recognize my own voice, what I'm saying. "You have to get your mom. She'll know what to do."

"My mom? This will ruin her business," Julia says, weeping, barely getting the words out as she begs me. "Don't tell my mom. Please don't tell my mom." But she's not making any sense. Don't tell her mom? Someone is . . . Harmony is . . . I can't say the word.

I lift Harmony's shoulders out of the water. The violet tone of her cheeks. It reminds me of that John Everett Millais painting from our Nineteenth-Century Lit class, of Shakespeare's Ophelia, her eyes wide open in the water, her face blank.

Ophelia who died of a broken heart.

We should have looked harder for her. We took Blue Honey instead. We swam in our expensive dresses while Kai took photos of us.

"Please, Julia, help me," I say.

Julia crawls over, sniffling in her tears, and we pull Harmony up on the hot tub stairs, Julia's sobs cracking. I place my mouth on Harmony's, breathe air into her, but her lips are cold. I do it again, trying to breathe life back into her. I took a CPR class once. The mom made me do it before I babysat her kid. The boy who throws the M&M's.

Now I'm here trying to revive Harmony. Her beautiful face. The way she hugged me that first time at the Femme gathering. Her face comforting and warm, so familiar. How do you explain the face of a person who's not alive? It's not the same person you knew, except it still is.

We lay Harmony down on the tile, and I can't take my eyes off her, her face so bloated and discolored, as Julia babbles.

"I couldn't sleep and you were passed out, so I just thought I would come down here and get in the hot tub, that maybe it would relax me. And that's when I saw her. I jumped in right away, and that's why my clothes are wet, my hair. I grabbed her foot, took hold of her, tried to turn her over, but then I realized . . . I realized, oh my god, Bean, she wasn't breathing. Of course she wasn't breathing; she was face down in the water."

Julia crawls into a little ball, rocking back and forth.

"We have to call the police. We have to call them now," I say. But Julia doesn't answer me. She's humming like I'm not there. And what would we tell the police? That we were supposed to help her, but we did drugs instead? My mom raised me to be supportive of my friends. To be supportive of people in need. And I failed Harmony.

What kind of person am I? I shouldn't have left her in that bathroom. I'm so ashamed.

"This is going to ruin Deena. It'll ruin Deep," Julia says, crying. "Why did it have to be in the spa? Why? Think of all those women who come down here in their fluffy white robes, all the products they buy. How is my mother going to ever go into this spa again?"

That's what Julia's worried about. The spa. The robes. The appearance.

I know people say all sorts of weird things when they're in shock. But this concern—*How is my mother going to ever go into this spa again?*—feels like the most deranged.

"Your mother will hire someone to sage the shit out of it," I say, snapping at her. I look at her in disbelief. She must be in shock. "This is Harmony we're talking about. And she's not breathing. And we're just sitting here . . ." I grab her arms. I'm screaming now. My voice outside my head. "Julia, we have to call 911. This minute."

But my phone. I don't even know where my phone is. I was blacked out when Julia got me. Where was I?

"Do you think she died of suicide?" Julia says, completely ignoring me. "She had been so depressed and weird. Even at the party, she wouldn't talk to me. She was in her own world." Something has changed in her face. She turns away and starts to walk up the steps. "I'm going to get my mom."

I think about what Harmony said to me. *Stay away from them, Bean. Don't work for Deep.*

"You can't tell anyone about this, Bean," Julia says, looking back at me. "We have to get our story straight. I found her down here, and then I woke you up to come down. And that's our story."

"What other story would there be?" I say.

My heart races. I have so many questions.

Why did I pass out? How did I end up in Julia's bed? What happened to Harmony?

I think about the newspaper articles that are going to get printed, the TV coverage and how bad it will be. I think about my mother and what she'll say. How she'll cry when she finds out that Julia and I had to pull Harmony out of the water.

"There's no other story," Julia says. "We found her like this. That's the story."

She wraps her arms around me, and whispers that she loves me. I recoil. I don't want to be touched.

"Bean. Please," she says. "We can beat this, me and you. We

can be like Bonnie and Clyde. Thelma and Louise. Just the two of us together against everyone else."

But her words are empty. Why do we need to *beat* this? We didn't do anything. We found Harmony. We didn't hurt her.

"I need air," I say. "I can't be down here anymore."

Julia cries. "You hate me, Bean. I know you hate me."

"Everything's going to be okay," I tell her, but I know that can't be further from the truth.

31

Julia and I wait in the living room under white llama blankets while Deena talks to the police on the phone. She's in a long white linen nightgown. I've never seen her look so tired. It's not just bags under her eyes. Her face is sallow, yellow, all the freckles and age spots showing through.

She sips on a matcha tea as she speaks to the police. "Yes, officer. Thank you, officer."

I stare at the mirror behind Deena, and my black eyeliner looks caked on underneath my eyes. I look away. I don't want to see myself. I want to close my eyes and sleep, but every time my eyes shut, even for a second, I see Harmony.

Deena hangs up the phone, her face so serious. Julia's crying, her shoulders shaking.

"Bean, I want you to know that Harmony was a very troubled girl." I nod uncomfortably.

"I would never ask you to lie, you understand that. In fact, I want you to tell the police everything you know about her. You knew her in high school, isn't that correct?"

"Only through my friend Ivy," I say. "I don't know what I'm going to tell my mom. She's going to be so upset I was involved in this."

"There's no involvement. You and Julia found her. That's very different than involvement," she says. "And I'm sorry I can't be more compassionate, but I have a girl, a woman, who was part of my family," she says with an ache in her voice, "and now she's dead. So that's what I'm worried about."

Deena Patterson is disgusted with me. Maybe Kai was right. Maybe I am a narcissist.

Julia crawls up in her mom's lap, and Deena strokes her hair as tears stream down Julia's face.

"Listen to me, girls," Deena says, her voice cracking, low. "Since Harmony is no longer with us, we have to make sure that we're *memorializing* her, not *demonizing* her with our actions. We have to make sure that Harmony is remembered with love and sanity. Do you understand? This isn't about me, Bean. This is about Harmony. How do you want to see her represented? For this reason, we don't want to speak to other people about what happened. Because it will hurt Harmony. If one person is in trouble, then we're all in trouble, remember?"

Through the window, blue and red police lights whiz toward the house, sirens blaring. An ambulance behind them. Deena kisses Julia's head and walks to the door to open it for them.

32

The police ask questions. Their voices banal and tired sounding, like a teacher you're trying to drown out.

Was there anything unusual about the night?

No.

Did Harmony seem unhappy?

She was upset about something, but I don't know what.

Would someone want to hurt her?

No.

Were you taking any illegal substances? Any alcohol?

No.

Julia and I decided we wouldn't say yes if they asked us any questions. She was terrified of being a suspect. She was terrified that our partying would make her mom look bad. We have to play it like we're so naive, she said. Play it like we went to sleep and then found Harmony like that. "I don't want us to be tied to this at all."

"But we are tied to it, Julia. We found her." *You found her*, I want to say.

"Do you know how they're going to tear us apart online, Bean? Do you know the things they'll try to pin on us? We have to keep it vague. We know *nothing*. Understand?"

I feel like I want to die.

———

The Pattersons' driver gives me a ride home, and I sit on my front steps for a few minutes before I open the door.

I don't know what to think. None of it makes sense. I don't understand how I saw Harmony alive just twelve hours ago and now she's dead. I don't know how to explain this to my mother. I don't know how to explain this to Ivy, who I'm not even talking to.

Just then my phone buzzes. It's from Brooks. At least I still have him and Nico.

How was the party? Did you OD on matcha lattes?

I shut my phone off and shove it back in my pocket before I walk in my house.

Everything those next few hours is a blur. I can't tell the chronology of it at all. I know that at some point, I tell my mom what happened, and she holds me, crying. "I can't believe you had to see someone like that, Bean. I'm so sorry you had to see that." I melt in her arms. She doesn't tell me I never should have been there. That I didn't belong there.

"Close your eyes, honey," she says. "Let me make you a smoothie. I'll rub your back to help you sleep. I'll do X marks the spot."

I lie down on my bed, and she does the X marks the spot over my shirt. She's trying so hard to make the hurt go away. "X marks the spot with a dot-dot-dot and a dash-dash-dash," and then she starts crying too. Through her tears, she presses on. "Spiders going up. Spiders going down."

I don't want to close my eyes too long, because if I do, I can see Harmony's dark curls, the light hair on the side of her face, floating in the water.

Julia calls me, and her voice sounds shot. "We have to act like everything is fine. Like we didn't do anything wrong."

"We've already done that, haven't we?"

"Going forward. If they ask us more questions, which Deena said they will."

"But it's not fine, Julia. How can we pretend like it's all fine?" I say, and hide under my covers.

"Bean, I don't even know if there's going to be a funeral."

"What do you mean? Everyone has a funeral." Don't they?

"My mother is listed as power of attorney for Harmony. My mom is her next of kin. And Harmony told my mom she wanted to be cremated. She doesn't have family. They were horrible people. She was closest to Kai and my mom. They want to cremate her and give her back to the earth. Kai thinks she should have a green burial instead. There's a place in New Jersey. They wrap your body in muslin. It cuts down the carbon footprint, he said."

There's something so awful about it, that Harmony's family won't have a say. I remember Ivy speaking about Harmony's family back when she was Ivy's peer leader, telling me how much Harmony admired her sister and how Ivy wished she was Harmony's sister too. Harmony. Harmony. My lips against her cold, wet mouth. I shudder thinking about it. Pull the covers up to my chin.

"Not even her mom?" I say, and I cry thinking about my mom, and if something happened to me, how devastated she would be. I don't know anything about Harmony's mom. I know Harmony told me that she felt like she was poisoned. But didn't her mom still love her? It all seemed so unfair.

"Deep was Harmony's whole life, Bean," she says. "It's fucking tragic."

It's a heavy weight that presses against my chest, like I can't breathe. Like someone is sitting on top of me.

"Bean, why don't you come back over to my house? Sleep in my bed with me. You didn't have to leave."

I put my phone down. I don't want to go anywhere near Julia's house.

I would have done whatever she said just twelve hours ago. I would have moved into her closet if she had asked me. Now it feels so different, as if there's a world between us.

I hear her crying on the other end of the phone, and I want to reach in and touch her hair, hold her so that she knows I still love her.

"It's all my fault," she says. "I should have gone to help her. We should have found her earlier." I wince hearing her say that. "Bean, you haven't told anyone, have you? You can't tell anyone."

"The police are at your house. Everyone's going to find out,

Julia. It doesn't matter who I tell. It's going to be on the news. Harmony went to Talentum. They're going to want to do a memorial or a vigil. At the very least, they're going to do an email. You do understand that, right?"

"But they don't have to find out details from *you*, do they?" she says. "I mean, we have to keep Harmony's spirit sacred and at peace, like Deena said. But she had been self-medicating, so maybe she slipped and hit her head? Maybe it was even purposeful?"

I can't deny that I thought the same thing briefly. But now, as I think about it, it doesn't make sense. Could she have really killed herself because something happened to her and Kai? You never know the darkness that eclipses people's minds.

"Outside of how upset she was with Kai, why would Harmony kill herself? She was happy except for that one night. If she was unhappy, I never saw it."

"Just because you never saw it doesn't mean she wasn't unhappy," she says.

She starts to cry again. I hear her sniffling over the phone.

Femme is a gateway, that's what Harmony said. What did that even mean? A gateway drug? A gateway to what? I have to work out some of what happened last night. I can't put it all together. I miss Ivy. This is something I'd go over with her.

I think about last year, when we were working on the historical-society scandal. Up all night on Ivy's carpeted floor with papers everywhere. Ivy replaying their interviews on her little tape recorder because it seemed more professional than using a recording app on her phone. The two of us jotting down questions. Why would they steal from the library, of all places? Was there a threat? Did they not think the library board of trustees, people who were trained on the Dewey-fucking-decimal system, were detail oriented? The rush of solving it together, she and I for hours, our heads like one.

"We make such a good team, Bean," Ivy had said. "You're like me. You never want to stop." I thought we made a good team, but it wasn't because we were alike. It was because I supported her blindly. I wasn't really like her. I didn't have that drive, that need to bite into life like she does.

I have so many questions about what happened last night with Harmony. What happened to me. When I was passed out, I heard someone's voice while I was on the floor, saying, *She's awake.* But who was it? A man's voice. The only man I can think of is Kai.

33

Nico comes over later in the evening. My room is dark except for the little night-light with the bunny ears on my wall near the closet. Nico slips off her pointy Victorian boots. Slides into my bed with me. All her red hair, the big beehive on top of her head, resting against my pillow. I miss Ivy. I crave Ivy. But Nico is so kind, one of those people who wants to smile at you and make all the bad things disappear.

"People are going to stare when I go to school," I say. "They're going to gawk. They're going to know I was there that night."

"They'll be kind and gracious. We'll make sure of it," she says. Nico pulls a tiny cotton woven-like quilt thing out of her bag. "I thought this could be a little security blanket for you. You know, you can rub it with your fingers when you feel scared."

I hug her tightly, my face in all her big hair.

"You haven't even asked me any questions about what happened. I figured you would have grilled me," I say, rubbing the mini blanket.

"I'm ready to hear what happened when you're ready to tell it. Don't worry about me."

"And then what happens after that? Ivy quizzes you, you tell her something because of some moral code that she makes you feel guilty about, and Ivy writes about it?"

"If you told me anything, Bean, I wouldn't tell a soul," Nico says.

I can't look at her. I don't know if I believe her.

"Don't worry about Ivy. Worry about yourself right now. Take care of yourself."

"But isn't that the wrong way to be? To always be thinking of yourself?" I say. I think about what Kai said. How he mocked me that night. *That would be a great poster for a narcissist, wouldn't it?* I felt so ashamed.

"Did you ever think I was too self-involved?" I say to Nico. "You know, before Deep?"

"What are you talking about?" she says, and lifts her head up from the pillow, looking at me strangely. "You'd come with me to pick up Brooks at the mall. You'd wait for me at the dentist's office, sitting there reading while I got my teeth cleaned because I was scared of that little hook instrument. You basically sat with Ivy during the historical-society investigation last year, glued to her desk, brainstorming with her. You think that we could have done that on our own, without you?" Nico says. "That's not a self-involved person, Bean. That's a supportive friend."

"I hardly did anything with that article. I brainstormed. I copy-edited. I looked at pictures. I never should have been at that award show," I say. "And I'd go to the dentist anytime with you. It's perfectly fine until you start gagging."

"Bean, you're an amazing friend. You have to see your self-worth."

But what does my worth even mean now?

34

Monday, I take off school. Deena wants us to meet at Deep. We should discuss what happened, to heal, and to release our pain, she texted us. When Julia and I get to the store, there are three news vans and a throng of photographers.

"The media is here?" she says. "How are we supposed to get in? Plow through them?"

"Just keep your head down and drive," I say, surprising myself with my command. She parks quickly, and we skitter into the building.

Kenny, Harlow, Grace, Katrina, and Imani are all sitting on white floor pillows in the back when we get in. "I told my mom I was going to be mourning Harmony for the rest of my life," Grace cries. Candles are lit, and there's a large picture of Harmony with white roses surrounding it. A huge amethyst crystal, about the size of a large coffeepot, is placed in front of the picture. An altar for her.

Deena walks in slowly, her hair pulled off her face, and Kai trails behind her. After about three minutes of chanting and prayer, Deena finally speaks.

"We're shaken. But we're standing," she says, and bows her head. "A moment of silence for our beloved Harmony."

Everyone bows their heads, but I keep my eyes open and watch everyone. From across the circle, Kai catches me, and I quickly shut them. My stomach turning, worried that he'll call me out.

"As everyone knows, there's going to be a lot of chatter from the press. They're already outside, as you all know. We have to keep our dignity intact and our hearts and heads centered. Rumors will be afloat. But this is not a rumor mill. We don't run on rumors. We run on reality. We run on spirituality."

Deena pauses and places her hands, all those rings dangling on her fingers, close to her face. Her hands veiny and crinkled, a terrible thought I wish I didn't have. It's the second time I've seen her look human. The first was the morning after. Yesterday, I realize. That was yesterday. Her eyes are bloodshot now, a night of crying. Julia crawls across the circle to her mother, wraps her arms around her.

"Let's do a healing session," Kai says. He instructs everyone to get tighter together, our thighs touching. "That's it," he says. "Huddle in. Soak in each other's energy." He turns to Julia, tells her to go first. "How do you feel right now?"

Julia takes a long breath. "Mom, this all happened because you wanted to help people. And I feel protective of you," she says, her eyes wild. "First everyone should know not to speak to the press. All they want to do is hurt us. I saw gossip sites this morning already predicting that Deep is going to go bankrupt by the end of the year. That is not going to happen."

"Julia's right. No one speak to the press. When you see them outside, you keep your head down and keep walking. No peace signs. No *pray for Harmony*. Nothing."

Everyone nods, understanding.

"The Dalai Lama said that if you lose a loved one, you should fulfill that loved one's wish," Kai says. "So that's what we're going to do. We're going to do this for Harmony. We're going to keep this insular. Because that's what she would have wanted."

I'm not sure that's what she wanted. Before she died, she wanted me to leave Deep, that's all I know. Kai strokes the long crystal hanging from his neck. It's a talisman, he told me a few days ago. It looks alive, like it has colors inside it.

"Bean?" he says. "Tell us what you think."

I stutter, not knowing what to say. "Me?"

"Yes, you're part of this group, aren't you?" There he goes again, stroking the crystal.

"I'm thinking about Harmony. How bad I feel for her," I say.

"Death is part of life. If you're thinking only about yourself in this moment, then are you thinking about Harmony?"

"I didn't say I was thinking about myself," I say, but it comes out more defensive than I'd like. "I said I was thinking about her."

"*I*, Bean. You started with *I*," he says condescendingly. "You don't even see it, do you? How the *I* came up so quickly for you."

"But you asked, how are *you* feeling?"

"Feelings don't have to start with an *I*, do they, Kenny?"

"No," she says, wiping away her tears. "Feelings should start with the emotion."

"You know what starts with *I*?" Kai says. "Narcissism. That's what starts with *I*."

Narcissism starts with N, I want to say, but instead I look over at Julia, who's still curled up with her mom. She's got both her hands crossed over her chest and her eyes closed. Where is she? *Come to my defense*, I want to scream.

I feel like I'm going crazy, but I nod, accepting what he said. Don't make it about me. This is about Harmony. This is about what she wanted.

Kai claps his hands together, hard, and it makes a loud smacking sound.

"The only way we can reach true enlightenment, be truly alive, is through pain," he says. "Death is a form of pain that we must deal with. We have to hold that pain close to us and use it to grow."

He stands up, his white pants dragging on the floor. "I want you to experience that pain when you first heard that she died. I want you to mourn her with as much pain as you can muster. Scream out at each other. Moan. Yell. Sigh. Make noise. You can feel safe here. You'll be protected. This is my promise to you."

I wonder if he's serious, if everyone is going to scream at each other. But I've learned something about Kai: he's never joking.

"On the count of three. Channel your pain." He walks in the circle behind us. "One. Two. Three."

The screams are bloodcurdling. Like voices that I've never heard before, bellowing deep from their bellies. These girls in their white dresses, the veins popping from their necks. Across at Julia, her body hunched over, her mouth open wide. Deena, staring up at the ceiling, her cries of anguish. Katrina and Imani, their bodies contorted, moaning.

Just as their screams and moans stop, they take deep breaths, start again. Kai nodding to all of them, encouraging them, counseling them between their screams.

"Let it go. Say the things that you feel. Use it to deal with your emotional pain. Don't be afraid."

I feel like someone is going to break a blood vessel.

I can't get my scream out. It's stuck in my throat. Kai sits down behind me. His hands on my shoulders as I tense up. "Channel your pain, Bean. Let it out."

"What if I don't want to scream?" I say.

Kai puts his hands out. "Everyone stop for a second. Hold back your process. I'm sorry to be so abrupt, I could hear you in your process, so deep, so committed. Thank you." He holds his hands in a prayer to his heart.

"Bean is having trouble connecting to her sorrow." I lift my eyes to meet theirs. They mouth to me, *It's okay, Bean.*

"We know. We *all* know how you feel, Bean," he says. "And we can feel that energy like a brick wall, like arrested development."

"You have the key to your own enlightenment," Deena says. It seems so simple, the way she puts it. I understand how people across the country, in other countries, flock to her.

"Let's try an exercise in pain. I think everyone can benefit from it," Kai says. "Let's manifest it in a physical form so that you can *be* the pain. What's the thing you're struggling with most now, Bean?" Kai says.

"That Harmony's gone," I say. I am very careful not to say *I.*

"To help yourself through the grief, you must become the grief.

You must use your voice to manifest that pain. Fill your whole body up with it. Start with a lower register, maybe? Then *be* the pain."

Kai lets out a growl that sounds like it manifested in his belly.

"That's my pain building. That's me harnessing my pain, you see?" he says. Everyone nods. All of them, mesmerized by him. Their eyes trained on his face. "Start low."

I close my eyes. A sound comes out of my mouth as a moan.

"This is silly," I say.

"You feel powerless, don't you?" Kai says.

I nod my head.

"You can do it, Bean," Julia says. She gets on her hands and knees and crawls into the middle of the circle toward me and meets my growl. Her eyes are closed, and she raises her head up to the sky.

"Harvest that pain," Kai says. "Raise your voice. Feel that anger of injustice. Your father's abandonment. Your mother's control. Harmony's death. Manifest it in your voice."

Julia growls at me again and raises her head, her shoulders wide, like a lion's roar.

"Julia, share with us why you're growling?" he says.

"I'm angry at Harmony. I'm angry at her for taking her own life."

I stare sharply at Julia. But we don't know that Harmony took her own life.

"And it's okay to be angry, right? But that anger needs a place to go. Dig into that feeling, Julia. It's okay to be afraid. I'm here for you. I'm not going to leave your side." Kai places his hand on her back, between her shoulder blades. Closes his eyes.

Julia growls at me again. Her face bright red.

"Do it back to me, Bean," Julia says in a low, deep voice. "We can heal each other."

I open my mouth, and a sound comes out that I don't recognize, high pitched and frightened. I close my eyes and raise my head, letting out a scream I've never heard before. I don't even know if it's me.

35

Afterward, Kai and Deena go to discuss the next-steps strategy with a public relations team. Julia is in the bathroom, and the rest of us sit in a circle.

"You look so pretty today, Bean, did I tell you that?" Harlow says. "I love your dress."

I'm so drained by that exercise. Almost every time I blink, I see Harmony floating in the water. I can't believe Harlow's talking to me about clothes.

I look down at myself. All the ruffles. "Thanks," I say. "I got it at a vintage store in the city." It's hard to believe Harlow's complimenting me on my dress at a time like this.

"Kai will eat that up. He loves it when we're repurposing," Katrina says. "He says Deena doesn't do enough of that, that there are so many landfills filled with clothes, and that the fashion industry should be shut down, or at least curtailed."

"Your dress looks like a birthday present. You know Kai is a Libra, right?" Harlow says. "Oh, he would love Bean all wrapped up in a little bow."

He would love me wrapped up in a bow? I must have misheard her.

Harlow looks over at Kenny and smiles. It's the kind of smile you give your best friend when she has a crush on someone.

"Yeah." Grace giggles, scratching the edge of Harlow's dress. "We could give her to him as a present for his birthday. Cheer him up a little. You know how Libras are."

I look around at Imani and Katrina, blushing.

"No, I don't know how Libras are," I say. I wonder where Julia is. This conversation is making me extremely uncomfortable. I don't know if they're joking, but I don't like it at all. Especially since Harmony was Kai's girlfriend and that picture of her is staring out at us, her innocent face, her beautiful curls. Those hazel eyes.

"Libras like order and symmetry. We can give you to him on the blue moon, which lands on his birthday," Grace says, giving me this pleased look.

Just then, Kenny smacks Grace's arm. It's a smack that's hard enough that I can see a red mark flash across Grace's pale skin. She flinches and gives a slight cower.

It's not the first time I've seen her hit Grace. But it's the first time I've seen Grace look upset, like there's a real divide between them. A fissure.

Kenny stares at Grace like she's going to hit her again. Grace doesn't move and gives Kenny a hard stare. Harlow sits there unbothered, saying nothing. It was hard to tell with all the matching outfits and the constant coordination who the leader of the three of them was, but it's clear now who is in charge. Grace is at the bottom. Kenny is not.

"What are you talking about, idiot?" she seethes at Grace. "Bean is with Julia."

Cars beep outside. Is it the press? The back of my neck itches from all the ruffles. I wish I weren't wearing this dress.

The girls are silent, not saying anything, staring back and forth at each other. I don't know what just transpired. What was the gift they were talking about?

I thought about what Julia said after I saw Harmony and Kai in the meditation room. That he was like Wendy was to the Lost Boys. And they were the Lost Girls. *He wants to spread love that he missed out on.* Were they talking about sex? No, it can't be, and I shiver. I'm just imagining things.

Julia comes back from the bathroom. Her face looks sullen. "Kai wants to speak with you privately," she says to me.

"This is a lot for you. I know it is," Kai says to me.

He waves to me to sit down on the big white couch in his office. The cushions are hard and clinical. I sit up straight on the other end. "I loved Harmony. And I know I don't do things in a typical way."

No, I think. *Nothing about you is typical.*

"There's something I want to talk to you about, that I think it's time you know about me," he says.

I wonder if he's going to tell me about his relationship with Harmony, maybe explain to me what she meant that night in the bathroom.

"I want to tell you about my father," he says, which surprises me. This is not what I expected him to say. "My father wasn't a good person. He isn't a good person. I've tried to really separate myself from him. But it takes a lot of work," he says, and pauses. "Do you know who my father is, Bean?"

"No," I say. "Someone that Deena was close with. That's all I know."

"My father is Antoine Gagnon."

"Oh," I say, and I should be stunned. Shouldn't I? Why wasn't I entirely surprised that Kai's father is this twisted French businessman who is now in jail for . . . sex trafficking? Maybe because he was sending signals all along? Signs I should have put together on my own.

Thanksgivings in Paris.

Summers in France.

The man in the garden who blew Julia a kiss and spoke to her in French. Her mom's financial advisor, she had said.

The men who worked for Gagnon's company who were at that second Femme gathering. Sebastian, the handsy one, he was one of them. And then what did Kenny say to me when I asked her about it? *Kai's brilliant like that. Getting these kinds of guys with shitloads of money to invest in new projects.*

How did it go completely over my head for so long? How could it not? Even with all those signs, why would it have occurred to me that Antoine Gagnon was Kai's father? What was I? A detective?

When I listened to Julia talk about her fantasy-like childhood, all those summers in France, how she met Kai, and they were like brother and sister, it seemed so enviable. Like the kind of life I wished I lived. Oh, Julia.

Now I feel so stupid, like I'm going to throw up. But I have to hold it together. I have to listen to what Kai has to say about his father. Then I have to talk to Julia.

"Kai, why are you telling me this now? I don't understand."

"I want you to know about me since I already know so much about you," he says. "My mother died when I was a child. Drugs, alcohol. My father was a criminal. So you see, we have a lot in common."

I know I'm supposed to have an aha moment right now. I can see this is what he expects of me. We should be connecting. We've both come from chaotic homes; this is what he's trying to tell me.

My father was a vulnerable man who was in pain. He had a disease. He suffered from mental illness. My father didn't want to be the way he was. My father didn't have access to yachts and mansions and powerful politicians. My father lived in a small house with little peach shutters and answered the door in sweatpants.

My father might have been a disaster, but he was no Antoine Gagnon. This guy was a disgusting man. He's in jail for sex trafficking. *Let's just say he wasn't a good person,* Julia said when she told me about Kai's father. *It's complicated,* she said. No wonder she kept it from me.

Kai pushes his hair back off his face with his hand. Those manicured nails. Something about him telling me this feels like a performance. It's the first time I feel this way about Kai.

"The reason I do this, Bean, the reason I'm so involved in Deep, is because I genuinely want to help people." He laughs at something, a passing thought, I guess. "Did you know I got asked to model? And I could have done it because modeling is easy. What's not easy is giving back to the world and making a difference. Deena taught me that. Deena and I could teach you a lot too."

"I've learned so much from you both," I say, trying to please him.

"I'm glad you feel that way. Because finding Harmony that night has obviously been traumatic for you. It's been traumatizing for me too." He reaches across the couch to hold my hand. I let him, even though I'm quivering. "We have a connection, you and I, that's different from the rest of them.

I nod. *Say nothing, Bean. Say nothing.*

"Bad things happen to rich people too, Bean. Rich people are the same as people who don't have money. They just have nicer clothes," he says. "I'm telling you this because I want you to know where I come from. Because I don't want to be like my dad. I've worked so hard to be the antithesis of him."

Kai smiles at me, takes a deep inhale. "Can I hug you?" he says, and even though the last thing I want to do is hug him, every part of me wanting to push him away, I let him. "We're in this together, Bean. I promise you, we're all trying to better ourselves here. That's the reason we work so hard at this place. That's why so many people across the country, across the world, want to be part of it. And can you blame them?"

I stand there, lifeless. He's got his hands on each of my arms. His eyes lock with mine.

"How do you feel now?" he says.

"I feel exhausted."

"I know that exercise was draining. It's good for your brain to let all that anger out," he says. "I promise you it'll get better."

How, Kai? How can it get better if Harmony is dead? How can I be okay with any of this, knowing what Harmony told me in the bathroom? How can I be okay with the girls talking about me like I'm something to be gifted?

If I have learned anything, it's that Kai has reserves of secrets. I'm sure of it.

Afterward, as Julia's driving me home, I ask her about Antoine Gagnon. "How could you not tell me he was Kai's dad?" I say.

"Kai told you?"

"Yeah. It's kind of a big thing to leave out, Julia."

"You would have had preconceived notions. You would have judged him," she says, and doesn't give me an ounce of emotion. Her face flat. "He has a lot of shame around it. I didn't want to embarrass him."

"Why did he tell me, then?"

"He sees something in you," she says, and stops at the red light. She slides her hand across the middle console, wrapping it over mine. "Don't you get it, Bean? Don't you?"

36

The first thing Tuesday morning, I go to the pressroom. Even though I'm still furious with Ivy because of that article, I'm longing to see her. My heart aches too much not to see her. She's always there, an hour before school even starts, before anyone gets there, reading over drafts, checking for grammatical errors, coming up with new stories for next week, creating an editorial calendar on the whiteboard.

When I knock lightly on the door, she looks up at me. Tired, her face drawn. Eyes bloodshot from crying. I can hear her sigh from the door. We meet in the middle of the room and hug. Her big black crinoline skirt smashing against my bare legs. I squeeze her tighter.

"I saw the news," she says, wiping away tears. "I was going to text you last night, but I thought you wouldn't want to talk to me."

"Has there ever been a time I didn't want to talk to you?" I say.

"Yeah, last week. And the week before."

"I was mad at you. It wasn't that I didn't want to talk to you," I say. "I still had to fight every ounce of my body not to call you."

She leans against the desk, her shoulders hunched.

"What happened?"

I want to spill it out to her, tell her what a horrible night it was, that I saw Harmony in the water and that I had to pull her out. Oh my god, I had to pull her out. I hold back a sob. But I don't know what Ivy is going to do with that information. And then once I tell her, she'll want to know details. I've seen her interview people who are trying to cover up something. If I say anything, she'll press further. She'll see the lies on me.

Couldn't she see them on me now?

"I can't talk about it. The police said not to," I tell her. "I can't tell you anyway, because I know you're going to write about it. I can't trust. And it kills me that I can't trust you, Ivy."

"You're here bright and early before class has even started, so clearly you trust me a little bit." She raises her eyebrows and widens her eyes.

"Are you going to write about this?" I say.

"How can I not, Bean? A former student died at a powerful wellness guru's house. She used to attend this school. Plus, she was sleeping with one of her bosses, also a Talentum graduate. How can I *not* write about this? It would be, as my mom says, *a shonda* if I didn't write about this."

"Since when did you start quoting your mother?" I say.

"You haven't been around in a few weeks. Things have changed."

I wince, and it takes all my restraint not to tell her about how alone I feel after finding Harmony.

"I am begging you not to write about this, Ivy."

"But why, Bean? Why? Julia's your girlfriend. She loves you. If she and her mom are not embarrassed about the way they behave, then why should they be upset by what I write about them?" she says. "And most importantly, why should they blame you?"

"I shouldn't be here." I walk to the door, feeling utterly defeated. I don't know what I'm going to do when this article comes out. It's going to be a nightmare.

"On the news, they said they think it might have been suicide, but they haven't ruled out other possibilities," Ivy says, still talking to me, though I'm halfway out of the room. "Obviously there were drugs involved."

"What are you, the police?" I say, and turn away.

"Why did you come here this morning, Bean? What do you need? Are you trying to get me to lie to you? Is that what you want? For me to tell you everything's fine?"

"I need my friend," I say, and I start to cry.

She shuffles over to me and holds me, strokes my hair. I can feel her shoulders going up and down, hear her sniffling. She's crying too.

"Your hair feels so soft," she says.

"Deep Hair Mask," I say, and it makes Ivy laugh.

"I don't want to leave it like this, so bad between us. But I feel loyal to Deep. I feel loyal to Julia," I say.

"You were loyal to me once," she says.

A moment passes between us, and I don't know how to respond. *Sit in the silence*, Deena would say. I pull away.

"I'm here for you, Bean," she says, calling after me.

I wonder if it's me she's here for, or if she's just here for the story.

———

In the hallway, Kenny, Grace, and Harlow stroll toward me, their arms locked together like they're going to a spring picnic or something. They're humming a song, like sweet and innocent little ducks. Like nothing happened. The first bell hasn't even rung yet.

They see me and squeal my name. "Beaaaan," they say in unison.

Then Kenny glances at the pressroom door and back at me quizzically. "Why were you in there? Were you giving the *Talentum Free Press* an exclusive or something?" She laughs like she's kidding, but I know she's not.

My heart beats quickly. "No, of course not. I was visiting my friend Ivy. That's all." Which is the truth. I didn't tell Ivy anything new, nothing about Harmony at least.

"So, did you see the letter that the Talentum staff sent out?" Harlow says.

"What letter?" I say, and Grace pulls up the letter on her phone. It's all about suicide prevention and a suicide-hotline number.

"Suicide?" I say.

"It's what the investigation found, Bean."

"But the investigation hasn't found anything yet," I say.

Didn't Ivy just tell me she saw on the news that the police haven't ruled out other possibilities?

"Oh?" Kenny says, her eyes sharp. "I didn't know you had the inside scoop."

Before the party, Kenny, Harlow, Grace, and I felt in sync. Kenny and I connected. At least I thought we did. Now I don't know who they are.

"It's all just so upsetting," I say, my mouth twitching slightly. All I want to do is disappear from this conversation.

"Isn't it so tragic?" Harlow says. "I didn't want to come to school, but my stepmother forced me to. My father's in London for business, and I can't stay home with her all day crying, she told me. Isn't she a monster?"

"But you were all just singing and humming," I say. No one was crying at all. I don't even see any tearstains on their faces.

"We're singing Harmony's favorite song," Grace says.

"Tell her what song we're humming," Kenny says.

"We're humming 'Gypsy.' You know, Stevie Nicks?" Harlow says. "Do you want to sing it with us?"

"No, I don't want to sing it with you. It's fucking morbid," I say; it makes me cringe. "Where is Julia? She's not answering my texts. Did you hear anything from Kai?"

"First of all, it's not morbid, Bean," Kenny says, snapping at me. "I was singing this to Kai last night to help him sleep. Harmony loved Stevie Nicks, so we were singing Stevie Nicks songs. There's no other way in the human condition to prove love without feeling pain," Kenny says. Harlow and Grace close their eyes and nod, like they're praying.

I have the urge to slap them. My fingers trembling.

"We're singing Stevie Nicks because it's painful. Because it reminds us of Harmony. It's the best way to remember her, to fall into that pain of her loss instead of ignoring her," Harlow says.

"It's awful about Harmony, Bean. We know how awful it is," Kenny says. "But some people just aren't meant to be helped. I've been meditating on it with the palo santo sticks and the sandalwood mist spray from the store."

"I love that new sandalwood mist spray," Grace says. "It's so otherworldly."

Students pass us in the hall, staring at the four of us like we're eternally connected. Except we're not, are we?

"We're here for you," Kenny says, and reaches out her hand. "Remember that. We're a unit. When you feel something, we all feel something."

37

I skip fifth period because I know that's the only time my mom has free time in her schedule. She's in there with a freshman, whose back is to me. I can hear the girl crying, talking about her parents and how they don't understand her. It should come as no surprise that my mom is spending her free period talking to a kid who needs her, who has problems at home. My mom, the eternal caretaker.

She gives me the signal of *one minute*, and I stand outside the door until the girl walks out. She wipes tears from her eyes. "Your mom is the nicest person," she says. "I wish my mom was like yours."

Funny, I said something like that to Julia once.

I can't stop thinking about what Harlow said to me about Kai at the meeting yesterday. *Oh, he would love Bean all wrapped up in a little bow.* And then Grace. *We can give you to him on the blue moon, which lands on his birthday.*

I try to catch my breath. Slow my racing mind. But it's not just the birthday-present comment. It was the way they were humming Stevie Nicks like it was karaoke night. How Kenny said she was singing to Kai last night to help him sleep.

Is it obvious?

Is Kenny sleeping with Kai? Are Harlow and Grace too?

Kenny and Harlow are seventeen. It wouldn't be illegal. But Grace is sixteen.

My mom waves me in. "How are you holding up, honey?"

"I'm okay," I say. "I mean, of course I'm not okay, but I'm okay right now. Anyway, that's not why I'm here."

"Talk to me, Bean," she says.

"I want to ask you a question," I say. "Do teachers ever date other Talentum teachers?"

"Yes, all the time. But I wouldn't know about it unless it got serious."

"What about principals and teachers?"

"I think it violates sexual harassment laws because the principal is the boss. It's sexual misconduct, I'm pretty sure," she says. "Where is this line of questioning going?"

"Wait, what about a teacher and a student? What if the student was eighteen?"

"No teacher should be dating any student. Ever. Ever ever ever. I don't care how old you are. That's an abuse of power. The teacher will always have the upper hand. It's an intimate connection to be teaching someone," she says. "And if the student was under eighteen, the teacher would be immediately arrested for child molestation."

I wonder if the same logic applies to someone like Kai. I'd have to find out what the age of consent is in New Jersey, but I'm pretty sure it's sixteen. I remember Nico having a huge crush on a senior, Taz Torres. She was fifteen, and he was eighteen. She was devastated when he told her that they'd have to wait until she was sixteen. He didn't want to get in trouble, he said. But he didn't wait for Nico. He started dating someone else instead.

"Bean, please tell me where this is coming from?" she says. "Obviously this worries me. Like, really, seriously, very much worries me."

"Oh, Ivy is doing an investigation," I say, lying through my teeth. "Just helping her out with some research questions."

"As a teacher, I have a duty to report child abuse," she says. "Do you understand?"

"I know, Mom. And I promise it's nothing like that. I would tell you if it was."

38

After school, Julia and I speed down Dalton Street in the center of town. She's swerving around cars.

"Jesus, Julia," I say, gripping on to the car door. "What's wrong with you?"

"Everyone looked at me at school today like I was some kind of pariah," she says. "Then Kenny, Harlow, and Grace told me that you were talking to Ivy this morning. Is that true?"

"I mean, I always talk to Ivy."

"I thought you were fighting."

"We were taking a break from each other," I say. "And what do you mean that they *told* you? Are they spying on me?"

"Stop being so paranoid, Bean," she says, and runs over a curb as she's making a turn. "They saw you in front of the pressroom. Obviously it wasn't some random conversation. I know Ivy is the editor in chief or whatever. You can tell me, Bean. Did she ask you any questions about what happened? Or did you tell her anything?"

My heart practically skips a beat. I can feel it in my chest, clamoring away at my breastbone. I don't want to share my new thoughts with her. Not yet. Not like this.

"Please slow down, Julia."

"Just say it. Tell me—you're going to talk to Ivy about what happened that night, aren't you? Can you at least tell me what you're going to do so I can be prepared for it?" she says. "I know she took down the historical society last year. And now she's going to try to take down Deep, too, isn't she?"

She's squirming in the seat next to me, choking the life out of the steering wheel.

"Take down Deep? That's absurd, Julia. She wants to know what happened to her friend."

She turns to me and screams, "Harmony wasn't even friends with her when she died."

I place my hand on her waist, reaching around to her lower back, an acupuncture point called the Sea of Vitality, which she told me about during a relaxation class at Deep one night.

"Slow down, Julia. Let's center ourselves, okay? Exhale, Julia. Exhale like you told me. Remember, exhaling will trigger your vagus nerve to activate the para . . . the para . . . I can't remember the name."

"The parasympathetic nervous system," she says.

She exhales a few times, and we sit in silence until she calms down and pulls into the Deep parking lot. It's practically empty, except for the news vans still around back. There's a Mercedes parked there too, with a license plate that says DEEP 1.

"Your mom is here?" I ask as we get out of her car.

"No, that's Kai," she says flatly. "He's borrowing her car." And something about her voice and the empty parking lot, devoid of the women and all the shoppers who are usually crowding around the store, feels strange. Or maybe it's Julia, and how angry she is, how disconnected she seems.

Julia walks in the building and waves to Kai with such calm, everything shifting within her, that anger in the car now gone. It's almost like she's slipped into a role.

I look between the two of them, his little prayer hands, the head lowering. Julia follows his lead. She went from rage to calm so fast. It practically makes my head spin.

Kai sits us in a circle—me, Julia, Kenny, Harlow, and Grace. There's a new girl, too, Marley. She looks younger than everyone else, with long dark hair, curly bangs. Bright, full cheeks. I think she's about fourteen. I don't know why she's at this meeting.

"Let's breathe together. Let's feel each other's energy so that we can solve whatever problems come our way," he says. Kai lights sage incense in the center and wafts the heavy gray smoke in the air, pushing it to loop around each of us. Then he turns to me. "Bean. Enlighten us."

I clam up. My throat tightens. "Enlighten you about what?"

"Tell us about your meeting with your friend. The one who's the editor of the school paper." He smiles at me like this isn't an interrogation. I look over at Kenny, Harlow, and Grace. They have the same placid look on their faces.

"I explained this to Julia already. She's my best friend. We had a falling out. I just went to see her."

"I thought you felt connected to us, Bean?" Kai says. "We don't want any secrets between us. I know Julia doesn't want any secrets between you and the rest of us. Is that what you want?"

"No, not at all. I feel connected to all of you," I say, almost desperate as I look around at all their faces, their eyes blankly staring at me. "I don't want there to be any secrets between us." I'm answering in fear now. I can feel it.

"Is your friend Ivy working on a story about us?" he says.

My heart is beating so fast, my breathing shallow. I lie.

"If she is, I don't know a thing about it."

"I'm asking because she called the offices telling us that she wanted to get a statement about Harmony," he says. "She called twice."

"Okay," I say. I look over at Julia for help, to say anything, something to give me an idea of where to go with this line of questioning. But she's looking down at her lap. "Maybe she just wanted a statement because she was writing a story about Harmony's death. It's public knowledge."

"Here's the problem, Bean," he says slowly. "Maybe you don't know this well because you're still new, but everything here at Deep is about the group. If you're going ahead and talking about private situations outside the group, then it sounds like—"

"Gossip," Kenny says. "It sounds like gossip."

"Kenny, let's move back into a neutral space. I highly doubt that Bean would be gossiping with her friend, the journalist, because we're her friends too. If Bean was engaging in gossip, it would mean she wasn't a loyal person. And I think you are, Bean, aren't you?"

"Yes," I say. "Yes, of course I am."

"I think there's a lot to improve on. I think we can turn this around," Julia says, and reaches over to take my hand. She's still not looking at me.

"I think what Kenny meant by gossip is that what we've created at Deep, and also in Femme, is very special. It's not just about gathering together to party or to make surface connections," Kai says.

Then he looks at Marley. I heard from Imani that Marley's parents had paid for private spiritual sessions with Kai. Now Marley's here with him. This doesn't seem like a "private spiritual lesson" to me.

"Marley, tell us. What is this about, do you think? What do you see? We want to hear a new voice, someone like you who is new to our group."

"Clearly, it's about living your best life," she says.

Kai gives her a big smile. He approves of her answer.

"So, Bean, if you're putting all that at risk, and if you're not interested in living your best life, then we have to know, are you actually committed to us?"

"She's committed, Kai," Julia says. "I told you she's committed."

I told you she's committed. Why did Julia have to convince Kai of anything?

"I believe that too," Kai says, and crawls over to me, kneels in front of me, and places his hands out for me to touch them. "Energy, remember. We're sharing energy. Bean, I need you to be able to show us that we mean something to you. Okay?"

"Okay," I say.

"Share your ideas with us. What do you propose?"

"What do you mean?" I say shakily.

"How do you propose to show us your loyalty? How are you

going to prove to us that you're part of this group?" He takes his seat back between Harmony and Julia. The three of them watch me with great care as if I'm about to say something insightful. I don't know how to explain this, but it feels so heavy in this moment, like everything is on the line, that whatever I do next will determine if I get kicked out of Deep or not. I don't want that. More, I don't want to lose Julia.

"I'll tell Ivy not to write the article," I say.

Kai lets out an overdone *hmmmm.*

"Do you think that's going to be enough, Bean? Because I get the sense that it won't be enough," Kai says. "Especially if the article is already in the works."

"Then I'll get rid of the article," I say, steely. I don't know where the idea comes from, but it's out there now. I see Kai's eyes light up. "I know it won't entirely solve the problem. I know she can write another one. But if I get rid of the article, then I'll be sending her a message."

I look over at Julia, who is nodding, encouraging me. If she's happy, then I've made the right choice. That's what I tell myself at least. Julia could be afraid to lose me too. She could be as desperate as I am to come up with a plan to appease Kai.

It's possible Julia wants me to say anything to make this all stop. I wish she would talk to me. I wish she would ask him to stop, to give us some time to talk. But she says nothing, only stares at Kai with her full attention.

"How will you do that? Sneak into the school?" Harlow says.

"Will you break into her house?" Kenny says.

"Girls," Kai says. "Let Bean speak. She has a mind of her own. Don't you, Bean?"

"I have Ivy's iCloud password," I say.

I do. I know her iCloud password the same way you know your best friend's phone code. Or her Instagram password. Or her crush's birthday. Ivy's iCloud account is where she keeps a backup of all her documents. Every single thing she's ever written. *Ever.* Plays from sixth grade. Short stories. Articles for the paper she never filed. Essays that she wanted to send in to the *New York Times* op-ed section. It's like a treasure trove of the most important things in her life, and it's all right there in the cloud. I watched her enter it so many times that it's been seared into my mind.

ZadieSmith420

Zadie Smith because she is Ivy's favorite writer. And four twenty because that's Ivy's birthday. No, it's not for the other reason.

I look at Julia, Kenny, and Kai, their eyes plastered on me. Waiting for me to speak.

"I'll go into her account and delete the document."

"Bean, I don't want you to feel like you've been forced to do this," Julia says with so much care in her eyes.

"You were so upset earlier. She shouldn't be writing a story. Ivy doesn't have to write a story. It's wrong of her to do that."

That's what I said to Ivy this morning, long before this meeting. I didn't want her to write anything, and she had to go and stir up so many problems for me. For everyone here.

"Are you sure, Bean?" she says.

"Bean needs to decide on her own what to do," Kai says. "If she wants this, if she wants to send this message, she's going to have to send it and own it. This is Bean's beef with her best friend. Everyone understand that?"

Everyone nods.

"I want to do it," I say.

"You're so brave, Bean," Harlow says.

Kai does it again. The exaggerated *hmmmm*.

"I'm wondering if it's worth it," he says. "If you get rid of one article, that specifically targets Deep, wouldn't she be suspicious? Wouldn't it be smarter to get rid of everything she has in her iCloud file?"

"Oh, yeah, that's such a good idea," Grace says. Grace, who will agree with anyone and anything.

"You really do have to delete it all, if you're going to do it," Kenny says.

I turn to Julia. I can feel the panic in my face. All of Ivy's work. Everything that she's ever written is saved in that iCloud. All her notes. All her documents. All her stories. If I got rid of it, it might cripple her. Goddamn it, why did she have to start this? Why did she have to write about them and put me in this position?

"This is up to Bean. If Bean wants to be part of Femme, if she wants to be part of Deep, she's going to have to make some tough decisions, right? She's going to have to really decide what's important to her and what's not. It's a commitment not only to us, to Deena, and to Julia, but a commitment to herself," Kai says. "Where do you stand, Bean? That's a question you're going to need to ask yourself."

Julia caresses my thigh, biting her lip.

"This kind of commitment is meant to empower you, Bean," Kai says. "Because when you first came to us, you didn't know where you belonged. And I can see you fading a bit. I've seen some fractures in you. But a decision like this, diving into the pain . . . well, if I've taught you anything, you should know that it'll help you to regain your power through love."

Julia holds my hand tightly, entwining her fingers with mine. Part of me wants to squeeze her hand and run out of there together. The other part wants to make her happy, to stop all this attention. Not too long ago, Kai's attention energized me. It made me feel so special. In spite of everything, I want him to focus on me again. To take pictures of me. Protect me.

"I want to do it," I say.

"You sure?" Julia says. I nod my head, and she takes my face in her hands and kisses me in front of all of them. Part of me wants to cry. I just want all of this to be better again and not so hard.

"Good girl," Kai says.

I go into Ivy's iCloud. It's so easy, takes me a minute to enter the password in my laptop. And I see all of Ivy, her whole life right there in front of me. I could erase every single one of her documents if I wanted to. It was a sick thought, and I didn't want to. I don't want to destroy Ivy. I don't want to erase her. But they're right. I should be angry about this. I should feel protective of Julia. I don't have to be so fucking supportive. My initial instinct when I heard about this article was to be furious about it. I need to stick with that feeling so Ivy feels the way I feel. Deceived.

What did Ivy think was going to happen if she wrote about

Deep? Did she think we could salvage our friendship? I can't even believe I went there this morning to talk to her. I had convinced myself I needed her. But she never needed me, did she? She was always going to do what she wanted to do without me.

I right-click on the folder that says WRITING.

I press delete.

It asks me: *Are you sure?*

But I am not sure. I am not sure at all.

I press delete.

39

My phone buzzes in the middle of the night. My eyes are swollen from crying myself to sleep. Ivy. I deleted all of Ivy's work. I'm a terrible person. I'm a terrible friend.

I look at my phone, and it's a text from Ivy.

Here's a question, she writes. Who suicides in a hot tub?

Nothing about her entire folder missing? Nothing about being hacked? I sit up, the white light from my phone too bright.

I don't know what you mean, I text.

She sends me a screenshot from the *Essex County Record* with an article about the investigation. Circled in red, it reads *Sources say the Essex County medical examiner has not ruled out suicide or an accidental drowning in the death of Deep employee, Harmony Williams* . . .

We already know this, I text.

If you're going to suicide, you don't drown yourself, Ivy writes.

Unless she passed out, I text.

Yeah, but that's accidental drowning, she texts.

A pause, those awful little dots.

Why would the article say anything about suicide?

I have to give her a little information because the guilt I have for deleting her entire folder is too overwhelming. My stomach gurgles, and I curl up in pain.

Harmony had been feeling depressed, I text.

Depressed about what? She had this amazing job at Deep. You told me when you saw her speak at the Femme gathering that she was inspiring.

I stare at my phone. Why can't she stop? Why does she always have to push everything so far? Why does she have to solve every puzzle, always be the one to fixate on the evidence? When I was sitting next to her brainstorming about how the historical society hacked into the library's accounts to steal the money, it was exciting because we were working on it together. The historical society was the bad guy. Now Ivy is coming after me. She's coming after my girlfriend.

Ivy just stop. I beg you. There is no story here.

Bean, she texts, what do you know?

I'm not sure how I fall back to sleep, but I do. And I go right into a dream. I'm in bed at my father's tiny house with the peach shutters, which is weird because I only slept there a handful of times. The house is like a gingerbread house, delicate, with pieces broken off. I have my own bedroom there, which wasn't the case in real life. The few times I slept at his house, I slept in my dad's bed and he slept on the pullout couch. Not in this dream.

Suddenly the ceiling opens up to the clouds, as if we were

camping outside. And a person appears in the clouds, but I can't make out the shape. It's a woman, and she's in a long white dress. It could be Harmony. Or Julia. Or any of the girls from Deep, even Deena herself.

She starts speaking to me even though I can't make out her voice or her face. *Why did you leave me?* she asks.

And I have the strangest response: *I didn't leave you,* I tell her. *I left myself.*

Left myself? What does that even mean?

All of a sudden, the girl in white morphs into my dad.

And I wake up. I'm drenched in sweat, and I'm crying. I'm crying so hard that I can barely stop. I cry and cry, to the point where I can't breathe. I blow my nose with my shirt, and it's gross, but it's either that or suffocate on snot.

My mom knocks on my door. "Bean, I can hear you crying. Please let me in?"

But I can barely speak. She opens the door, and I'm under the covers, my face in the pillow. She sits on the edge of the bed and holds me in her arms, telling me it's okay.

"I had a bad dream," I tell her. "I blew my nose in my shirt."

She grabs another T-shirt off the floor and hands it to me so I can change.

"What was it about?" she says, wiping the sweat off my forehead.

"It was about dad, I think," I say. "I miss him. Except I don't miss him. It's weird to miss someone that you barely had in your life to begin with."

"It's part of the mourning process, Bean," she says. "Nothing you feel is wrong. Even if it's missing the relationship you never had. You still loved your dad, honey. And remember, just because he wasn't able to make healthy choices for himself, it doesn't mean that you can't. You can make the right choices in your life, okay? You're not him. You're not me. You're your own person."

She wraps her arms around me and shushes me softly like I was a baby.

40

In the morning, I feel wrecked. My head is heavy, and I can't eat a thing. When I look in the mirror, I have dark circles under my eyes.

At school, Nico and Brooks lean against my locker. "How are you?" Nico says. "We're worried about you."

I want to cry. I want to cry so badly. I want to fold myself into Nico. I want the two of them to hold me and tell me that it's going to be okay.

"I'm tired. Weird dreams."

"Listen, we have to tell you something," Brooks says. "Ivy's computer was hacked."

A nervous jolt shoots through my belly. "Oh my god," I say. "Do they . . . How does she know?"

"An entire folder was gone. All of her writing. Everything," Nico says. "It's really bad."

I can barely talk. My left eye twitches, and I can't control it. What did I think would happen today? Did I think it was going to be normal? That I thought I could come to school without anyone saying anything about Ivy's files was completely delusional, as if the whole thing didn't happen at all. As if I wasn't the one to erase my best friend's work. There was something wrong with me, very wrong. I briefly let myself slide back into my old role as Ivy's best friend, the one who'd come into her house and look through her pantry for snacks without asking for permission. The one who'd slip into her bed while she showered. Who helped her mom put away dishes.

"That's insane," I say, shaking. "That's all of her work. It's going to break her."

"Nothing breaks Ivy, you know that Bean," Brooks says. "Anyway, she's got like three other backups."

"Three other backups?" I say.

Of course she has three other backups. Maybe somewhere deep in my mind, I knew about the backups. That deleting that folder wasn't more than a symbolic gesture. A fake sacrifice. Maybe all along I knew Ivy was going to be okay. I must have known.

"Yeah, so that's not a problem. But the fact that it was done is really scary. Her dad made her go to the police," Brooks says.

"We didn't even know she has an external hard drive that automatically saves like every three minutes or something," Nico says. "Did you know?"

"I had no idea," I say.

"Plus, she has two other secure spaces her parents set her up with last year after the historical-society scandal," Brooks says. "Her dad was worried about her getting hacked back then."

"Yeah, turns out powerful people don't like it if you write about them," Brooks quips.

I want to melt right there on the floor, fall into a wave of relief that Ivy's work wasn't fully erased. Ivy would never be that careless about her work. It has to be why I did it so easily, turned on my best friend without a second thought. Because I knew she'd be protected.

Still, I did it. Still, I'm a terrible person.

Kai and Julia. Why would they want me to do that to my best friend? Except, it wasn't their idea, was it? It was mine. *How do you propose to show us your loyalty?* Kai said. I could have picked a million other things, couldn't I? I don't know what those other options might have been, but I didn't have to target Ivy.

The hallway slopes a bit, my locker at an angle as I try to grasp on to what happened last night. Didn't Kai threaten to kick me out of Deep? Or did he just imply it? Kenny, Harlow, and Grace staring at me, waiting for me to come up with something so bold. Snippets flash at me.

I start to feel lightheaded, and all of a sudden I can feel my legs give out from under me. My body drops, and I can't stop it. I feel two arms under me, and I look up. It's Brooks and Nico, their worried faces.

"We got you, Bean," Nico is saying. "We got you, and we're not letting go."

"Are you sure?" I say.

"One hundred percent," she says.

The three of us sit on the hallway floor together as I get my balance back. People stroll by staring, and I try to keep a calm look on my face, but there's no hiding anything when you're on the floor.

"We should get you to the nurse," Nico says. "At least for an ice pack. Some applesauce."

"I'm okay," I say. "I have a Deep Power Bar in my bag, and I promise to eat it."

Brooks hunts through my bag and finds the bar, then opens it. He puts it in front of my mouth. "Take a bite, Bean. I don't want to have to baby-bird-feed you."

I take a bite and let the sugar, the protein replenish me. I ache thinking about Ivy, how I could have ruined so much for her.

Slowly, they help me stand up.

"You sure you don't want to go to the nurse?" Nico says.

"No, I just need to get to my lit class. I have to talk to Julia."

41

"I guess I'm having a hard time understanding why Jane would run away and go into the forest with nothing," Julia says. We're sitting across from each other at our shared desk.

"She had a perfectly good position at Thornfield. She loved Mr. Rochester. I'm sorry, Bean. I don't get it."

We're at the part of *Jane Eyre* when Jane runs away from Thornfield, where she lives and works for Mr. Rochester, the man she's supposed to marry. But Jane just learned that Mr. Rochester was *already* married. And worse, that he's locked his wife, Bertha, on the third floor of his home.

"What's not to get?" I say.

Julia gives me a blank look.

"Jane left because Rochester lied to her, Julia. Because he manipulated her. Because he imprisoned his wife, Bertha, in the attic and tried to keep it a secret."

"You make it sound so simple, Bean," Julia says. "Rochester had to lie to Jane about Bertha, because Bertha was mentally ill. It's not like he had any Xanax in the house to give her while she was having wild outbursts. It was the 1800s."

Julia reads from an underlined passage. "Here, listen to this. 'No servant would bear the continued outbreaks of her violent and unreasonable temper or the vexations of her absurd, contra-dictory, exacting orders.' I mean, she was mad. She wasn't well," Julia says.

"According to *him!*" I say too loudly. "How do we know she was mad? Because he told us? What if she wasn't mad at all? What if he was just a manipulative asshole and she went crazy because he was trying to control her?"

"Jesus, Bean, what has gotten into you?" she says.

"Fight. Fight. Fight," Scotch chants in a low voice, his chest hovering over his desk.

"*Shut up,*" Julia and I snap in unison, and he slides back down into his seat.

I turn back to Julia and take a deep breath. *Focus on the story*, I tell myself. *Collect your thoughts. Figure out what you want to say, Bean.* But she looks at me with wide, confused eyes. This is the person I love, isn't it? Yet she's also the same person who told me it was okay to turn on my best friend. I feel sick.

"I want to ask you about something that happened at that first meeting we had after Harmony . . ."

"Okay," she says wearily.

"The girls said something to me while you were in the bath-room. It was probably just a joke, but it was weird."

"What did they say?"

"That they wanted to *gift* me to Kai. They were giggling and being silly and saying that he's a Libra. What does that even mean?"

"What does it mean that he's a Libra?" Julia says. "Well, it's an air sign. Libras can be very passionate, giving their whole selves to someone."

"Not the Libra part, Julia," I say, trying not to sound irritated. "The gift. What did that mean?"

She shakes her head and runs her fingers through her hair, exasperated.

"You know I told you Kai loves very intensely."

I'm aching to ask her. I just have to spit it out. I need answers.

"Is Kai sleeping with some of the girls?" I say.

Julia bites her lip and nods her head yes.

"I thought Harmony and Kai were together? I thought they were in love? Why would he be sleeping with anyone else, especially people who are much younger than him?"

She scoots her chair in even closer to the desk. Our heads down, whispering.

"You have to understand something, Bean. Harmony and Kai, they didn't have that kind of relationship. They didn't believe in monogamy. They believed in open love. Kai felt love for Harmony, but he feels a lot of love for the other girls too."

"Hold on. Which girls does he feel a lot of love for, Julia?" All the thoughts I had about them. They're all true.

Ms. Taylor walks toward us, and Julia quickly opens up the book to a page with a little pink sticker. She reads out loud to me:

"'No one will ever love me so again. I shall never more know the sweet homage given to beauty, youth, and grace—for never to anyone else shall I seem to possess these charms.'"

Her eyes flicker back and forth, watching me.

"Jane loves him, Bean. Don't you see how much she loves him?"

"I see it, Julia, but what about this?" I say, and I scan down the page, just a paragraph down. "Jane says, 'Yes; I feel now that I was right when I adhered to principle and law,' which means Jane is glad to leave him, because she knows she made the right choice."

Oh, Julia, Julia. Can't you get this? Can't you understand?

"She did this because she knew Rochester wasn't a good person," I say. "Because Jane had principles."

Julia's eyes are so weary.

"Julia? Frances?" Ms. Taylor says. "How's your *Jane Eyre* project going?"

"Excellent," I say with no emotion.

She squats down next to us. "I know that this is a hard time for both of you. I know you're feeling so much sadness, and I want you to take the time you need," she says. "But maybe you can share your thesis statement? Let's get it down on paper, and we can slowly go from there."

I turn to Julia, who is blank. She has nothing to say.

"It's about the madwoman in the attic," I say.

Julia stares at me, surprised. "I thought we're doing it on free will. Or how Jane isn't subservient?"

"I changed my mind," I say.

Ms. Taylor looks back and forth between us. "Okay, talk to me. What about her?"

"Was Bertha actually 'mad' because she was mentally ill? Or was she 'mad' because people kept telling her she was mad? What if they wanted to get rid of her? Is it possible that we don't know what her mental state was? All we know is what Rochester has told us. That she went into drunken rages and that she was promiscuous. What if she was suffering from trauma? What if she had anxiety? Depression? We know she suffered from mental illness because Rochester at least tells us that." I flip through the book, shuffling between my marked-up pages. "'. . . She came of a mad family; idiots and maniacs through three generations!' he says. What if Bertha had bad menstrual cramps? What if she was a tortured artist and she hated her husband? What if she wanted freedom, but this man trapped her in his house?"

My hands shake. Julia and Ms. Taylor look at me like I'm possessed.

Maybe I am.

"Of course Bertha went mad," I say. "Bertha was a prisoner. She doesn't have anyone to talk to, and she's locked in an attic. The only person she speaks to is the housekeeper for one hour a day. What kind of life is that? She was deceived by her husband, the person she was supposed to trust."

Julia looks at me blankly, then rubs her face, her eyes shut tight.

"These are profound thoughts," Ms. Taylor says. "Sounds like you two have a lot to discuss."

42

After class, Julia and I go to the library. We can be alone there, in the Alcove, a little space on the second floor.

Julia takes both my arms in hers. "What's going on, Bean?"

But I don't want her to touch me. I scoot the chair back, away from her.

"What's going on?" I say. "Let's see. First, I pulled our dead friend out of the water because you refused to call the police. Second, I deleted my best friend's writing folder—illegally, might I add—to appease you and Kai. Third, Kai, a twenty-four-year-old, is sleeping with a trio of high school girls. How's that for a start?"

She grimaces, puts her head down.

"Are you going to say something?"

"It's not like it's nonconsensual between Kai and the girls," she says, so certain, as if she's annoyed at me for even suggesting it. "They love him. Stop acting so repressed."

"Repressed? The things we've done together are pretty . . . I'm not repressed. And I resent you saying that."

Her eyes finally meet mine.

I scoot closer to her. "Don't you want to know why Harmony was so upset that night?"

"The *Essex County Record* is saying that police haven't ruled out suicide," she says. "You don't know how unstable Harmony could be."

Who suicides in a hot tub? Ivy had texted me.

"Right, maybe she got into a fight with her boyfriend and it made her want to hurt herself in a hot tub. Sorry, I don't believe that for a second."

"Kai isn't *anyone's* boyfriend," Julia says.

"Oh, excuse me. Kai is a free bird. Gotcha."

"You sound so snarky when you say that, Bean. I'm sorry if you can't handle a less traditional lifestyle, but the reason my mother is so successful is because she's unconventional."

"Are you telling me you want to see other people?" I say. "That you want to be like Kai? That you're like Kai—and that you're not anyone's girlfriend?"

"What?" she says, leaning in to me, kissing my cheeks, my forehead, my chin, my mouth, all over, everywhere she can reach. She's saying my name over and over. "Bean, Bean, Bean."

"I just want to be with you, trust me," she says, her head on my shoulder, squeezing my hand so tight, like she might break a finger. "Remember what my mother said? We have to make sure that Harmony is memorialized with love and sanity. That's our only goal. You have to trust me on this. And Kai, well, you have to understand the way he grew up."

"He told me about the way he grew up, remember?" I say. "I know all about his dad."

"But that doesn't mean Kai is bad. You know that, right?"

I think about the photo shoot with me in the nap dress. How

Kai told me that I have the power to make my life go the way I want it. *You have to accept your self-worth.*

Someone who could make me feel that special couldn't be that bad, right? Or is that *precisely* the reason he's so bad? All that charm? All that beauty? *You have to allow yourself to shine. Do you know that about yourself, Bean?* I felt so beautiful that day.

Was all of it fake? All of it.

"Are you mad at me, Bean? Because I feel like you are. Now I feel like it's directed at me."

"I would like to know how I passed out that night. I'd like to know what happened to me," I say. "Wouldn't you?"

"What do you think happened to you?"

I stare straight at her without hesitation. "I think we were drugged, Julia. And I don't mean on drugs. I mean, someone put something else in the Blue Honey." I can't believe I said it. I can't believe I *had* to say it. It erupted from my mouth as real as the day.

She inches closer to me, looking around to make sure no one else can hear us.

"That's crazy, Bean. That's just too crazy. Why would anyone drug *me*?"

"I don't know," I say, and I lean in closer to Julia, my voice so low, the lightest whisper. "Why was Harmony down there in the spa? Was anyone else with her? Harmony rarely did things alone. She was surrounded by people. Why would she have gone there by herself?"

Julia raises her eyebrows at me, her face tightening, looking at me like a terrified animal.

"I just want it to go back to being what it was before," Julia says.

"I want that, too, Julia. But I don't know how to do that. I don't think we can do that."

I close my eyes, and I see Harmony's face. Her hair floating around the hot tub. The moment I dragged her body to the tile. How I pressed my mouth against hers. How Julia crouched in the corner, shaking violently.

"We need to see Ivy," I say. "You have to come with me."

"What for?"

"Because we need to figure out what happened that night. And we need her to help us."

43

We meet up with Ivy, Nico, and Brooks at the Meat Locker after school. The Meat Locker is a shitty basement with a few black vinyl booths. Goth kids in South Brent go there to play music. The floor is greasy, it's dark, and it smells like moldy socks. Ivy, Nico, and Brooks are sitting at a circular booth at the back drinking soda.

I think Ivy can see my agonized expression, because she nods her head calmly and gives me a compassionate look. I can't hold it back anymore. I feel so horribly guilty.

"I hacked into your computer," I say, blurting it out.

"Huh," Ivy says. No reaction.

"Actually, I didn't hack anything, that would take work. I just went in with your password." *Do you think that's going to be enough, Bean? Because I get the sense that it won't be enough,* Kai had said to me. "We thought it would be a way to make you stop."

It comes out of me so wooden, like I have no attachment to it.

"That's not true, Bean. Kai had nothing to do with it," Julia seethes. Her face enraged. "You did that on your own."

I ignore what she's saying and face her. I do the opposite of spiritual emanation, I realize. Because Julia is wrapped up in her reality and I'm pretty sure I'm wrapped up in the one the rest of us are in. At least, I'm trying to find my way back there.

"Julia, I love you," I say. I'm speaking softly now, gently. I don't want to hurt her. I want her to trust me, to know that I wouldn't lead her down the wrong path. Too many people have clearly fucked with her mind up to this point, including Kai and including her mother. "But there is no reason a manager of a wellness company of Deep's stature should encourage one of their employees to break into someone's computer without permission and delete information just because it seems damning to the company."

Ivy, Nico, and Brooks look at Julia sorrowfully. One thing my friends have is compassion.

"This is ridiculous, Bean. No one encouraged you."

"He didn't stop me. He didn't say, 'You shouldn't do this because it's breaking the law.'"

"I'm not listening to any more of this. You can do what you want, but I'm leaving." Julia stands up from the booth, shoving at the table.

"We're all here because we want to know what happened to Harmony," Ivy says to her. "It's your choice to stay if you want that too."

"You don't know a thing about Harmony," Julia says. "She was part of my family for the past two years."

"Maybe you could tell us more about her, Julia?" Nico says gently. "We only knew Harmony when she was Ivy's peer leader. We looked up to her."

"I looked up to her too," Julia says, her voice shaking. "I don't want to believe that she tried to . . . that she hurt herself."

I can feel it bubbling in my stomach, the need to talk. To tell them about how Harmony acted in the bathroom. I can't hold it back anymore. No matter how angry Julia gets at me, even if she thinks I'm betraying her family.

"She was unhappy that night," I say, softly.

Julia turns to me, her whole body, lurching like I've killed someone. "Bean, stop."

Ivy ignores her. "What was Harmony unhappy about?" she says.

Julia bites at her lip, her dry, cracked lip, and it starts bleeding. Drip drip drip, a streak down her chin. I go to wipe it with my finger, but she swats me away. She takes a tissue from her bag and dabs her skin, getting the blood off. She pulls a tube of Deep Lip Repair out of her bag and smears it on her lips, making all the cracks disappear.

That's what they do at Deep: they cover up everything.

Cracked lips. Bad skin. Death.

"We need more space to process this," Julia says to me. "Please, Bean."

"I've had plenty of space. Too much space." *All I am is alone with my thoughts*, I want to tell her. "I need to hear from people I trust."

"Oh, you trust them over me?" she says incredulously.

"You met us here to figure out what happened. No one is trying to hurt you, Julia," Ivy says.

"I don't think you understand, Ivy. If someone's trying to hurt Deep, or anyone involved with Deep, then they're trying to hurt my mom. Everyone talking about this, everyone speculating and pointing fingers and writing articles is trying to hurt me. This whole conversation hurts."

I am so uncomfortable seeing the pain in Julia's face. She might not ever be willing to accept anything bad about Deep. She's too close to it, like she said. I'll have to come to terms with that somehow.

"Julia, your mother should be worried about protecting you, *her daughter*," Nico says. "Not the other way around."

Julia looks down at the floor and shakes her head. "This was a mistake to come in here. This place is gross, and it smells like feet," she says, then looks directly at me. "I'm taking an Uber home." She storms out, and I don't stop her.

"I should go follow her," I say to them, except I don't actually want to and I don't move.

Nico stretches her hand across the booth. From the outside seat, she gets up and scoots next to me. I can't get out unless I climb over her.

"Bean, don't leave," Nico says, her voice so gentle. "Give Julia a second to process."

"There's something else, Bean," Ivy says. She takes a picture out of her bag and slides it toward me. "Did you know that Deena Patterson and Antoine Gagnon were connected? There's a picture of them kissing in the South of France like years ago."

I stare down at the photo of Deena, at least a woman who looks like Deena, on a cobblestone road in a string bikini, her arms around an older man. Deena looks so young in this picture, her tiny frame, her big cheeks. Like a teenager.

"I knew Antoine Gagnon was Kai's dad. He told me," I say. "I knew the families were connected. But this . . ." I look down at the photo again. "Deena Patterson looks like a child."

"I don't think they've been straight with you," Nico says.

"You've gone through some serious Bean-washing," Brooks says.

We all start to laugh because the joke is so terrible yet maybe a little true.

"You came in so brave, so honest to admit that to Ivy. That took a lot of courage," Nico says.

"I haven't been brave," I say, flashes of me and Kai in that circle, the way he prompted me to erase her files. "I'm so ashamed. Ivy, I can't even believe you're sitting here with me after what I did. What's wrong with me?"

My whole body starts to shake and feel tingly, my brain like mush. I'm tired and confused. I just want to sleep and for all this to go away. I lay my head down on the table and start to cry.

"Bean, we think you're in a cult," Brooks says. Just blurts it out, straight-faced.

"You always have to be so bold, Brooks." Nico rolls her eyes. "That's not what he means."

"I actually do."

"What are you talking about? You think Deep is a cult? Why? Because they don't do things that are mainstream?" I say.

"Bean, they've exploited you. They've exploited the other girls. They promote and sell things based on fake research," Ivy says.

"That was just the beesting thing, and it was only in California with some crazy beekeeper," I say.

"Listen to you defend them, Bean," Brooks says.

"Meanwhile, Deena Patterson knows that whole beesting thing

is shit and she still promotes it on the Deep website," Ivy says. "They're distorting information, and they're exploiting people financially so they can promote bullshit products."

"But the worst thing so far," Nico says, "is how they convinced you to do something illegal against someone you love."

"You don't get it—that was my idea. I'm the bad one," I cry.

"How did this idea come to you?" Ivy says. "Because I know you weren't sitting there one day saying, 'Oh, I should try to destroy Ivy's life.'"

I want to defend myself, but why should I? It could have destroyed her life. I could have sunk her for good if she wasn't smart enough to back up all her work. I search my brain and think about that day. All the days, the hours, since Harmony died, since we fished her out of the water. It all feels like it's merged together.

"Kai started getting worried, you know, after hearing about how I met with you in the pressroom Tuesday morning, and after you called the Deep offices to get a statement. We had a meeting, and he said to me, 'How do you propose to show us your loyalty? How are you going to prove to us that you're part of this group?' And that's when I came up with the idea."

Brooks scratches his hair so violently that I think he's going to pull chunks out.

"That's textbook emotional control, textbook manipulating you to submit to a higher authority. I mean, this checks so many fucking boxes I'm surprised they don't have a sign WE'RE A CULT hanging outside their door," Brooks says.

"When did you become some kind of expert?" I say.

"I watched a lot of cult documentaries," he says. "Especially in the past month."

"I'm going to move from the topic of cult documentaries and get to something real," Nico says. "Bean, tell me this. What would have happened if you didn't come up with the idea to delete Ivy's writing folder?"

The answer is so clear. "I'd be kicked out of Femme. Fired from Deep. I'd lose Julia."

And all at once, so quickly, the whole thing settles in. That I chose to hurt Ivy so that I didn't lose Julia. That I chose to hurt Ivy to convince Kai of my loyalty.

Flashes of the past month come to me in spurts, me in the nap dress, cuddling with Julia in the grass in her backyard, the candle-lit ceremonies at the barn, the lymphatic-drainage facial, the sea of white dresses.

How I fell in love with Julia, the way she looked at me made me feel so important. How I trailed them all, Kenny, Harlow, and Grace, amazed by their closeness, their positivity. Katrina and Imani, how they folded their lives into the sanctity of Deep.

They all seemed like they belonged someplace, and didn't I finally feel the same? Didn't I want the same? The way they spoke and how they acted made me feel like I was part of a community, like I was building toward something.

We were lost, and Deep made us feel found.

"Tell me how to fix this," I say, my hands trembling. My mind numb. I don't tell them how scared I am. I don't think I have to. They can see it in my face.

"Why don't you tell us more about that night," Ivy says softly. "You said Harmony said something to you."

"Harmony told me that Femme was a gateway. She told me to get far away from Deep. She warned me, and I didn't listen. She was crying that night, not making sense, except it makes complete sense now," I say. "Kai is sleeping with the girls."

"Kai Edwards? Other than Harmony?"

I nod. I might pass out. I just might.

"How many of them, Bean?"

"I don't know. Kenny, Harlow, and Grace. Maybe more. Maybe all. Except for me, of course, and definitely not Julia." I think of all the girls at Femme, how he protected us that night from those awful men. How he protected *me*. I know my friends won't be able to comprehend that in their minds. That's something you can comprehend only in your heart. I looked for protection. And I found Kai.

"Grace Champlain is only sixteen," Nico says. "And Kai is like, what, twenty-four?"

The three of them are so quiet. The hum of the fluorescent lights above us rings in my ear like a worm.

Ivy jots down notes on a place mat with half a blue crayon she found stuck in the booth seat. I've trusted Ivy since the seventh grade, and I'm going to go on that trust. Because I know that's all I have.

"Walk me through it, Bean," she says.

I tell her how one minute Julia and I were in the pool, and then the next minute I passed out and woke up in Julia's bedroom. How I heard voices. That Julia's hair was damp.

"Did they drug you?" Ivy says.

"Who's *they*?" I ask her.

"Well, that's the question of the evening, isn't it?" Brooks says.

"Wait a minute," Ivy says. "Tell me exactly what happened when you woke up?"

"I was in Julia's bed. We went to the spa. And we saw Harmony. She was down there."

"You found Harmony?" Ivy says. "*You're* the one who saw her there?"

They don't even know the worst of it. How I dragged her out of the hot tub. How I gave her mouth to mouth. I want to tell them the details. I can see in their faces how they want me to, but I can't get the words out.

44

We decide that the only way to move forward is to see if we can get Julia involved in this. My heart feels like it's sinking inside itself.

But first, I'm called to the police station. Two officers sit across from my mom and me, a woman and a middle-aged detective. He's bulky and looks like he goes to the gym every morning, his muscles popping out of his police shirt, which is clearly too small for him.

"Just tell us what you remember," the woman says.

I explain how I found Harmony. How her arms were floating in the water. How we heaved her out of the spa.

I don't tell them that I didn't know a dead body filled with water would be that heavy. That I didn't expect her to look so beautiful, her eyes clear and open. I leave out that she looked like Ophelia because I doubt they'll get the reference.

I also don't tell them how Julia woke me up. That I was drugged, I'm sure of it. How Julia didn't want me to come clean about any of it because she was terrified of her mother's business going under. Julia's not a monster. They wouldn't understand fear in that moment. They'd see guilt. But I don't know how long I can protect Julia. And what am I protecting her from?

"Frances Bean, huh?" the man says. He strokes his chin.

"Yes," I say.

"Like Kurt Cobain's daughter?"

I get this a lot, when people see my middle name, but I usually get it from people much cooler than this cop.

"Yeah, like that," I say.

"Here we are now, entertain us," he says. "Remember that line?"

"Everyone remembers that line," the female officer says. You can tell she's sick of working with him.

He shuffles forward in his seat like there is a remote possibility for him to connect with me. There is not.

"What was he trying to say in that song? Was he trying to tell us that we're blind to entertainment? Or that we can't see what's right in front of our eyes?"

"Kurt Cobain is talking about the apathetic youth of Generation X," my mom says, unflinching. She literally wrote papers on this in college.

This has always been part of my identity. I can't avoid my name, Frances Bean. That name, my name, isn't just a part of my identity; it is my *whole* identity. I've always been someone else. The girl with the dead rock star's daughter's name. The girl whose best friend carries around a parasol. The one with the platinum-blond hair. The girl whose mom works at Talentum. A scholarship student. The girl whose father died.

I think about what Kai said to me about my name when I first joined Femme.

Do you like *being called Bean, or is it just something you've accepted because that's what people have decided to call you?*

It struck me, that question. Is that what I've done for so long, allowed people to dictate who I was? Did I really have no say? I wanted to run away from myself for so long. I didn't want to be me, and it was so easy to slide into Deep. So easy to slide into Julia. To love her and let her love me. But was it real? If it was real between us, wouldn't she tell me more about that night?

My memory all starts to unravel. Why were Kenny's and Harlow's clothes wet when I woke up in that groggy state? Who moved us from the pool to inside, to Julia's bedroom? And why didn't Julia want to know what happened to her? Take Harmony out of the equation. Why was I the only one concerned about us passing out after we ate that Blue Honey?

"Do you know if Ms. Williams was in contact with her family?" the female officer says, waking me up from my daze.

"I don't think they had a great relationship. At least that's what Harmony told me," I say. "She told a lot of people that." A flash of her rant in the bathroom hits me. I'm afraid of saying too much.

"Did she say why?"

"She said they were toxic. She said that Deena Patterson was like a mother to her."

"Is that what you observed? Or did you see another side to their relationship?" I look over at my mom for help.

"My daughter only worked there for four weeks. I don't know if she saw multiple sides to people," my mom says.

"We're just trying to get a full picture," the male officer says.

"Because Ms. Williams's mother and sister say Harmony—uh, Ms. Williams—was told not to speak to her family anymore. Is there anything you know about this?"

"I don't exactly remember." Harmony also told me her mother was a bad person. *I was dying inside. I had to let go of toxic people who were bringing me down.*

I think about what Harmony said to me one night. *We help so many girls, girls like me and you. Girls who need us.*

Is that what he makes them all think? That they *need* him? Isn't that what I thought too? That I *needed* Kai. That I *needed* Julia? Is that what they wanted me to believe? Is that what they want everyone to believe—that Deep products will cure you, save you, guide you, cleanse you?

Deep is a business just like everything else. And if Kai's job was to sell sell sell, could he have gotten rid of Harmony because she refused to sell? Because she didn't want to share him with all the others? Because she would have gone public with that information—that he was sleeping with underage girls? Because she wanted to disrupt his plan?

He was driving the car with the license plate that said DEEP 1. Why would Deena let him drive her car when he has his own?

Kai always makes it about Deena. Deep is Deena's baby. This is Deena's company. Everyone needs to listen to Deena.

But who is doing the day-to-day ins and outs? Who is running the behind the scenes?

Kai.

Could Kai have been done with Harmony, and then he . . .

The woman looks at the buff guy, and she closes up her notes.

"Thank you, Ms. Ellis. We'll be in contact if we have any more questions," he says. Then a sly smile. "So tell me, does that stuff really work? The face cleanser? You know, for your skin? Because my wife has been wanting to try it, but it's so expensive."

"Deep Glow? Is that what you mean?" I say.

"Yeah, that."

Deena Patterson and her lifestyle have even seeped their way into the South Brent Police Station.

Look at his eager face.

"It really brightens your skin," I say sweetly, representing the company as Deena would want me to.

45

I text Julia over and over. I want to tell her about the detectives questioning me, but she doesn't get back to me. I walk to Deep after school in hopes of finding her. A customer follows me in the door, a woman in her midfifties wearing piles of gold necklaces.

Kenny, Harlow, and Grace are there. Little white linen skirts with lace tops. Dressed like triplets.

"Hiiii," the three of them say, and glide toward the woman, their sunshiny faces dying for customers. The news trucks are gone, but the store is empty.

"Do you have anything for headaches? Something natural. My daughter told me you have tinctures for everything," she says.

"Oh, we know about headaches," Kenny says. "We have an assortment of tinctures."

"Deena had headaches, too, but she totally cured herself," Harlow follows.

Grace says nothing, but her eyes, those expressive eyes, say to the woman: *Poor you.*

You want to be like Deena? You want your daughter to look like us? You want to feel better? You want to feel better about yourself? We can help you.

I was one of those girls too.

That's when I realize what Deep sells. Not spiritual guidance. Not wellness. Not glowing from within.

It's hope.

Your body surrounded by crystals, your eyes taking in the purity of their white costumes, their beautiful faces. Kai, their beautiful boy. Deena's beautiful house. Everything is so beautiful here. Don't you want to be part of it? Spiritual emanation, your face smothered in Deep Glow, your body brimming with the buoyancy of life. If you have hope, then you're living. If you have hope, you have possibilities. If you have hope, you belong.

I stand in the corner, watching in horror.

"My daughter would love something like what you're wearing. It's so ethereal," the woman in gold chains says, and Grace dances around in a little circle, twirling her skirt.

"Can I spray you with a spirit mist?" Harlow says. "Frankincense and citrus. It opens your heart."

She sprays the mist through the air, and it smells like sour lemons.

"You should sign your daughter up for one of our Femme gatherings," Kenny says. "It's a program for young girls who want to get more in tune with themselves. We're all in it. It's a special group. Kind of like a youth group but wellness-focused."

"Plus, you get to go to Deena's house," Grace says.

Because Grace knows that's the hook.

"Wait, we get to go to Deena Patterson's house?" The woman looks like she won the lottery.

"Oh, yes. But not you. Just your daughter," Kenny says, reeling her in, following a script that I know so well. The woman nods, looking utterly disappointed.

I wander to the back to see if I can find Julia but run into Katrina in the hallway, her arms filled with boxes.

"Bean! I'm so glad you're here. Can you help me with something? No one else is around to help. Except that new girl Marley, and she's off with Kai somewhere doing some training."

"How did Marley get involved, again?" I say. "She just seemed to show up one day."

"Her parents were getting spiritual-guidance lessons from Kai. And they loved him so much that they sent Marley here to learn from him, to be part of the Deep family. Isn't that amazing?"

"She left her family in Mexico to live here in New Jersey?"

"She's here with us now."

I follow Katrina to the meditation room, where someone has written on the chalkboard wall:

MALE ENERGY HEALING
Tonight @ 8 pm

"Male energy? Is this new?" I say, taking some of the boxes from Katrina's arms.

"Oh, yeah, it's really powerful. It's for men who, you know, wrestle with their masculinity. Kai wants to help them. He's not happy with how some of the businessmen have been acting at the Femme gatherings, as you know. The inappropriate behavior."

Katrina and I place the boxes down on the ground. Inside, there are new slip covers for the cushions. Stacks of candles. A package of silky eye pillows. Musky hemp fragrances.

"Kai's doing such an incredible thing with these men, you know? He's teaching them how to be vulnerable to their emotions. This is the third one of these that he's done. I've seen the most macho guys come in here and cry. So many of them are so suppressed."

"Sounds intense."

"You know Kai. He listens to people no one else wants to hear."

It makes all of us sound like rejects.

"We're so lucky, Bean," she says. "You know. As women."

"Lucky?"

"You can commit yourself to Kai, and then you don't have to worry about men out there in the world who might hurt you. I know you have Julia, so you might not understand. But I never had a home before I met Kai. I would do anything for him. The rest of the girls would too."

"What do you mean *anything*?"

Katrina stares at the doorway, then motions to it.

Harlow. She pops her head in, a big sunny smile on her face.

"Hey, Bean, I thought you were here, you sneaky girl." She turns to Katrina. "Sorry to interrupt. But Kai wants to talk to Bean."

———

Harlow and I walk down the hallway toward Kai's office. "So have you talked to Ivy? Did she say anything to you about missing documents on her computer?"

"Oh, no," I say. "I guess she didn't notice."

"Kind of impossible not to notice a big hole like that, huh?" Harlow says. "Maybe it taught her a lesson."

I say nothing. Swallow hard. I don't know what Kai wants from me. I don't know what any of them want from me.

She runs her hand through her hair, turns back to me, and smiles. "I can sense that you're nervous, Bean. You can trust me. I've got your back on this."

"It's fine," I say.

"Kai says the word *fine* is code for pain. Sometimes, you have to sink into the present moment to escape the pain. I've been finding myself in the shadows lately. Do you feel that way?"

I look down the hallway and see Kai and Marley meditating in his office. They're facing each other with their eyes closed, so close that he could reach out and kiss her.

Reach out and kiss her. My shoulders tense up.

I think about how the detectives told me that Harmony's mom was heartbroken. That she thought Harmony was brainwashed.

If I went into Kai's office, what would I say? Would I accuse him of being a predator? Would I ask him why he's sitting so close to a fourteen-year-old like that? Would I accuse him of hurting Harmony? And what would he say back? He'd have something smarter. Something more calculating. No, nothing good would come of confronting him. Not now.

I always trusted my instincts. My mom raised me that way. She always told me my choices had to be my *own* choices because she wasn't always going to be there for me. *That's how you build instincts, Bean*, she always said. *By following your own path.* Right now, I don't trust my instincts when I'm around Kai. He confused me, made me doubt myself, and deemed me a narcissist. I don't want to go anywhere near him.

"You know what, Harlow," I say, trying to smile. "I have been chugging down so much Deep Beauty Drink, and I have to pee so bad. How about I use the bathroom and I'll meet you in his office."

"Coconut water," she says.

"Excuse me?"

"Coconut water, you know, to replenish yourself if you feel dehydrated."

"Right," I say, and quickly head toward the bathroom, but make a right at the delivery room door, exit out to the back parking lot, and run.

46

A few blocks away from Deep, down a side street, behind a school, I call Nico. She, Ivy, and Brooks pick me up in her minivan, and we drive around until we end up at the place we always end up: Don's parking lot.

I put my phone on silent in the front seat while Nico squirts ketchup over my fries the way I like it. I've got no appetite. She hands me a soda, and I sip it, but it lands like a rock in my stomach.

"We need to talk numbers," Ivy says between bites. "So here's the big thing that I found when I did some digging. We know Deep hasn't been profitable in four years."

"How is that even possible?" I say. "They have tons of products coming in. All the parties, the mediation sessions, the male-energy-healing gathering that I saw tonight. They're making twenty thousand dollars a night off some male-energy shindig."

"That might be true," Ivy says. "But the reality is Deep is a public company, which means their finances are public."

Ivy pulls her laptop out of her bag and opens it up, then hands it to me from the back seat. It looks like a mishmash of numbers with yellow highlighted columns.

"I've got a literature brain, Ivy," I say. "Please tell me what I'm looking at."

"You're looking at the Deep numbers from the past five years. Deep was profitable for five years. Out of the gate, they did everything right. Quadrupled sales. They were making a ton of money off their products. Paid their taxes. No audits."

Then she tells me to scroll to another group of numbers, highlighted in pink.

"This is when they expanded. They did well, so they opened other stores, they introduced other brands. That's when they started having Femme gatherings. That's when Kai got involved."

"That's probably when Harmony joined," I say.

I scroll to the next slew of numbers, highlighted in red.

"This is when they went downhill. One year they lost one point nine million. Then a year later, two point one million."

"What happened?" Nico asks. "I thought they were doing so well when they opened the other stores?"

"I'm going to call it the Instagram effect," Ivy says. "They made it look like they were doing well, but in reality, they probably expanded too fast. Maybe they paid themselves big bonuses. Maybe Deena Patterson can't really afford a spa in her basement but does it for looks. I'd have to really dig into their records."

"So they're bleeding money?" Brooks asks.

"Yeah, and here's the weird part. They didn't take any loans from banks. There's no infusion of money. How are they surviving if they're running on a deficit? It's certainly not from their profit."

"Who's funding Deep?" Brooks says. "That's the question."

"Well, let's see," Ivy says. "They're either stealing it from the customers or they're getting it from unnamed investors. Like . . . those creepy men at the party you told us about."

But this is very hush-hush, Bean, Kenny told me at one of the Femme gatherings. *Two of them are from Antoine Gagnon's company.*

"I have a question. Can you still access your money when you're in jail?" Ivy asks.

"I'm pretty sure you don't have access to your money," Brooks says. "But rich people don't have to have access to their money to control it. He can have some financial person control it for him while he's in prison. Maybe Kai's getting money from his dad and then he's infusing money into Deep?"

"And what does he get in return?" Nico says.

The four of us stare at each other, like we've uncovered a horrible stench that we can't put away.

"Jesus, this isn't some sex ring, like a Jeffrey Epstein thing, is it?" Brooks says. "You don't think he makes the girls from Femme have sex with the businessmen?"

"Please, let it not be that," Nico says.

"No," I say firmly, remembering distinctly that night when those two men—Sebastian and James—were all over Kenny and me. "Kai protected us when those guys came on to us. He made it very clear that wasn't acceptable behavior."

"Yeah, because he wanted the girls all to himself," Nico says.

I groan, my stomach turning from the fries, but also trying to digest all this. How could it be unfolding the way it is?

"That's probably why they don't let the moms in. So Kai can manipulate the girls without interference," Brooks says.

I think of Marley, how her parents are in Mexico. How he convinced them to send her here. Promising them he'd take care of her. "I feel sick."

"Do you think Deena Patterson knows about it?" Nico says.

"She has to be turning her head the other way to some degree. The question is how much?" I say.

"If Kai is infusing Deep with his dad's dirty money, then Kai gets to call the shots. Not Deena," Brooks says.

I think of Kai's borrowing the Mercedes with the DEEP 1 license plate.

I think of what Katrina said to me earlier at the shop. *You can commit yourself to Kai . . . I would do anything for him. The rest of the girls would too.*

I feel like an anvil has been lowered on my head. Something strong and suffocating, like I can't breathe. Like I've done something that I can't undo.

My phone buzzes. It's a text from Kenny.

Hey Bean everyone wants to know where you went.

I don't answer. Then another text, seconds later:

There's going to be a last-minute Full Moon Party tomorrow night. On the small side because we need to be respectful of Harmony's passing. Kai thinks it'll be good for all of us to go through a rebirth under the moon.

Have they absolutely lost it? Have they really lost their minds? I want to get out of this white linen skirt, its itchy fabric chafing my calves, and I stretch the fabric over my boots, tearing the delicate lace.

"Get it off me," I'm saying all of a sudden, like it's a swarm of insects attacking me. "Get it off me. I don't want any part of it." I strip off my white lacy camisole, too, so that I'm just in my sports bra, toss the camisole to the ground. I shiver in the front seat, my knees to my chest, my lips chattering.

I stare out at the white lace top lying on the pavement, underneath the glow of the golden arches. Someone in a silver car backs up, rolls over it, and there it goes, all that beauty crushed in a McDonald's parking lot.

Brooks peels off his long black sweater and hands it to me. I wrap myself in it, my fingers through the holes by the cuffs.

"This is all my fault," I say, rocking back and forth. "I did this to myself. I was weak." I jump out of the car. "I'm walking home. Don't follow me."

47

Nico drives slowly next to me as I hoof it down the street. Me in Brooks's oversize holey sweater, which goes down to my knees, and my boots.

"Bean, you can't walk around like this. It's dangerous," she calls out the window.

"If I had said something that night Harmony opened up to me. If I had called any one of you. If I had done something," I scream. Headlights swipe past from the other direction, blinding me. Cars beeping at Nico, who's driving five miles an hour to stay next to me.

"I'm weak," I say. "I'm a weak person."

"I'm sorry. Who's weak?" Ivy yells out the back window.

"Me!" I scream. "*I'm* weak. Look at me. I don't have a fucking backbone. I'm a follower. I just follow what everyone tells me to do. Even our whole getup, the four of us walking around like vampires, like we were dark Victorian lords."

I stop walking, and Nico pulls the van over to the side of the road, then turns her hazards on. Red lights flash on and off over my face. All three of them get out of the van.

"What?" I say, and kick the tire. "What do you want from me?"

"Everything's okay, Bean. We just want to talk."

Ivy comes around the side. Takes my hand. "Bean, those outfits we've been wearing, my parasol, our Victorian clothes? Whose idea do you think that was?"

"I don't know," I say, really blanking out. Trying to recall that first time. "Yours?"

"Me?" she squeals. "That wasn't me."

"But the parasol. You found that on a trip with your mom," I say. "I remember you calling me about it."

"Yeah, I sent you that picture of the parasol on that trip. I asked you if you thought I should get it, and you said, and I remember this clearly, you said, 'Buy them all. We're changing our look.' You were impassioned," Ivy says. "My mom was so annoyed. She kept telling me we were going to have to pay a customs tax. But I told her, 'Bean said to bring them all home.'"

"It was just a thing I said," I say. "I didn't even mean it seriously."

I think of Ivy twirling her parasol in her bedroom when she got home from that trip, and how quickly it became a fixture. The two of us staring at ourselves in the mirror, laughing. Me dressed in her mother's long black lace slip. Black feathers in my hair.

"But *I* took it seriously. After that, I started researching afrogoth, Bean," Ivy says. "Do you remember me learning how to draw a cat eye on you in black eyeliner? Do you remember that? Your eye burning from the makeup remover? Sticking scotch tape to your face right at your waterline?"

I nod, remembering me searching for the right technique to draw the perfect cat eye. That's when it all started coming together. The sparkling black eye shadow palette I bought at CVS.

Me in the black lace stockings I picked up from Amazon. Wet n Wild black lip liner. We called Nico and Brooks over and played dress-up.

"It felt like something magical was happening to us," Nico says. "Like we were under a spell."

"Yeah, Bean's spell," Brooks says. "The way you grabbed the chubby black eyeliner and covered your eyelid, thick and heavy, all the way up to your eyebrow, smudging it with your fingers so it looked raw and dark. 'Fuck a perfect cat eye,' you said."

They didn't realize that it was all because I wanted to be someone else. Not the teacher's daughter. Not the alcoholic's daughter. Not the smart girl's best friend.

"After that, you were unstoppable," Brooks says. "You found my iconic velvet military jacket."

"You found my black crinoline floor-length skirts at that vintage store. You wouldn't let me walk out of there without buying them," Nico says. "You turned to us, and said, 'This is who we are now.' I was mesmerized. All four of us in the costume of your creation."

"I remember thinking, 'It's Bean's dark little world. We simply live in it,'" Ivy says.

Some guy yells out the window as he zooms by, "Get the hell out of the road," and the four of us, without hesitation, spin around and give him the finger.

"Let's get back in the van. It's very dark out here. I don't feel like dying," Nico says.

"When you name someone Frances Bean," Brooks says, and rubs my shoulder, "you're birthing an icon."

48

That night, Julia comes over to my house. She wants to talk. She wants to tell me things. We sit on my front porch, the wind blowing. The moon almost full.

"I spoke to the detectives earlier," I tell her.

"I don't understand why they wanted to talk to you. They didn't ask to speak to me."

But that doesn't matter. I didn't tell them anything. And I need answers from her. I need the truth.

"Julia, why did we black out? We ate the Blue Honey, we got in the pool, and that's all I remember."

I hear the words in my head from that night. *Shhhh*, someone was saying. *Shhhh*. It was a man's voice. Was it Kai?

Then a flash of Julia asleep on the floor.

"Kai told me that Harmony was the last one to have the Blue Honey. Earlier in the night, apparently she gave it to Kenny, Harlow, and Grace. She told Kai that she put something in it."

Finally, Julia is admitting that we were drugged.

Except it's not the right answer. It's another lie. It doesn't fit. There's no way Harmony would drug us.

"Harmony? Why? Why would she? She wasn't even around them. She was in the bathroom . . ."

"I told you, Bean. Harmony was crazy. She struggled with delusions. Mental illness. We tried to tell you that night. Well, now it turns out she was out to get me and my family. So she gave Kai the Blue Honey, and he realized she put something in it."

"You can't possibly believe this, Julia."

Julia wraps her hands around her bare arms. I can see her skin pucker up with goose bumps from the chill.

"Kai was trying to protect us. Don't you see? That's why he dragged us into the bedroom," she says. "He's always trying to protect us. You know that."

"You and I were supposed to be Bonnie and Clyde, Julia. Remember?"

Then it comes to me. Bonnie and Clyde were on the run because they killed people.

"Julia, did *you* do something to Harmony?" I say, my voice low. I can barely get the words out.

"Me? My god, Bean, what do you think I am?" she says, a tremble in her voice. "You think I could hurt someone?"

All the sadness about that night, searing into me, like sharp pains. No, I don't think she could hurt someone. But she lied to me. And she's lying to herself if she believes anything Kai has to say. I want her to be truthful, but I'm not sure she knows how. Her brain is so damaged from these people she thinks are there to protect her.

"You think you knew her, and you think she was a good person, but she hated all of us, Bean," Julia says. "The only person she wanted attention from was Kai. She loved him, but it wasn't love. It was obsession. She wanted him all to herself. She hated the girls. Kenny, Harlow, Grace. All of them. All those girls who used to come in from out of town looking for guidance from my mom. She despised them. And my mom too."

"But she knew we were together," I say. "She knew she didn't have to be jealous of me, or you. You and Kai are like brother and sister. Julia, this doesn't make sense. Why would she drug me?"

Julia stands up, her white dress sways in the wind. Something cracks in her eye. A look of fear.

"I'm not like you, Bean."

"Like what? What's that supposed to mean?"

"I'm not confident like you. I might look it, but I'm not," she says. "I'm not like you and your friends. The four of you always looked so badass. And then we became partners for the *Jane Eyre* project. I would stroll in late, and there you always were, staring at me with those big bright eyes, with your cool black costume on. *That girl*, I would think, *she could be anyone she wants to be.*"

Not anyone, I think. I barely wanted to be myself.

"When I slipped the invite to that Femme gathering in your locker, I didn't think you'd come. I thought you would think that Femme, or anything that had to do with Deep, was too mainstream. That it was beneath you."

"I came because of you, Julia."

"Doesn't it seem like forever ago?"

I have to pull her back into the conversation. I need to know more about what happened that night, and she's deflecting. That's what Kai taught her to do. And she does it well.

I think about the girls who came in from LA, and how enamored they were by the white leather hammock, the sixty-five-thousand-dollar hammock.

"Julia, tell me about the connection between Kai and his dad. I know who his father is. He told me. Tell me about the money. How much money does Kai have?"

"Sometimes we lie to ourselves. I don't think you really understand that, Bean, because you're a truth-teller."

"That's not an answer, Julia." I'm angry, and I can't hide it.

Julia rises from the porch, then sits in the grass on my front lawn and pulls up weeds left over from the summer. I kneel down next to her.

"Why did Harmony tell me that Deep was a gateway?" I say.

But she's not even looking at me. I've lost her. Where's the Julia I first met? The girl who pranced around Talentum like she owned it. Who plucked me from obscurity, from my dark goth clique of friends, into Deep, into her white, sparkling world. She has to be in there somewhere.

"Julia, I can help you, but you have to talk to me," I say, and take her hands. Kiss them. She finally glances at me. Her eyes bloodshot and watery.

"It's Kai. All the girls get passed around like dolls," she says. "I wanted to always believe that he loved them. And maybe he does. But every new girl came in, and it was like an indoctrination, how they all fell in love with Kai. I had an assumption, the way they would talk about him as if he was a god, and then I heard some of the girls talking about being in love with him.

"But it was Harmony who told me that he considered himself everyone's boyfriend. That he loved so hard, because of losing his mom at a young age, that he had to spread his love this way. She made this all seem okay. I guess she willed it into being okay."

"Does your mom know?" I know the answer to this. I know Deena must know everything.

"I don't know how much she knows," she says. "I'm guessing she turned a blind eye. If it didn't affect me, then she could tolerate it."

"So she didn't mind if other girls were being abused as long as it wasn't you?"

"All those mothers, they pushed their daughters into Femme, didn't they?" Julia says. "Don't they have to take *some* responsibility for it? I mean, that one woman tried to break into my house during a Femme gathering. It wasn't just Kai trying to lure people in."

No, it wasn't all Kai; he had the girls making his sales pitch for him. But to blame the parents? You can't blame them—at least, you shouldn't—because Kai groomed the mothers too.

Truthfully, they didn't need to do much to lure the mothers, the daughters. They had the store. The Deep Glow. The Deep Beauty Powder. The nap dresses. The sound baths. The beesting treatment. They had the celebrity element. The viral social media photos of the girls looking into the camera with longing. Then they had Deena Patterson, the glamorous Deena Patterson.

I remember what Kenny said to that woman the last time I was at the Deep store. *You should sign your daughter up for one of our Femme gatherings.*

The woman was tickled; she even asked if she got to go to Deena Patterson's house.

Not you, Grace had said to the woman. *Just your daughter.*

Then there were the invitations to the Femme gatherings. How beautiful was that card sticking out of my locker that day? Kenny had made it, Julia told me. She's an artist, Julia said. *Might as well be an invite to a coronation*, Brooks said. *Embossed lettering*, Nico said. How could anyone turn down that kind of attention? Why would they?

I think of all the other cards that Kenny must have made in the name of full moons and how she and the others would lure more girls to come into Kai's lair.

Kai got those girls to do all his dirty work. Kai was in control all along.

"Julia, how long has Kai been funding Deep?" I say.

Julia doesn't say anything. I don't know how many lies they must have told her throughout the years. I don't know how many lies she's told to me. Countless.

"Long. Too long. Social media can make a business look incredible from the outside, can't it?" she says.

"Is anyone actually buying those expensive nap dresses?" I say.

"Of course they're not," Julia says. "Why do you think all the girls are walking around in them? Because Kai hands those things out like they're candy." A dark thought crosses her mind; I can sense it. "Maybe that was his plan all along, Bean. Maybe Kai wants Deep to run at a deficit. Maybe . . ." she says, and trails off.

If Deep runs at a deficit, it benefits Kai. Because then Deena remains indebted to him. And if Deena's indebted to Kai—then he continues to get access to all the girls.

That's why he "rescued" us from those creepy men. Because it's all a show.

"What am I supposed to do, Bean?" Julia says, her voice cracking, so scared. "Kai is still like a brother to me. I grew up with no family, I always felt so alone. But I always had him. Him and the girls."

I understand what Julia means, about being alone. She craved brothers and sisters. She craved a place to belong. For that reason, the girls became her family. Kai became her family.

But it doesn't take away from what I know is true: Kai put some kind of sedative in the Blue Honey to get us out of the way. Then he killed Harmony because she was going to talk about what was really happening with Deep. That he was funding it, that he was sleeping with all the girls, that he was keeping them repressed so he could get some control fix. It was a cycle. Market Deep products, recruit more girls. In sequence.

Then Harmony figured out Kai was using all of them, including her. Or she decided one day that she'd had enough. She wanted more for herself, the makeup line that she talked about, maybe more control. But Kai wanted to keep her under his thumb. He doesn't share the power; that's what she found out too late.

"We have to talk to your mom," I say.

She looks up at me, her face in terror. "If I don't have my mom, I have nothing. You have Brooks and Nico. You have Ivy. You have your mom. The only person I have is you."

"That's why I'm sitting here with you," I say. "That's why I haven't left."

"What if my mom knows more than she should, Bean? Do I really want to uncover that? Do I really want to get to the bottom of it?"

"I don't think your mom is a malicious person. She wants to help people. That's how this started, isn't it?"

But I don't know if I believe that about Deena anymore.

There's a chill through my chest because all of this reminds me of something: me.

Julia reminds me of me when I was dealing with my dad. How I'd stand in front of that little house with the peach shutters, not wanting to know what was going on in there because it was too painful to witness.

I talk to her like the people at Alateen talked to me, little Bean with the broken little heart.

"You don't have any control over what your mom does, Julia. You can't stop it. You didn't cause it, and it's not your fault."

She pauses for a minute and wipes the tears from her eyes.

"What would our heroine Jane Eyre do now?" Julia says. "She ran away from Thornfield. She ran away from Rochester. I can't remember where we are in the book. My mind is spinning."

Julia rests her head in my lap, and I stroke her hair. "Her cousin St. John, a clergyman, wants to marry her and bring her to India as a missionary."

"I shouldn't admit this to you, but I didn't read up to that part," she says. "Don't hate me. Tell me what happens. Tell me a story, Bean. Take me away from this horrific reality."

She rests her head in my lap. I stroke her hair. "Jane realizes that St. John is her equal. He's as flawed as she is as a human. 'He had held me in awe because he held me in doubt,' she tells herself."

"How do you remember all these quotes so perfectly?"

"Ivy used to ask me the same question."

"Go on, tell me more. Does she marry St. John?"

"No, because she wants to be equal to him. If you married in the 1800s, you basically became a man's property. She doesn't want to marry him and be part of him," I say. "She doesn't want to be under his rule. 'Abandon your scheme of marriage,' Jane tells him."

"Free will," Julia says. "Jane Eyre's like you, Bean, she doesn't need anyone. She rejects what society thinks she should do, and she does what's right in her heart. Unlike me . . ." Julia starts to cry again, and she grasps on to Brooks's ripped up sweater as I hold her.

I remember one of the first conversations we had about *Jane Eyre*, back in September.

I am no bird; and no net ensnares me.

"It's not true that Jane Eyre doesn't need anyone, Julia. It's not true that I don't need anyone. I need you," I say. "But they've lied and manipulated people."

I think of Julia's speech about the nap dresses when they first arrived in the shop.

And then when they see photos of us in this dress, they'll want to make time for sleep.

This was Julia telling me this. I didn't even flinch when she said it.

They used my face to sell those dresses. My body.

Something twists energy and anger into me while Julia sobs in my lap. All this time, she's been lying to me, to herself.

I feel so stupid. So incredibly stupid. I think about what Brooks said to me in the van about emotional control and textbook manipulation. *Thought control. Information control.*

"We need to crash the full moon party tomorrow night," I say to Julia.

"We?"

"Yeah, me and my friends," I say, and clasp her hand. "I need them. We have to do this together."

49

That next night, I doll myself up in white. It's the last time I'm going to see these people. The last time I'm going to let them hurt me. It's the last time I'll let them infect my brain. I have to wear something white because I have to look like one of them. I have to fit in. I have to belong.

Nico picks me up in her van, and when I open the door they all light up, glowing in their white clothes.

"Oh my god," I say. A laugh comes out of my mouth for the first time in days.

"If we're going to arrive like the Greeks in the Trojan horse," Brooks says, "then we have to dress the part."

My heart jacks up a notch.

There aren't any sidewalks where Julia lives, just acres of grass leading up to the houses. Nico parks down the road so that Julia can sneak us in. Then Julia appears at the gate wearing a white nap dress. The one I wore for the campaign. The way the dress blows behind her in the night, she almost looks like a ghost as she runs through the grass.

She leans into me, her breath on my face. She kisses me, then kisses me again. Her lips are so soft. I feel like once we do this, once we go into her house and confront these people, she'll never kiss me again. She strokes the side of my face by my eyes, and then we quietly walk up to the house.

There's no security. There's no one holding a list at the door. No valet. Just a few cars.

I wonder if Julia is really ready for what comes next. If she can drive this wedge into her family, into this group of followers, until she finds the truth.

"What's the plan?" Julia says to us, wild-eyed.

"Your mom. We should talk to her first," I say. "Where is she?"

"The spa," Julia says. "She's in the spa."

Ivy, Nico, and Brooks wait in the living room while Julia and I go down into the spa.

The last time we were down here, I could see Harmony's hair floating at the surface of the water. *Big steps forward, Bean. You can do this*, I tell myself.

As we step down onto that warm handmade tile, all those memories come rushing back. White robes hang on brass fittings, so welcoming. The first time I was here with Julia, how we stripped down to our bras and panties, how we made out in this same spot.

Then the last time, how I lifted Harmony out of the tub. The way her eyes sank into the back of her head. Her lips blue.

Deena's in there now, the steam rising, her hair up in a bun on top of her head. Her eyelashes long and luxurious. Her gold bracelets jingling in the water. The dim lights cast a glow across Deena's naturally high cheekbones, and there's not one wrinkle across her neck. Not one.

It's all high-end dermatology procedures. I'm sure of it. There's only so much Deep Glow can do, and I know it doesn't turn back time. If you're selling miracle cream to women all over the world, swearing by your products, but you turn to surgical procedures, that doesn't make you a revolutionary. That makes you a liar.

Deena opens her eyes when she hears us walking in, then sits up straight.

"Julia," she says, pushing any stray hairs off her face. "I told you that I didn't want any one down here. Not after . . ." Then she looks at me, like she can't believe I'm standing here.

"Frances, I promise that the spa was not only cleaned by professionals with bleach, but also cleansed by spiritual healers. I use someone very special. She's a top shaman from Sedona. A real mystic."

Harmony has been dead for a matter of days, and all Deena Patterson is thinking about is spiritually clearing the space so she can use it. She doesn't care who might have killed Harmony.

"Mom, please. We need to talk."

Deena pulls her shoulders back like she's going to tell us something very important, but then stands up. "Tiles hold grief, did you know that, girls?" she says, and steps out of the tub in a white one-piece bathing suit. "Especially with handmade tiles like these are. You have to roll the clay, the earth in your hands, flatten it out, then shape it. It's an intimate process. It comes with baggage, history, like we all do."

All her handmade tiles were most likely made by underpaid workers who rich, careless people like her call "artisans." She pretends to care about people's health and wellness, and family, but she uses everyone to make a name for Deep, to help boost her reputation. Just like she used me.

She runs her fingers over the tiles, her long nude manicured nails, like fire spreading.

"They were overdue for a spiritual cleansing. *I've* been overdue for a spiritual cleansing," she says. "It's like that old adage, the bus driver's kids never go on vacation. Or the cobbler's children don't have any shoes. Well, guess what, darling? The spiritual guru needs a spiritual reawakening."

"Deena," Julia says. Her voice devoid of emotion. "Kai is doing things that aren't healthy. With the girls. All of them."

"It's funny, because he said you were doing unhealthy things too," she says. "And I tend to think Kai has a very insightful thought process."

"What unhealthy things have I possibly done?" Julia says with a mouth full of rage.

"Do you understand that people are always going to demonize me?" Deena says. "There are lonely people in this world. Lonely women who struggle with their identity. They want to feel better about themselves, they want to heal from the inside. And they come to me to do that. They need me to spiritually connect."

"Spiritually emanate," I say. It just comes out in a snarky way like I'm making fun of her. I don't care anymore.

"Yes, Frances. Spiritual emanation. I'm glad you were paying attention," she says, her angry glare trying to sink into me. I'm not afraid of her.

"You see, girls, women need, no, they *want* my approval. If you get rid of me, do you understand how many women will lose out?"

"No one is getting rid of you, Mom," Julia says, and then kneels down on the wet floor. "I just want the truth," her rage turning to sadness.

"Do you, Julia? Do you want to know how I get people to follow their own minds? Do you want to know how I get them to buy the products that I sell in the store? Do you really want to know how Deep operates? Because I think *you think* it runs on unicorns and crystals," she says, and raises her voice. "People don't *have* to be around me. They *choose* to be around me. The girls in Femme, the people who work at Deep, the people who commit themselves to me, to us, to this company, they don't *have* to stay here. No one is forced to be here. *You* are not forced to be here."

"Mom, what are you saying?"

"Get off the floor, Julia," she says, her voice commanding now, like I've never heard it before. Julia doesn't move.

Deena steps under the large brass rain shower and turns it on. All that water, washing away her wrongdoings, all that darkness. I can't take my eyes off her. When she's done, she wraps herself in one of her fluffy robes. Ties the waist tight. She looks so small with her hair wet, with her skin damp.

"You'll never be in a position to lift yourself from the ashes, to build yourself from nothing. I've given you everything, Julia. I've created a sanctuary for you. I've insulated you probably too much. That's why you've never been able to see what it takes to run this place. Because you've always been in this golden bubble of your own, and I helped create it."

I know what Deena means. That's how I used to see Julia too. So out of reach, gliding through the hallways of Talentum, through life with such wonder, so carefree and confident. The way she'd glide into lit class late every day with no care. It breaks my heart witnessing her digest all this, that the curtain has been pulled back on her. That none of it's real.

"You and Kai lied to me. You said he wouldn't be anything like his father. That's why he wanted to do this, to help girls because Antoine had ruined so many of them."

"We *did* help the girls!" Deena says, shouting now. She stops herself, slicks her wet hair back again. "Don't you understand?"

"You turned your back on them, that's what I see. You told me Kai was a special person. That he wasn't like regular men. That he could lead girls my age because he was spiritually elevated. You told me that," Julia says, her voice shaking.

"Because it's true. He is," Deena says, shifting in her robe. She turns to the mirror on the wall, admiring herself. This woman, what could she be thinking, seeing her reflection? Is there any hope for Deena Patterson at all? I don't think so. "Kai didn't build this company," she says stoically. "I did. And I'm aware of *everything* that happens at Deep. For better or for worse."

"You made them prisoners, Mom. You told them you were going to give them a new life away from their shitty childhoods and their shitty parents. And then you let Kai do whatever he wanted to them," Julia says. "And Harmony knew about it. And she was going to talk, and he killed her, Mom. Do you understand this? Kai killed Harmony."

It comes quickly, and I barely see it, like a blurred vision, Deena takes two steps toward her, leans down like she might kiss her. Julia looks up at her mother, so willingly, like she's been trained for this all her life, and of course, she has. Then Deena smacks Julia across the face.

"Mom," Julia says, holding her cheek, crying harder now. "Mom—"

"The problem with you is that I've always treated you like an adult. You never learned real respect. You never learned what it is to be a child who is supposed to keep her goddamn mouth shut for once. I encouraged you to a fault. I should have treated you like these other girls, with their unstable homes. All they wanted was to be part of what we had. Don't you get that? I took them from their sad, pathetic realities, and I made them like you, Julia. I tried my hardest to turn them into *you*."

She knew all along that these girls slept with Kai and that they did things for him. Harmony. Kenny, Harlow, Grace, Katrina, Imani, Marley, and the countless girls who came into Deena's palatial house as a safe haven. They're the girls who belong to Deep. They're her possessions as much as they are Kai's. Deena Patterson is not one of the good guys. She's calculating and conniving. For all the spirituality she preaches, she only cares about one person. That's herself.

"You have no idea what it means to lift yourself out of nothing," Deena says. "You have no idea what it means to survive. To raise a daughter with no help from anyone." Then she looks at me. "Your mother is like me in that way, Bean. I know your mother would understand."

"My mother is nothing like you," I tell her.

Deena makes a sound. A *humph*, as if it was the most ridiculous thing I could say.

Julia stands up and takes a deep breath. Straightens out her skirt. Bites her lip so that it's raw again.

"You should know," Julia says. "I told Bean everything."

Deena's face looks crushed. "Kai wasn't around Harmony that night. He had a specific plan to stay far from her because she was accusing him of such awful things."

It's like Deena's about to tell us something.

"Who was around her, Mom?" Julia says.

Deena stretches her head back and closes her eyes, almost like she's giving up.

"The girls," she says. "It's always the girls."

50

Julia and I walk to the barn. Kai is there holding hands with the girls. Kenny, Harlow, Grace, Katrina, Imani, and Marley. Marley looks like a little girl from back here. There are a few others I don't recognize. We linger in the door, unsure of what to do next, but Kai sees us.

"Don't look at him," I say to Julia, and lower my head so he can't make eye contact.

But Kai signals Katrina, who skitters over to us. "Bean? You're here too?" she says. "What are you doing standing out here like this? Come inside."

Julia stares at me with a blank face.

"Deena sent us out here," I say. It's the first thing that comes to my mind.

"Deena?" Katrina says. "I heard she's in the spa."

"Yeah," Julia says, looking away.

"I'm concerned about Deena," Katrina says.

"You don't have to be concerned about Deena," Julia says.

"That's not what everyone else is saying," she says, and looks back carefully at everyone in the group, all still active in their prayer circle.

"What do you mean?" Julia says. "What's everyone saying?"

"Julia, I love your mom, but maybe it's time for Kai to be in charge. Look at him in there."

"My mother started this company," Julia says curtly. "She's not about to give it up."

Katrina shrugs. "After what happened to Harmony, how can the store survive? People are scared, and understandably so," she says. "Kai is the spiritual side of the whole company. Everything else at Deep is immaterial. He's never needed Deep, but he certainly doesn't need it anymore."

Kai is a college dropout who had access to his criminal father's money and then hitched himself to a visionary like Deena Patterson. Kai isn't a leader of anything.

He's just another man who found a strong woman to latch on to.

"I need to get back inside," Katrina says. "Please, come with us. Please, join hands with us. Kai wants us all to heal. You could use it, Julia. So could you, Bean."

"I don't think so," Julia says.

"Your loss," Katrina says, and starts to walk back into the barn, but I grab her arm and she stops. She looks back at me, startled.

"Katrina," I say, still holding on to her. "That night when Harmony died, we all took Blue Honey. Did you take it too?"

"Oh, no, I don't do any drugs. Julia knows that. Not even natural ones like psilocybin."

"Do you remember that Harmony was upset?" I say.

"Yes, of course, that poor thing. She made it so clear how upset she was. It affected all of us," Katrina says. "You know how it is. One person—"

"Right," I say, cutting her off. "Did the girls like Kenny, Harlow, and Grace help her at all when she was feeling sad?"

"Oh, yeah, they sat with her," Katrina says. "I think you two went upstairs already because you were tired. Kai told me he was taking you to bed."

"Wait, Kai told you he was taking us to bed?" I say.

"I assumed you drank something, or maybe did too much of the Blue Honey, because he asked me to help him get you upstairs. We had to practically drag you up to the guest bedroom. Kai said you just needed to sleep it off."

The guest room. So that's where we were. I remember seeing all sorts of legs around me, but I don't remember Katrina being there. Maybe it was her crawling past me. Her lace dress in tatters, like a disassembled wedding train, I remember thinking until I blacked out again.

"And then what?" I say.

"And then I came downstairs. And the girls came down with Harmony."

"What do you mean *came down*?"

"Harmony was upstairs too. Walking around crying and screaming. It was an absolute mess. Like she was having a breakdown."

So that's what I heard that night. The screaming and crying. The echo of a woman's voice. It was Harmony.

"Kenny told me they were going to take her down to the spa. That they were going to do a long sauna with her, release all the toxins. Get her cortisol levels down. She needed to be centered," Katrina says. "She needed clarity."

It was the girls who brought her down to the spa. *The girls,* Deena told us. *It's always the girls.*

The memory comes to me: Harmony's dark hair, like it had a life of its own, pooling like hearts. The way she floated in the water.

"Where did Kenny, Harlow, and Grace go after they were in the spa with Harmony? Did you see them again?" I say.

"Yeah, running up the stairs. Their clothes were wet. They said Harmony wanted to be alone. That she was meditating. They were going to check on you and Julia," Katrina says.

That must have been the second memory I had—the three of them, wet in their dresses, circling around us. I thought it was sweat from dancing. But it was water.

"And you didn't go down there to check on her?" I say.

"Why would I go down there?"

"She was such a mess, you said. She was having a breakdown, you said. Maybe you'd go down there to see if she was okay." I'm trying not to raise my voice. I'm trying to stay calm, but I'm finding it impossible.

"The girls told me she wanted to be alone. So I gave her space. Kai told me that Kenny, Harlow, and Grace were going to fix everything. But maybe something changed. I guess that's when Harmony decided to end it all. It all seemed to happen so fast."

I used to think Katrina had it all together. That she came from so little and how strong she was. But she is as brainwashed as the rest of us.

It all flickers into focus now. The way Ivy called them the

Manson sisters. When Ivy said it, she had no idea how real it would be. Susan Atkins, Patricia Krenwinkel, and Leslie Van Houten, three of the Manson girls who murdered at least seven people in 1969 because Charles Manson exploited them. Kai had the same playbook. He made the girls feel loved in a way they never felt before. He made them feel like they belonged. He groomed them. Abused them. Kenny, Harlow, and Grace. Girls like Harmony and Katrina and Imani.

Me.

"I have to go back inside the barn," Katrina says, and takes Julia's hand. "You look lost. And, Bean, you seem angry. Please come in, it will ground you. Nothing to fear when you're with family." Then she runs back inside.

I turn to Julia. "Do you think Kenny would hurt Harmony if Kai told her to?"

"I think she's capable. Out of everyone, Kenny sees Kai most like a savior."

We stand there in shock, staring at the group of them, watching as Katrina whispers in Kai's ear.

He looks up at us and smiles.

51

Kai makes his way to us, playing with his prayer beads as he follows us into the house. Ivy, Brooks, and Nico are there in the living room watching us, and I should have been scared. But seeing my friends sitting there, having them by my side, I force myself to hold it together.

"You know I love you both," Kai is saying to us. "I see a lot of sadness between the two of you. A lot of confusion." He places his hands in front of our faces as if he's going to read our auras or something. I want to smack him.

"Stop the bullshit, Kai," Julia says. "It's my house, and I want to know what the hell is going on."

Just then I feel a buzz in the pocket of my dress. It's my Instagram notification. I open the phone to see what it is, and there we are, right on my screen, all of us on white cushions. The ones from Monday at the Deep store. The first meeting we had after Harmony. Scream therapy or whatever he wanted to call it.

I hold the phone up to his face. "You said this would be private, Kai. You said this would be a safe space. But you put it on social media?"

"It was a scheduled post, by Katrina or something. Just a mistake. It'll come down in a minute . . . Let me just tell her."

The more he tried to make excuses, the more I hated him.

You can feel safe here. You'll be protected. This is my promise to you.

That's what he told us.

I stare at the photo. All of us in midscream. Kenny with her mouth wide open, Harlow too. You can't see my face, but I'm there, my head down, my blond hair standing out like a streetlight. Kai's arms are outstretched as if he's a conductor.

Underneath, the caption reads:

We are mourning our loved one, Harmony, with this practice.
Scream therapy is an age old practice, bodies crouched,
voices loud and large. It's how the body dispels trauma.
#Harmony #Deep #Grief

Underneath, comments pile up, and the post has been there for less than a minute.

How do we find out more about scream therapy?

I lost my mom when I was 12 should I scream?

I love Deep Glow it makes my skin look so good!

"Hashtag 'grief'? Is this a fucking joke?" I say.

"Calm down," he's saying. "I didn't write the caption. I'm going to take care of it."

But there's something I don't get.

"You were sitting there with us. How did you even get the photo from that angle above us?" I say.

Julia glances at the photo. "Drone," she says. "He's got drones in the meditation room."

You can feel safe here, Kai said to me.

Liar. Liar. Liar.

"Let me just get Katrina and it'll come down," he's saying. "Turn your phone off, Bean."

But it's too late for that. If he knows anything about teenage girls, he should know we can slide through a phone carousel faster than a goddamn speeding bullet and come to a rapid-fire conclusion.

First, I land on the video, all nine of us screaming, including Deena. Our voices in operatic screeches. It's terrifying. As if we're killing someone.

"Just give it to me," Kai is saying, but Julia, she's too quick, and she blocks him with her body.

Next, I'm on a third slide, so different from the other two. Clear and concise. A registration page that reads *Click on the link in the bio for more information on scream therapy.*

Suddenly, Kenny, Harlow, and Grace march into the house like a little army. "Why are you doing this?" she says, her voice going higher and higher. "Why are you doing this?"

"Kenny, go back into the barn," Kai says. "I need to speak with Julia and Bean."

She looks wounded. "I thought there were no private conversations. I thought we share everything. We should be talking as a group." She stares at him, her face longing so badly for him to give her the right words. To say the right things.

"Kenny, come with us," Julia says softly. "I need to know what happened the other night with Harmony. You'll be safe with me."

But those are the wrong words. Those are Kai's words, and I can see Kenny's eyes flitting back and forth, how confused she is.

"Kai? What's happening?" she says. "Why does Julia want me to talk to her?"

"Come on, Kenny," Julia says, and takes her hand. "We can walk out of here together. We can talk. Remember how we used to talk, me and you, and Harlow, and Grace? Remember how it used to be us for such a long time together, you working at my mom's store before all these other girls started coming?"

I try to picture the four of them in a more innocent time. In a friend group like mine. I blink at Ivy, Brooks, and Nico as they sit on the couch, the three of them unsettled in the way they shift.

"Do we need to get help?" Ivy says. And I shake my head. *Not yet, Ivy*, I want to tell her. But I don't know what I'm waiting for.

"Everyone except for Bean and Julia, back into the barn," Kai says starkly, ignoring Ivy.

"Don't tell me what to do in my house," Julia says, and she glares at Kai with hatred I've never seen from her. "You might own my mother, but you don't own me." The way she's always looked at him, with such love, such admiration, such hope. That's all gone.

Everything feels so real, so alert like we're on the edge of something very bad. The quiet of the room, the full moon shining through the windows like a menacing spotlight.

Julia picks up a large amethyst crystal that sits on the table in the middle of the room, grunting as she lifts it, and heaves it at Kai. We all scream as it hits the side of his face and his hands, even though he tries to block it from hitting him, part of the crystal jutting out like a dagger, slicing his cheek, and knocking him down.

Kenny and Harlow fall to their knees to help him. "Kai? Are you okay?" Then their terrified stares over at Julia. "Why, Julia? Why?"

Grace stands still, staring with wet eyes and twirling a strand of her strawberry blond hair. Like a little girl.

"I'm calling 911," Ivy says frantically.

I know an ambulance will be here in a few minutes and the police will follow. I have to quickly get answers from Kenny and Harlow.

"Kenny, tell us what happened that night with Harmony," I demand, and kneel in front of her.

Kai moans, rolling back and forth on the carpet, the blood dripping from the gash on his cheek.

"Look what she did to him!" Kenny is screeching.

But I ignore her. Push forward. It takes so much effort to stay calm. "Kenny, did he ask you to do something because you love him? Were you trying to protect him?"

"You know how much I love Kai," Julia says, trying to appeal to Kenny. "But he's trying to hurt all of us. Don't you see?"

"You attacked him, Julia. You're not loyal," Harlow yells at her. She places Kai's head on her lap and rips off some of her white dress to stop the bleeding across his face, strokes his hair as he moans.

"Kai makes us feel strong. He pays attention to me. He helped me go up against my mom, the way she always pushed me down. He helped all of us. I can't do anything without him," Kenny says.

"Kai only loves himself," Julia says, moving toward her. "I finally see that now."

"That's not true," Kenny says, her face a ball of red. "Everything is about you, Julia. Julia the golden child. *Julia is the one you should look like*, he always said." She turns to me, points directly in my face. "How come they didn't make *you* look like Julia, huh, Bean? They let *you* be whoever you wanted to be."

Julia stands there, her mouth open in shock.

"What? That comes as a surprise to you? You didn't know you were the doll we were supposed to follow?"

I think about that for a moment. Maybe they would have turned me into Julia if I had stayed longer. If Harmony hadn't been killed, I might have been as trapped as they are. I would have been equally as programmed.

But it doesn't matter now, because Harmony's dead.

There's a seething hum in my ears, my heart throbbing still, but now it's with anger. I've had enough.

"We need to know what happened to Harmony, Kenny. Did he tell you to hurt her?" Everything snaps forward so quickly. "Tell me now, Kenny. I can help you."

The words fly out of my mouth like on a crime procedural. *Enough of the bullshit*, my face says.

And Kenny looks down at Kai, the bloody crystal, his face, Julia crying on the floor. And she lets it all out.

She lowers her forehead so it's touching his, his breathing more labored. "We started off that night trying to help Harmony. I followed her to the spa, and I was trying to connect to her. To calm her down. But she was trying to ruin us. I know you wouldn't understand this, Bean, because your mother actually cares about you. Her students. Not like our parents, right, Harlow? We don't have anything. All we have are Kai and Deena. All we have is Deep."

Harlow, who's barely said a word this whole time, looks straight at me. "It never made sense to me why you were part of Deep anyway."

I look at my friends. Ivy, Nico, and Brooks, the absolute pain in their faces. I say nothing. Kenny strokes Kai's head, coddles him like a baby. I can see something letting go in her. Then she tells us what happened.

Harmony was upset all night because of the argument she and Kai had gotten into. Harmony was being demanding of him, wanting more of him, Kenny tells us. Harmony hated Kenny, Grace, and Harlow. Hated. She was tired of the businessmen and their groping hands. She was tired of being under Deena's control. The new girls seemed so desperate to her, their home lives worse and worse.

Kenny says that Harmony fantasized about running off to Mexico with Kai and having kids together. "Harmony wanted to start a new makeup line under Deep," Kenny says. "She was delusional. She was unstable. Then she threatened him. She threatened to leave him—to leave us. She was going to spill details about our relationships, and they wouldn't understand. Kai said Harmony wasn't loyal. That she wanted to hurt us. That she was going to try to get us away from him. And I wasn't going to allow that to happen. None of us were."

The glimmer in Kenny's eye, it seems to disappear, and she stops talking. Like her own words scare her.

I must have seen Harmony right after that fight. That's why she was so wildly upset, trying to lock me in the bathroom.

"Kai saved my life," Harlow says. "In those pain sessions with him, the scream therapy, it would help me get rid of the anger toward my parents. So much anger that I had built up inside. But then he told me to stop talking to them. That they were abusing me. That they were psychologically damaging me."

I look down at Kai. He's right here with us, moaning in pain, but starting to move around. I place my knee on his arm, keeping him still.

"He said it to me. He said it to Harmony. We all got the same monologue," I say. "But you wanted to protect him because you looked up to him. Because you loved him. Because you looked up to Deena."

Kenny, Harlow, and Grace nod. I look behind me, and I see Katrina, Imani, Marley, and some of the other girls watching us. I'm not sure when they entered the house. I'm feeling dazed. Their hands are covering their mouths.

"Then what, Kenny?" I say, my teeth clenched. "Give us the rest of it."

"Kai didn't know what to do about Harmony falling apart like that, threatening him. He was so upset. He wanted to send Harmony away forever," she says. "Then he told us he wanted us to prove our loyalty. He wanted Harmony to go away. And he wanted us to help him. We wanted to show him how much we loved him."

"Prove your loyalty?" Like the day I erased Ivy's folder from the cloud. That's what Kai wanted me to do, prove my loyalty.

"Kai didn't want to get too involved because he said we had to prove our loyalty by repairing Harmony's negativity," Harlow says, then glares at me. "And you, Bean. You were attached to her hip."

"The easiest thing to do," Kenny says, "was to drug you two, because we knew you had planned to find Harmony later on so you could talk to her. It wasn't going to be anything that hurt you, but Kai slipped something into the Blue Honey. It was that easy."

I shake my head, look back at Ivy, Brooks, and Nico. Their mouths wide open. No one says a thing.

So many lies. So many manipulations. My mind is everywhere.

"Kai told us to take Harmony down to the spa to calm down. Me, Harlow, and Grace. But Harmony doesn't want to go," Kenny says. "So we lead her there. You need a mind-and-body detox. That you're poisoning yourself with all these thoughts. Which she was. Spiritual emanation, right?"

Julia groans loudly, and the pause between us is so heavy it might kill us all.

Kenny says that finally, *finally* after pressuring her, consoling her, they get her to the door of the spa, but she wouldn't walk down the steps.

"Do you know how annoying this was? Being responsible for Harmony? Harmony, who thought she owned Deep. Harmony, who thought she was owed something. And we got into an argument. Harmony slipped," Kenny says.

I can hear the sirens. They have to be close to the driveway. "Keep going. Tell me the rest. Quickly, Kenny."

"Harmony was complaining about her head. We got her into the hot tub."

"We got on top of her," Harlow says. "We held her down."

The emotion sucked out of her like a vacuum had been clamped to her head. Harlow, the same girl I've seen countless times skipping and singing and holding hands with her friends, strolling down the hallway like she's some Pollyanna. Now nothing. Vacant. Admitting to being a murderer.

"You drowned her?" I say, the dread in my voice. "You kept her under?"

"We did it for Kai."

Julia wraps her arms around Kenny. I'm surprised that she would comfort her at all. But I can see the guilt in Julia's eyes. I know Julia well enough to know she feels responsible, like it's her fault that this happened. *This is on Deena*, I want to tell her. But doesn't she have to take some onus too? Don't I?

"I'm so sorry. I'm so sorry," Kenny's saying over and over until the police barge in through the door.

TALENTUM FREE PRESS

Deep Leader Kai Edwards and Teenage Girls Indicted for Murder of Former Talentum Student

by Ivy Cohen-Smith

Kai Edwards, a former employee of the wellness company Deep, was indicted today by the Essex County grand jury for the murder of Harmony Williams, a former Talentum student and Deep employee.

The star witness was Kamakshi "Kenny" Khatri, 17 years old, who was also indicted. Khatri was a member of the exclusive girls group Femme that was created by Edwards to conceal his sexual, physical, and psychological abuse of women and girls.

Khatri testified that she and two other teenagers, Harlow Kennedy, 17, and Grace Champlain, 16, were under a "hypnotic spell" from Edwards at the time of the killing.

Deep was once a multimillion-dollar wellness corporation, but since the indictment, the company filed for bankruptcy. Deep was a portmanteau of the name of its former owner, Deena Patterson.

Patterson had once been known as a champion for women's wellness, and along with Edwards, she insisted she could help women through alternative healing practices. Customers all over the world flocked to Deep for spiritual guidance, wellness practices, and organic clothing and skin products.

But prosecutors say Patterson "assisted, facilitated, and contributed to" Edwards's crimes by helping him recruit, groom, and abuse girls who were under 18.

Patterson's lawyer maintains that she had no knowledge of the crime or of Edwards's predatory behavior and refused to make any comments.

Prosecutors say Williams was killed because she was going to uncover the abuse at Deep.

Epilogue

It's picture day at Talentum. Senior year. Everyone's dressed in pink. Clouds of pink. A sea of pink.

"It's tradition," everyone keeps saying, but I look at them all with my new skepticism because now I know things. I know how groupthink works. I know about thought control.

Change their outfits to white and we could be right back there at a Femme gathering. Instead of our dean waving his hands around to get us in line, it could be Deena or Kai in the barn. There are a few rebels, like me, Ivy, Brooks, and Nico. No one will make us wear pink. Not ever.

"Wouldn't it be ironic if I decorated my entire dorm room pink once I leave Talentum?" Nico says.

No one wears white. There are no more Femme girls. No nap dresses from Deep. No one wants that around Talentum anymore, not after what happened.

You couldn't avoid the story, no matter where you looked. It traversed walls. Our town was taken over by an army of news trucks. People would whisper *cult*. I'd hear them in the hallways, in the bathroom, in the news reports.

But it's not like you wake up one morning and decide to join a cult.

You fall in love with a girl. You're enamored by her and her dedication to her mother. You see so much of yourself in her, that you're both girls, alone in this world with your struggling single mothers who are just trying to raise you the best they can. You get caught up in this world of beauty, with answers and possibilities, so many ways to make you feel better, to look better.

While we stand there smiling for the photo, I search for Julia. It's a Pavlovian response after so many years of watching her, that blond hair, her easy looks, her glow. Of course, she's not here.

Reader, we didn't stay together.

How could we? I want to say we tried. I want to say that when she went off to boarding school, that I promised to talk to her always. But we drifted apart after that last night. She didn't want to remember anything. She didn't want to have connections to people who knew her then. She wanted a new life. She wanted to find herself. How could anyone blame her?

Sometimes I watch for Julia on the news, and she ducks her head from the cameras, her blond hair falling in her face. I expected a white suit, something. But it's gray. A steely tweed blazer and washed-out gray pants. Her hair pulled back into a tight ponytail.

I miss her touch. I miss her mouth. I miss the way she'd look at me. My heart aches for her. I will always love her.

At first, I used to gaze at her through the television, wondering if she'd look up into the camera to see me. I imagined that our eyes could traverse through TV land. And then it would happen, her eyes would gaze up, looking at me through my television screen.

The media kept referring to Julia as Deena's coconspirator. Ivy, Brooks, and Nico felt like she was just as much to blame. But it's so much more complicated than that.

I see Julia as a victim. I see all the girls as victims.

I heard some production company is making a movie about Deep. I wonder who will play Julia. She can't just be someone beautiful. She has to be someone with compassion.

I want to tell you about the girls, how broken they are. They're being prosecuted as adults. Kenny and I write letters to each other. Ivy doesn't understand this. "She killed Harmony," Ivy says brutally. And Ivy's right. She did.

But Kenny was a girl. Just like Harlow. Grace. Katrina. Imani. The fourteen-year-old, Marley, whose parents believed that Kai was going to help her get closer to some spiritual center. Marley's parents believed Kai was the smartest man in the world.

All Kenny wanted to do was belong. She wanted someone to belong to. I understood this more than anyone.

After the school photo I go to a meeting with a group of eighth graders. I was made head of the peer leaders in the spring after a long application process. It's a lot of responsibility considering that I'm also taking a Victorian-fashion-design class at FIT in Manhattan, but I like being busy. I like having a purpose. It doesn't keep my mind off Julia, nothing will. My mom says heartbreak can last for a lifetime.

I thought the school would protest it because I used to work for Deep, but no one did. Even Scotch Steiner came up to me after the announcement. A hangdog look on his face. All those months of being harassed by him in Nineteenth-Century Lit. "You're uniquely qualified to help people," he says, as if he never said a bad thing to me, not once.

I don't respond. It's a nice sentiment, but just because someone decides to be nice to you, doesn't mean you have to let them in your life. Also Scotch Steiner will always suck. I'm learning about boundaries in therapy.

The rest of the peer leaders, six of them, lean against the wall like bricks, their bodies slack and lifeless. You can see on their faces they want to be anywhere else. They stare at me, wishing I wasn't so invested, resentful of my enthusiasm. But I want to be better than the less-than-average peer leader I had. Jacobson Delmar and his bogus speech about how Harvard was his lifelong dream. I will never tell these kids not to feel anxious about college. I will never tell them how to feel.

I want to be like Harmony was to Ivy. Inspiring. A good listener. Someone who makes you feel welcome. I want to be the kind of person who the kids can confide in. *Peer leader* isn't just something to stick on your college résumé.

So I play a game with all of them. We sit in a circle and throw a ball to each other, calling out someone's name; then we ask them a question.

One of the kids asks me, "What's the best advice you've been given?"

I stare at this circle of fourteen-year-olds, their faces, most of them so young, pimply, stare at me in awe. A rush of power overtakes me. Is this how it felt for Kai, for Deena? To confidently stand in front of people who seem to look up to you? Do they see me as that person, knowing that I was once part of it?

"The best advice I've been given?" I say. "Drugstore products work just as well as anything else," I say.

I know I should have said something more serious, more thoughtful. But I can't be preachy. Not after listening to Kai. Sometimes, when you're meeting new people, it's okay to make a joke.

The kids laugh. "Didn't you used to work at Deep?" one girl, small, short blond hair shaved on one side, says to me.

"Used to," I say.

"My mom has some old Deep Glow. But it's rotting in the closet," the girl says. She smiles at me. I smile back.

After the session, the same girl with the short blond hair shaved on one side, comes over to me. "Thank you," she says. "I'm a late-year transfer student, so this has been a little weird for me. I don't know anyone."

"Well, now you know me," I say, and smile.

I mean to go to the pressroom, where Ivy is banging away at follow-ups to the Deep story, but I have to catch the train into the city for my class. Ivy's going to win more awards, of course. She wants to share them all with me. "Without your bravery," she keeps saying, "we wouldn't have a story." But I don't want anything to do with it. I don't need to shine under Ivy. I need to shine on my own.

On the train, I sit across from a girl wearing a white dress and I think of Julia. I always think of Julia. No one looked at me like her before, and it feels like no one will look at me like that ever again. She made me a different person, someone who felt part of something big.

We never needed Kai, she and I. That was the difference between us and the other girls. It's not just because we were in love with each other, or because Kai is a man.

No, it's not that. It's because we had our own center. We had our own sense of being.

No matter where I am in my life, a part of me will always belong to Julia Patterson.

And I realized recently that no matter where I am in my life, I will always belong to myself.

Acknowledgments

Thank you, Simone Roberts-Payne, my brilliant editor, for your contagious enthusiasm, endless brainstorming sessions, and smart insight. You helped me create a diverse and well-represented universe, and I appreciate you deeply. Thank you always to Emily Sylvan Kim, my cheerleader, my partner in crime, for always lifting me up with the most positive words. Thank you to the entire team at Putnam Books for Young Readers for getting my book into readers' hands. To Natalie Vielkind, the lovely managing editor who keeps everything running; to Alicia Lea, for your sharp, eagle-eyed copyediting; to Christine Doran, for proofreading with such precision; and to cover designer Jessica Jenkins, who came up with such a fresh take to represent this story.

Thank you to the YA community, to every single reader and YA author I've met who has supported me since my first book, *Something Happened to Ali Greenleaf*.

Thank you, Meridian Hinton-Cooley, for your beta read and your sensitive feedback. Thank you to all of my family and friends who have listened to my anxiety-ridden phone calls about writing. Having a writer in your life is no joke! As Erykah Badu said, "I'm an artist and I'm sensitive about my shit."

Research has always been important to my writing, and this

book was no different. I listened to countless podcasts about cults like *Sounds Like a Cult, The Gateway: Teal Swan, Infamous: NXIVM's Inner Circle*; watched documentaries like *Stolen Youth: Inside the Cult at Sarah Lawrence*; and read books by cult victims like *Member of the Family* by Diane Lake.

I've always been fascinated by the inner workings and psychology of cults. I wanted most to convey in this book that cult members can be both victimizers *and* victims. I'd also like to say this about the wellness community: I worked at a health food store in San Francisco in the '90s and have long been a fan and "cult member" of the wellness world. It's so easy to want to find answers when you feel vulnerable and even let down by life. As much as we'd like for it to be true, there's no secret potion for life, love, or beauty. If something feels wrong, it probably is. And though my title is *You Belong to Me*, the only person you belong to is yourself.

This book is dedicated to Andy, who has seen me through each of my books with love, support, laughter, and respect.

Resources

If you or a loved one are in an unsafe situation at home, here are some resources available for you to seek confidential support.

CHILDHELP
National Child Abuse Hotline
Call or text: 1-800-422-4453
ChildHelpHotline.org

LOVE IS RESPECT
National Dating Abuse Helpline
Call: 1-866-331-9474
TTY: 1-800-787-3224
Text: "LOVEIS" to 22522
LoveIsRespect.org

RAPE, ABUSE & INCEST NATIONAL NETWORK
National Sexual Assault Hotline
Call: 1-800-656-HOPE(4673)
RAINN.org

NATIONAL SEXUAL VIOLENCE RESOURCE CENTER (NSVRC)
NSVRC.org

LOOK AHEAD FOR A SNEAK PEEK AT HAYLEY'S YA DEBUT, A CRUCIAL AND COMPLEX PAGE-TURNER.

"Full of truth, hope, and empowerment, this story is one you'll be thinking about long after you've finished."

—Amber Smith, *New York Times* bestselling author of *The Way I Used to Be*

1

BLYTHE

Some nights it seems like the world has its arms wide open, that the future sizzles with possibility. White streetlights glare in your eyes like disco balls as you whiz down the road. Stars glitter in the black sky. Your favorite song bursts out, and the bass shimmies the car under you as you and your friends chant along.

This is not one of those nights.

We get to Sophie Miller's house and right away my boyfriend, Devon, and his best friend, Sean, leave me alone inside so they can smoke cigars with the rest of the soccer team. "Cigars are for old men," I say to Dev as he kisses me.

"I promise to chew some gum before we make out," he says. Another kiss and he's off.

Sean, the beatific Sean Nessel, is the reason we're here. Sean has a thing for a junior girl—Ali Greenleaf. She's tonight's focus. "She stares at me a lot," he said earlier, back at Dev's house. "Who doesn't stare at you a lot, Nessel?" I wanted to say, but it would have come out awkward.

Sean and Dev are still close—I hear them and the other guys roaring about their win yesterday. State Champs, all because of Sean's winning goal. In the school paper since day one. Front page every day. Like they don't get enough attention since the football team disbanded last year. Now the football moms and the entire town have put all their attention on the soccer boys. Their groveling attention. Outside, the guys are chanting a primal call. DE-FEAT. DE-FEAT. It makes me uncomfortable, all that male animalistic bonding with their claps and their stomps. Everyone at the party is tuned in to it; you can tell by their heads turned toward the windows where the sounds are coming from. Even when they're not in the room, the boys' growls take over.

My crew of girls—we're known as the Core Four: me, Donnie Alperstein, Suki Fields, and Cate Sandoval—should be here by now, but they're not. People aren't used to seeing me alone. I bury my head in my phone and text Cate.

Where are you

Be there in 2

"Oh my God, Blythe Jensen!" A girl I don't know hops in front of me. This happens a lot. When people get drunk, they introduce themselves to me. I nod politely.

"We're in chemistry together," she says.

"Where's the keg?"

She stumbles over directions. She's actually *describing to me* where the keg is. So I stop her before it gets too irritating.

"You would be so useful if you could just find the keg and get me a beer," I say.

"Oh! Sure!"

Ali Greenleaf, the girl Sean wants to hook up with tonight, walks in the door about a minute later. She's with Cherie Mizner, Raj Patel, and another girl, who I think is Cherie's sister. Ali is a scrawny chicken. A goose neck. A pasty-faced pumpkin. Full lips. Like a baby. Her hair with a loose curl. Bangs, which aren't easy to pull off. She has nice hair. Some cute freckles. Wearing a bunch of bracelets up her arm. I like the bracelets. I'll give her that.

Chemistry Girl is standing right in front of me again, twitching. She says "thank you" when she hands me the beer.

But I want to watch Ali. I want to see what Sean sees in her. She turns to her friend, her face glowing in that innocent way a face does. She's the kind of girl who doesn't realize how pretty she is. I can see it in her eyes. That scared look. One more oblivious girl who has no idea what's coming to her. Because I've been through this many times with Sean. Ali will come crying to me, wanting to know what happened between them. *I know you thought he liked you so much, and he does like you, sweetie, except Sean just isn't the commitment type.* It'll happen a few days from now. A week from now. This is textbook Sean. And these stupid girls, forever thinking they're the one he's going to be different with.

I text Dev: *Nessel's girl is here. Better come back in.*

Cate marches in with Suki and Donnie following. She pushes through the crowd to get to me, and the other girls follow. No one says a word about being pushed by them. They just step out of the way.

"So, so, so sorry it took us so long to get here. My mother was giving me a hard time," Cate says.

"Oh, *mothers*," I say, my words dripping.

Cate's mother is originally from Puerto Rico. She still

makes Cate's lunch every morning. Feeds us when we eat at her house. Pours us wine. Wants to fatten us up.

My mother is not this way. I wish I didn't have to help my mother sort her pills or deal with fielding my father's phone calls because he's so worried about her, but that is how it is at my house.

"Plus it took Donnie forever to leave," Suki says to Donnie, who is wobbling a little already. She's been stealing her sister's Vicodin lately, left over from a running injury. And maybe she took too much. She's wearing an oversize army jacket with a short white shirt showing off her brown belly and black skinny jeans. Her tight black curls are wild tonight—the bottom half is a washed-out blue.

Donnie twists around and trips over her foot. I catch her elbow.

"You gonna be okay, Don?"

"B, I'm sooo good." She licks her lips, wiping her hair away from her eyes. She pulls a blue strand out of her mouth.

ALI

Sammi, Raj, and I sit in a little circle drinking beer and smoking Raj's Lucky Strike cigarettes, which are destroying the back of my throat. These Lucky Strikes are Raj's grandfather's. The old man has emphysema and Lucky Strikes aren't easy to find, so he has Raj Google tobacco shops where they sell them. The two of them make a monthly pilgrimage, his grandfather with his portable oxygen tank. His grandpa stockpiles them. As long as Raj keeps it a secret, he'll throw Raj a pack or two.

Raj has been on varsity soccer since he was a sophomore. Which means he's friends with Sean Nessel, which means he's often in *close proximity* to Sean Nessel.

We play the Who Has Had Sex? game and focus on Blythe Jensen. Sometimes I wonder what it's like to be her. In the hallway at school, she's always staring straight ahead, like there's a light at the end of the hall, or a camera, or something else, much further away and superior. As if she's looking anywhere other than here.

"I don't think it's a question of *if* Blythe Jensen's had sex," I say. "She's been going out with Devon Strong forever. It's *how much* sex."

"Actually, the discussion is whether she's got a whip and handcuffs," Sammi says. "She looks like a punisher."

"Okay, Raj, your turn. What about him?" I point to a super-thin hockey player whose shoulders are bigger than his feet.

"I don't even know why we play this game," Raj says. "Half of this room has had sex."

Raj has wavy brown hair; it's soft and puffy and kind of hangs over one eye. All that softness, plus those brilliant green eyes and his skin, a mellow brown from his father's side, whose family is from India, goes against this intense glare, his eyes squinty, even behind his black-rimmed glasses, like he's angry, or thinking too much. "I'm just perpetually skeptical," he told me once when I asked him about it.

Then Sean Nessel glides past a window. Sean Nessel and his silky blond hair to his shoulders. I'm just going to say it: Everything in my life revolves around Sean Nessel. This is no secret. Raj and Sammi understand the full weight of my Sean Nessel obsession.

Even this stupid game. It's just a diversion. We're here at this party for a reason.